Also by Lee Collins

The Dead of Winter

LEE COLLINS

She Returns from War

ANGRY
ROBOT

ANGRY ROBOT
A member of the Osprey Group

Lace Market House,
54-56 High Pavement,
Nottingham,
NG1 1HW, UK

4301 21st St., Ste 220B,
Long Island City,
NY 11101
USA

www.angryrobotbooks.com
Ride a fast horse

An Angry Robot paperback original 2013

Cover art by Chris McGrath.
Set in Meridien by THL Design.

Distributed in the United States by Random House, Inc., New York.

ISBN 978-0-85766-275-0
eBook ISBN 978-0-85766-276-7

Printed in the United States of America

9 8 7 6 5 4 3 2 1

For my parents,
who gave me Narnia, Middle-earth,
Hyrule, and the Starship Enterprise
as playgrounds

ONE

Their eyes appeared first, floating in the night like orbs of yellow flame. One minute, the Oxford countryside was cold and still beneath an early April moon; the next, canine shapes ran alongside a certain backwoods lane. Tongues black as ink lolled from phantom jaws. Though they rose to the height of small horses, their feet made no sound on the young spring grass. They might have seemed like illusions – playing at the edge of sight only to vanish when looked at directly – but for their eyes. Saucer-sized, they smoldered like pits opening into a blazing furnace, silent beacons lighting the road ahead.

Victoria Dawes pulled her scarf up over her chin. Beside her, her mother wore a look of exasperation. The motion of the carriage threw their shoulders together time and again, but the seat left the two women no room to move apart.

"Come now, my dear," came her father's voice from the driver's seat. He had given their usual driver

the night off so he might enjoy the nighttime countryside with his wife and daughter. "It isn't as though
we are asking you to marry a chimney sweep or sta-
ble boy. Roger is a fine young man."

"A fine young man, a fine huntsman, and heir to
a fine estate," Victoria finished for him. "Fine hair,
fine teeth, and fine smallclothes."

"Really, Victoria," her mother said, "no need to be
crass. Your father and I simply want what's best for
you. Roger Grey will take good care of you and your
children."

"Assuming he could see us around that beak nose
of his."

Her father glanced over his shoulder. "I hardly
think a large nose is reason enough to decline a marriage offer, especially for a woman your age."

"You make it sound as though I've one foot in the
grave already," Victoria said. Her scarf tickled her chin
as she spoke, and she pushed it down. "I'm only just
twenty-three."

"And the last of your friends to be married," her
mother reminded her.

Victoria folded her arms and looked away. They
could say what they liked; she would not marry
Roger Grey. Even if he had a proper nose, the man
was still too simple by half. She didn't want her children to carry on his legacy of dull-witted comments
and friendliness with hounds and hawks. Roger
seemed to prefer the company of such animals to that
of people, but she couldn't fathom why. Her own father's hounds held little interest for her, and although

she had learned to ride at a young age, she'd never formed any special friendships with her horses. She had no pet cats or canaries. Animals were animals; dumb beasts bred to serve, not sit at table. Were she to wed Roger Grey, she would no doubt find herself breaking her fast with his favorite riding-horse each morning.

A flicker of light in the distance caught her eye. Leaning forward, she squinted into the darkness. A shadowy line of trees stood at attention across an open field, their crowns forming a jagged horizon against the night sky. The moon, just past the first quarter, flooded the field with silver-blue light. Despite the rumbling of the carriage beneath her, Victoria could still see well enough to make out an odd shape running over the grass. It looked as though it might have been a horse, but she couldn't make out a rider. The shape was also wrong, somehow, but she didn't know what else it could be. No other animal that size lived in this part of the country.

"Father, what is that?" she asked, pointing at the strange shape.

He glanced in the direction of her finger. "Just a fellow out for a ride, the same as us."

"No need to change the subject, Victoria." Her mother sat up as straight as she could. "I've half a mind to–"

The carriage swerved to one side, throwing Victoria against her mother. The older woman let out a grunt as they collided. Before they could disentangle themselves, the carriage veered again. Victoria's lungs emptied as her mother's elbow landed on her midriff. Struggling for breath, she tried to roll out from under the weight, but her mother clung to her in a panic. She was dimly aware of her father's surprised exclamations as he regained control of the horses.

After a few agonizing seconds, Victoria managed to climb out from beneath her mother and reclaim her seat. "What on earth was that?" she asked.

"I haven't a clue," her father replied. "The girls must have spooked at a fox, I suppose." He took a deep breath to steady himself.

Victoria reached down to help her mother up. Before their hands met, the team let out a chorus of frightened whinnies and broke into a gallop. Caught off guard, her father tumbled backward into the buggy, landing squarely on his wife. She cried out in pain and desperately tried to shove him off. The carriage shook and rattled as the horses picked up speed, and the motion kept knocking him off balance as he tried to gather himself. His struggles only provoked further cries from his wife, who started crying.

Climbing over her fallen parents, Victoria pulled herself into the driver's seat. The reins bounced along the floorboards, coming dangerously close to sliding out of the buggy completely. She made a grab for them and missed, nearly tumbling off her perch. Righting herself, she tried again. This time, a bump on the road shook the buggy's frame, knocking the reins into her outstretched hand. Clenching the leather strips in a white-knuckled fist, she pulled herself upright. Grunts and scraping sounds came from behind her as her parents struggled to regain their balance.

Without thinking, Victoria pulled on the reins with all her might. The heads of both horses snapped to the right. The rest of the frightened animals followed, pulling the buggy off the road and into the grass. Panicking, Victoria continued to fight with the reins, causing the buggy to swerve violently from side to side. Stealing glances ahead of them, she saw flashes of bright yellow light looming ahead in the darkness. She pulled the reins to the right again. The horses whinnied, fighting her. Looking right, she saw the reason for their terror, and a powerful shock of fear slammed into her stomach.

Beside the carriage, not three yards away, was a huge black animal. At first she thought it might have been another horse, but its gait gave it away: it was an enormous dog. Dumbstruck, she stared at it, the reins slack in her hands.

Before she could understand what she was seeing, the monster turned its head and looked at her. Eyes like tiny suns seared trails of liquid fire across her vision. Victoria jerked backward, instinctively pulling the reins to the left. The horses eagerly followed her lead, pulling the buggy headlong toward the waiting trees. The black creature slipped from view as they turned, bringing her a moment's respite. Turning her attention back to the team, she coaxed it into running at an angle toward the tree line. She could still feel those terrible eyes on her. The creature was chasing them now, she was sure of it. With any luck, she could turn the buggy in a slow circle, bringing them back to the road and a chance at escape.

Two more creatures charged out of the trees. Their eyes flashed in the shadows as they ran straight for the buggy. The terrified horses veered sharply to the left. The buggy's wheels skidded along the ground as it pulled through the turn, but it stayed upright. Victoria clung to the reins in desperation. She thought she could make out the road ahead of them. Just a few seconds and they would reach it.

"Victoria!" her father shouted from behind her. "What's happening?"

"I don't know," she called back. "Now hush!"

Victoria could feel the monsters behind them, but she forced the thought out of her mind. If she lost control now, she would kill herself and her parents. She had to focus on keeping the horses under control. In their present state, not even her father's driver would have had an easy time of it, and she had little experience with driving a buggy. Still, if she could take herself in hand and guide the animals in the right direction, they might just live through the night.

The road appeared ahead of them much sooner than she anticipated. As luck would have it, however, they were running along it at an angle. She gave the reins a short, sharp tug to the right as it passed beneath them. The horses responded, pulling the buggy out of the grass and back onto packed earth. Victoria looked to the right, expecting to see monstrous yellow eyes bearing down on them, but the field was deserted. She allowed herself a small smile of relief.

"Are you all right?" she asked over her shoulder.

"Yes, I think so. Your mother's fainted on us, I'm afraid," her father replied. She felt his hand on her shoulder. "Well done, my dear."

Victoria nodded her thanks. Ahead of them, she could see a bridge. The river it spanned was at least thirty feet across. She didn't know if the creatures chasing them could swim, but the bridge itself was narrow. If they could get across, they might be able to lose their pursuers. She clapped the reins across the team's back, but the animals needed no encouragement; the buggy thundered toward the river at a breakneck speed. Leaning forward, Victoria watched as the bridge loomed closer in the moonlight. Her fingers curled around the reins. They were going to make it.

A black shadow leaped up from the river. Fierce yellow eyes glowered at them as it landed on the road just before the bridge. Victoria slapped the reins again, urging the horses to charge through the creature. Instead, the animals panicked and veered to one side. Ahead of them, the surface of the water spread out like a vast pane of black glass. She pulled on the reins, desperate to steer the buggy away from disaster.

When they jumped the bank, Victoria found herself weightless. Horses, buggy, and passengers seemed suspended in midair, floating above the moonlit water like ghosts. She could see each white-tinted ripple and count every reflected star. The driver's seat drifted downward toward the river, but she remained aloft, sailing through the night. Looking down at her hands, she realized she had let go of the reins. Her father's voice reached her ears from a great distance. He was carrying on about something, but she couldn't make out what. Not that it mattered. She'd discovered she could fly. Closing her eyes, she tilted her head skyward and smiled, letting the cool air kiss her face.

The shock of icy water numbed her arms and legs as it closed in around her. She gasped at the impact, pulling a mouthful down into her lungs. Spasms shook her body. Her arms clawed frantically at the darkness, seeking a way out. The weight of her dress and coat pulled her downward, away from the surface and its life-giving air. She began kicking. Her shoes slipped off her feet and floated away. After a few more agonizing seconds, she felt her toes scrape against something solid, and she pushed against it with her remaining strength.

Frantic splashes filled Victoria's ears as her head broke the surface. She filled her lungs with night air and was rewarded with a violent coughing spell. Beating her arms against the water, she managed to keep herself afloat long enough to spot the closest bank. It wasn't far. She forced her legs into action and made for it.

Pulling herself up onto the riverbank, she collapsed as another coughing fit wracked her frame.

Fire scorched her throat, making each breath a sweet agony. Her dress clung to her legs as she brought them up to her chest, but she barely noticed its cold, clammy touch. The world consisted of nothing beyond her aching lungs.

When the coughing fits finally subsided, she pushed herself up into a sitting position. The night was still and quiet around her. With a start, she remembered the shadowy creatures and the frantic chase, and an ocean of panic welled up inside her stomach. Victoria struggled to her feet, eyes sweeping up and down the river for the buggy or her parents. The water flowed past her, dark and placid. She wrapped her arms around herself with a shiver. Standing there, dripping wet, she suddenly felt very cold and very alone.

Upstream. If her parents were anywhere, they would be upstream. Victoria shook herself out of her stupor and began walking. It was slow going. The wet folds of her dress wrapped themselves around her legs with each step. She kicked them away as best she could. Her toes sank into the cool mud that lined the riverbank. As she walked, she kept her eyes on the river, searching for any sign of the ruined buggy.

A splash in the river behind her made her jump. Looking toward the sound, she saw a set of rings expanding outward across the surface. A fish, or maybe a frog. Not one of those dog creatures. The thought of them sent chills skittering across her body. She turned in a slow circle, watching for any telltale yellow eyes, but the fields around her were empty. Taking a deep breath, she continued the journey upstream. Her renewed fear added urgency to her steps. Every sound, real or imagined, turned her head and halted her progress. Unwelcome thoughts of the nightmare hounds kept forcing their way into her mind. She found herself imagining what their jet-black jaws would look like up close, the fetid smell of their breath, how their teeth would feel as they sank into her arm or leg.

A dark shape in the river caught her eye, and she froze. Her breathing became shallow, soundless. Every muscle in her body tensed itself for flight if the shadow so much as twitched. Moments passed, punctuated by the thumping of her heart, but the shape didn't move. As the initial fear loosened its grip on her, she realized that she recognized the object in the water.

It was the buggy.

"Father!" she called, the shadow creatures forgotten. "Mother! Can you hear me?"

No reply came from the wreck. She began running along the bank, yelling her parents' names. Twice, her dress coiled around her legs and sent her sprawling in the mud, but she didn't stop. When she reached the point where the riverbank came closest to the buggy, she waded out into the water. The river rose to her waist, but she couldn't reach the wreck. This close, she could see the upturned rear wheels rising out of the water. The buggy had completely capsized, and there was no sign of the team. Anyone still inside would be trapped. Shivering, she called out again. Silence.

Helpless, Victoria waited, hoping for an answer or movement or any sign at all that her parents were still alive. The silence became ominous, sending waves of fear through her mind. As her panic grew, she pulled off her overcoat and tossed it behind her. Her fingers began tugging at the laces crisscrossing her back. She hesitated, wondering what a fool she would make of herself if she had to return home in only her wet smallclothes. If her parents were still alive, they would be too humiliated to show their faces in public after such a display. Any hope she had of finding a halfway-decent husband would be dashed.

She shook herself. What on earth was she thinking? Pulling the laces free, she peeled her dress away from her shoulders and down over her hips. The current played with the laces as she stepped out of it and rolled it into a lumpy ball. She tossed it toward the bank, where it landed with a soggy splash. Now free of the crippling weight, Victoria started toward the wreck.

The river swirled around her in dark eddies as she waded toward the drowned buggy. As the water rose to her shoulders, she realized she would have to swim to reach it. She'd never been a strong swimmer, and even this light current made her uneasy. Survival instinct had fueled her earlier push to shore; if the current swept her downstream, she wasn't sure she could make it to the riverbank a second time. Still, if her parents were trapped under the buggy, she had to help them.

Taking a deep breath, she pushed off with her toes and began swimming. The current picked her up immediately, pushing her away from the wreck. She fought against it, kicking upstream until she caught hold of a wheel. The buggy shifted slightly beneath her weight, but it didn't come loose. Hand over hand, she made her way toward where the opening should have been.

Swinging around to the side of the wreck, Victoria got her first good look at what remained of the upper half. The entire top had broken loose of the wheels and fallen forward. Most of the cab was submerged, anchored to the riverbed by its own weight. Victoria sucked in a breath and pulled herself along the frame, submerging her head. Keeping her eyes closed, she felt along the buggy's side. Her fingers found a metal edge, and she pulled herself toward it. The riverbed brushed up against her shoulder. The opening was barely wide enough to accommodate her arm, but she plunged it in anyway. Fingers spread out, she groped for an arm, a leg, anything that might be her mother or father.

Something bumped against her outstretched hand, and she clutched at it. Wet cloth slid between her fingers. It was an arm. She shook it, hoping to feel a twitch or flex in response. Nothing. Frantic, she began pulling it toward the opening. The arm came easily enough at first, but it stopped short before she could pull it through. No matter how she pulled, it refused to come any closer.

Her chest heaved. She needed air. A flurry of

bubbles escaped her mouth as she released the arm and swam to the surface. Making a desperate grab for a wheel, she climbed on top of the ruined cab. Victoria beat on it with her fist twice, then paused to listen for a response. Nothing. She tried again. Only the quiet gurgling of the water around the submerged buggy answered her.

A fit of despair swept through her. Lifting her head, she screamed at the night sky. The echoes rolled back to her from the trees. She screamed again, pounding her fist against the metal husk that had become a coffin. The cold steel shifted beneath her as she rolled onto her back. Her third scream broke down into sobs. Warm tears trickled out from beneath her eyelids and traced new tracks of wetness across her face. If only she could have brought the horses under control. If only she'd learned how to drive and swim instead of spending her time reading those silly novels, her parents would still be alive. The knowledge that the evening drive came about as a result of her refusal to marry twisted her insides with guilt until she felt like vomiting.

She didn't know how long she lay on top of her parents' tomb. When at last the storm subsided, she shivered and lifted her head.

Yellow eyes peered at her from the riverbank.

Victoria's despair vanished beneath a white-hot flame of rage. The creature stood at the water's edge, lantern eyes fixed on her. It knew exactly what it and its kin had done to her. She pulled herself into a crouching position, waiting for the monster to leap across the water. It might kill her, too, but she refused to be easy prey.

"Come, you coward!" she called, beckoning to the shadow.

The hound made no reply. Its eyes glowed large and grotesque in its dark face. Beneath them, black jaws worked in silence. Victoria returned its gaze, hands curled into fists, ready for anything. Another shadow joined the first on the riverbank, but neither one made a move toward her.

"Filthy beasts!" She rose to her full height, balancing on the wreck. "I'm right here!"

The creatures turned their heads, their eyes looking downstream. Victoria glanced in the same direction but only saw the moonlit water. Turning back to the creatures, she beckoned to them again, but whatever they saw downriver held their attention. She yelled and waved her arms. They ignored her. After a few moments, they turned and ran into the night, vanishing into the shadows along the river.

Victoria watched them go, her defiant posture deflating. Exhaustion flooded her body, and she collapsed into a sitting position atop the wreck. Her parents were dead. Those creatures had driven their buggy into the river and drowned them. The realization left her numb, as cold and unfeeling as the river beneath her. Somewhere in the back of her mind, she realized what a sight she must be, sitting on a ruined buggy in the middle of a river in naught but her wet underthings. It would certainly be the talk of Oxford if someone found her.

She put her hand against the cold metal, intending to push herself back on her feet. Her palm slipped, and she found herself lying on her side. A breath of wind made her shiver. She needed to get up, to go back into town for help, and she would. Just not yet.

"Hallo! Are you all right up there?"

Victoria's eyes snapped open. Where was she?

"Miss? Can you hear me?"

Maybe they were talking to her. It would be polite to answer. She opened her mouth to speak, but she could only produce a hoarse croak. Stiff with cold, her arms creaked in protest as she forced herself upright. Blinking away the haze of sleep, she looked around for the speaker.

There, on the riverbank: a shadow was holding a lantern in one hand. The yellow light sent a thrill of fear through her body, and her eyes snapped wide open. Her legs were under her in an instant, ready to fight, ready to run.

"You're awake," the shadow said. "Can you tell me what happened?"

Victoria swallowed. The monsters hadn't talked to her before. "Um…" she managed, her voice thin.

"I'm sorry?"

"There was an accident," she said.

"I can bloody well see that," the man said. "Are you all right?"

She felt along her own body, hands burning with the cold. "I think so. A bit chilly, though." She wrapped her arms around herself, suddenly remembering that she had left her dress on the riverbank.

"What's your name?"

"Victoria." Was that all of it? "Victoria Dawes."

"Henry's girl?" The shadow lifted its lantern higher, letting her see the outline of its face. "It's me, Edward Brown. Do you remember me?"

"I can't see you," she replied, "and anyway, my father's dead."

The lantern twitched to one side. "I beg your pardon?"

"Yes, he and my mother both," Victoria heard herself say the words, but she couldn't understand what they meant. "They drowned."

"Here?" The shadow named Edward pointed toward the half-sunken buggy. "Are they still inside?"

"Yes. I tried to pull them out, but I couldn't. I never was a very good swimmer, and it's so cold."

"Good heavens," Edward said. "Did this just happen?"

Victoria's forehead wrinkled. "Not too long ago. I've been here for a little while." Her voice sounded dull and leaden in her ears.

"Can you come down? You must be frozen half to death."

"I'll try." She stood up. The buggy shifted beneath her, and she nearly fell.

"For God's sake, do be careful," Edward said. "Here, let me help you." The shadow's feet splashed into the shallow water. It came on until the water rose to its waist, then held out a hand. "Climb on down, my dear. I'll help you back home."

"That would be nice," Victoria said, grabbing ahold of a wheel and lowering herself down. "I think I'd like to sit by the fire for a moment."

"You can do just that, I promise. We'll make one nice and big for you."

Victoria gasped as she lowered a leg into the water. The touch of the icy river jolted her out of her stupor. Suddenly, she could feel her parents' hands reaching out for her from inside the buggy. They needed her help, and she was just going to leave them behind.

"Oh my God! They're still in there!" She pounded on the side of the buggy and heard a knock in reply. "Did you hear that?"

"That was just the echo, love."

She stared at him. Had there been an echo before? She couldn't remember. But if there hadn't been one, her parents must really be dead. Now she was alone in the world: no parents, no husband, no siblings. Only a few family friends who certainly couldn't take her in. How would she make her way?

What strength she had left abandoned her, and her legs threatened to drop her down into the inky water. Maybe it would be better that way. She could join her parents in Heaven. The good Lord must have meant for them all to perish in the crash tonight, but somehow she had avoided that fate. It wasn't too late, though. All she had to do was drop into the river and let it carry her away. She felt half-dead from cold and damp already; the end wouldn't be long.

"Victoria," Edward's voice cut through her confusion, "take my hand. We'll see about sending someone for your parents when we get back to Oxford. Let's get you home, dear."

After a moment's hesitation, she wrapped her shaking fingers around his outstretched hand.

The lacy black veil offered little protection from the pastor's kind glances, nor could it block out the murmurings of the other mourners. Victoria could hear them whispering the same words her neighbors, friends, and own mind had been hammering into her for the past five days. If it had been proper, she would have stuffed black handkerchiefs into her ears to drown out their endless condolences and apologies. Most of them were strangers, acquaintances of her parents who came to pay their respects. Victoria suspected that some of the tears falling were not quite sincere, those shedding them secretly wishing to be elsewhere. She stole a glance over her shoulder. Near the rear of the chapel, she spied a cluster of men in expensive suits. Business associates of her father's, no doubt. Henry Dawes had had the sense to invest in electric power when it first came to England, and his business had quickly expanded into a small empire. Men such as these envied him his success even as they worked with him. Had they the choice, they would surely be toasting her father's death in their offices and studies. Still, etiquette demanded their presence in the cemetery chapel, bidding farewell to a man they had thought was beneath them.

Victoria herself felt only a great emptiness. At times, the void seemed cold and lifeless, a great dead thing lodged inside her ribs. She looked at the wooden boxes lying side by side on the bier and felt nothing. No wails tore themselves from her lungs; tears lingered in her eyes but did not fall. Had they seen her behavior, her parents surely would have found it improper. It wasn't the way a young woman grieved for her parents. They wouldn't expect her to carry on like a drunken wench in the gutter, but she ought to have the decency to weep. She could almost hear her mother's voice scolding her while her father looked on in his solemn way. Her blue eyes grew defiant behind her veil as she mouthed her rebuttal and watched their faces crease with frustration.

All at once, the hard lump in her chest became brittle as glass. Her breath caught in her throat, and she held it for a moment, afraid to breathe too loudly lest she shatter. A single tear trickled downward, tracing a line through the powder on her cheek. Clutching at the handkerchief in her hand, she squeezed her eyes shut and willed away the gathering storm. Even if it was proper, she wouldn't start blubbing like some infant. She was now Ms. Victoria Dawes of Oxford, heiress to her father's estate and mistress of her house. The young girl who had let her parents die because she could not save them had died in the river. A new woman had emerged from the wreck of the buggy.

"Now, let us commit the bodies of Henry and Abigail to their final resting places."

The pastor's words brought her back to her present surroundings as mourners began leaving the chapel.

They would proceed to the Dawes family crypt, where the bodies of her parents would be laid to rest. Wood creaked softly as the pallbearers lifted their burdens for one last journey. Keeping her eyes lowered, Victoria followed her aunts outside.

The April air was chilly beneath grey clouds as the procession wound its way toward the crypt. Weathered headstones stood at attention to either side of them, their mossy crowns lifted in silent salute to the ones joining their ranks. Stone angels wept into crumbling hands, still grieving for men and women only they remembered. Victoria studied them with a detached fascination, wondering if angels really did weep for the passing of mortals. Were the lives of men so valued in the heavenly realms? It seemed absurd. Surely these statues, carved with such skill and care, represented nothing but the vanity of those buried beneath them.

When the procession reached the tomb, the crowd parted to make room for the pallbearers. Victoria watched them pass, uncles and cousins she didn't know, but they didn't meet her eyes. They carried her parents into the cold shadows of the mausoleum. The stone walls of the structure were milky-grey, matching the hue of the clouds overhead. Moss wormed its way along the stone in fluid shapes, but it lacked the venerable serenity of the neighboring crypts. Her father had it built when she was a young girl to house himself and his descendants, but he had been too ambitious in its size. The sons he had envisioned lying next to him in eternal repose never arrived. Victoria's only sibling, a younger sister who had died in infancy, was the sole occupant of the family crypt.

Until today.

Tradition dictated that she should wait outside with the other women while the men followed the dead for the final interment. Had it been an aunt and uncle in the coffins, she would have gladly complied, but these were her parents. It was her failing that had brought them to this place. She owed it to them to see their bodies to rest herself.

The air inside the crypt smelled musty, of stone and soil and water. Men holding lanterns had gone in ahead of the pallbearers and now stood by the corners of the waiting sarcophagi. Eerie shadows danced to the rhythm of the flickering light like fey spirits. The sound of dripping water echoed in the shadows.

Victoria drew in a sharp breath. Her vision swam as a long-forgotten fear welled up inside her. She suddenly felt as though she was trapped inside a nightmare from her childhood. In them, she would always find herself lost in a maze of dark alleyways. Rain-slick cobblestones were cold on her feet as she ran, terrified, always just a step ahead of some unseen terror. Bleary gas lamps floated in the haze around her, but their light gave no comfort. Instead, they only served to confuse her, drawing her ever deeper into the labyrinth. Sobs filled her throat, choking off her cries for help. And still she would run; she knew that stopping meant certain death.

A hand touched her shoulder. She whirled toward it, arms rising. The haze lifted from her eyes, and she saw the face of her father's brother looking down at her. Concern creased the skin around his eyes.

"Are you still with us?" he asked, his voice quiet.

Victoria felt a hot rush of blood burn her cheeks. She nodded, lowering her eyes to the dusty floor. Her hands trembled. She forced them to be still and turned back toward the lanterns. The shadows still frolicked in their mischievous dance, but they no longer hid the monsters that haunted her dreams.

The pallbearers lowered her father's coffin into the sarcophagus. Echoes filled the small space as they slid the stone lid into place. Two lions, standing on their hind legs and grasping a sword hilt between their forepaws, adorned the heavy slab. The Dawes family crest. It was supposed to be her heritage and her pride, but she'd never felt much like a lion. A fox, sometimes, when she had done something clever, but never a lion.

The crypt grew colder as the men paid their final respects and left one by one. Soon, Victoria stood alone before the beautiful stone boxes. The lantern-bearers stood in the doorway, throwing shadows and light across the relief carvings in the walls. Victoria laid a hand on each sarcophagus, feeling their chill through her thin black gloves. Letting herself return to that night and its harrowing memories, she called to mind an image of the black dogs. She willed herself to stare into their glowing eyes. Rage flowed through her like liquid fire, and she let it spread, filling every fiber of her being. Her eyes glittered like distant stars.

"Father." Her voice was dark and hard like the granite walls around her. "Mother." She drew herself to her full height. "I'm sorry I failed you. I know it can't help you now, but I vow to you that I will hunt down those beasts. I will hunt them to the ends of the earth and back, and I will kill them. I know I may not have been the daughter you wished for, but I will make you proud in this. No matter the cost, no matter the distance, I will give you justice."

TWO

Victoria felt the curious eyes of the fellows all around her as she stood beside the coach. Aspiring scholars in flowing robes strode along the paved avenues in groups of two and three, oblivious to the grandeur of the buildings around them. Their conversations gave way to mute stares when they caught sight of her. Although Oxford had just established their first women's college, she imagined it had been a good while since many of the students here had seen a young woman of marriageable age without an escort. Stray strands of hair peeked out from beneath her hat, gleaming like gilded steel in the sunlight and catching the golden thread woven into the bodice of her dress.

She straightened her back and allowed her bosom to thrust forward a little. Might as well give these poor shut-in schoolboys something to remember. Her mother had been a shapely woman, and Victoria had inherited her good fortune. Combined with her father's piercing blue eyes, she'd stolen many a young man's heart since growing into womanhood. She found it quite tiresome at times, waiting for a smitten messenger boy to deliver his message or seeing round, gawking eyes follow her from doorways and carriage windows. Still, she couldn't resist the modest flaunting of her charms from time to time.

Today, however, she couldn't linger to tease passing students. Pulling a slip of paper from a coin purse tucked in her bodice, she compared the name written on it to the building in front of her. Blackfriars Hall. This was where she was supposed to meet him.

Victoria approached the front entrance with an air of caution. Unlike the other buildings that comprised the various colleges at Oxford University, Blackfriars Hall was a squat, simple construction that had fallen into some disrepair. Two rows of windows stared gloomily out across St. Giles, and a third above them was nearly lost in the sloping roof. It boasted no sweeping arches or towering spires, and even its front doors were plainly carved. It seemed a poor choice for the professional edifice of such a renowned scholar.

Her hopes dampened, she pulled open the old oak door. Inside, the floor groaned beneath her, announcing her every step. A man ensconced behind a massive desk looked up at the sound, candlelight dancing in his spectacles.

"Excuse me, miss," he said. "Are you lost?"

"No," Victoria replied. "I'm here to visit a friend of my father's."

The man smiled and rose to his feet. "You must be mistaken. You see, Blackfriars Hall has not been in use by the university for a very long time. We keep it open for historical purposes, but I'm afraid there are no offices here."

"But I'm certain he told me to meet him here." The paper crackled in her hand as she held it out to the man. "Blackfriars Hall."

The man took the paper from her and inspected it. "Yes, that is what it says. Perhaps you misunderstood?"

"Perhaps not," Victoria replied. "I'm quite capable of reading, sir."

He offered her a thin smile. "With whom were you exchanging letters?"

"A Mr. Townsend, an acquaintance of my father and scholar of some renown."

Behind his spectacles, the man's eyes widened. He looked back down at the scrap of paper and swallowed. "Mr. James Townsend?"

"Yes." Victoria stood up straighter. "He requested that I come visit him, and he instructed me to meet him in this hall."

"Of course," the man said, returning the paper. "If you'll follow me."

Surprised but pleased by her host's sudden acquiescence, Victoria fell into step behind him. He led her down a long corridor lined with closed doors. Some had names and titles carved into their ancient wood, but the doorman's pace was too brisk for her to get a good look. Their footsteps echoed through the empty building. Despite herself, Victoria pictured a procession of ghastly scholars with black robes and pale faces following them. Her skin prickled, and she pushed the thought away. She was here to speak with this James Townsend and learn from him how she might avenge her parents. Whoever he was, she was sure he wouldn't be impressed by a young woman who was frightened of echoes. He expected the bold, determined woman from her letters, and that was who she must be.

Her silent guide led her up a flight of stairs and down another corridor. Dust danced about his shoes in tiny swirls. The back of Victoria's throat began tickling something fierce. She tried to swallow it away, but it persisted. Lifting her hand to her mouth, she coughed as quietly as she could. The sound seemed to fill the building like a locomotive in a tunnel, but the porter did not turn or even seem to hear.

Some distance down the hall, he turned and approached a door indistinguishable from the others. She half-hid behind him as he rapped on the door with his knuckles.

"Yes? Who is it?" The thick wood muffled the voice behind it.

"You have a caller, Mr. Townsend," the man in the spectacles replied. "A young woman."

There was a muted exclamation of surprise, and the door opened. The man on the other side was small and stout. Light from behind him glinted in his glasses as he smiled and extended his hand. "Mr. James Townsend, erstwhile professor of religious studies, University of Oxford."

Victoria didn't smile as he kissed her hand. "Victoria Dawes of Oxford, daughter of the late Henry and Abigail Dawes."

"Yes, of course," James replied, placing his other hand on top of hers. "My sincerest condolences for your great loss. Your father was a remarkable man, and your mother a most worthy wife to him. Please, come in." He stood to one side and waved a hand toward the room beyond.

Victoria smiled her thanks as she stepped through the door.

"Thank you, Benedict," James said to the other man. Benedict nodded without replying and began retreating down the hall, his footsteps fading into the darkness. Closing the door, James turned back to Victoria, who stood with her hands clasped in front of her. Her face must have reflected her distaste for the strange porter, because James let out a chuckle. "Oh, don't mind him. A queer fellow, to be sure, but harmless. You'd be hard-pressed to find a man in this building who wasn't a curious sort."

Victoria's smile felt shaky. An uneasiness had been growing in her since she came into Blackfriars Hall, and neither Benedict nor this James Townsend made her feel any more comfortable.

"Please, have a seat." James motioned toward a pair of high-backed chairs facing the fireplace. Victoria obliged him, settling gingerly onto one of the thick cushions. Electric lanterns filled the small room with a dingy yellow light, mixing with the sunlight glowing through the single window. The remains of a fire blinked at her with a dozen red eyes. Shelves on either side of the hearth sagged under the weight of the innumerable books piled on them. Victoria started searching for familiar titles, but quickly chided herself for expecting a scholar to own any of the Gothic romance novels she fancied.

James went to the desk and rummaged through the drawers. After two failed searches, he produced a dark green bottle and a pair of snifters from a third drawer. Glass clinked against glass as he filled the snifters. Crossing over to the other chair, he offered her one of the glasses before sitting.

"In memory of your parents," James said, lifting his glass. She touched hers against it and brought the liquid to her lips. Checking to make sure James was occupied with his own drink, she gave the contents a quick sniff. It smelled of apples and cinnamon. Satisfied, she drained her glass. The cider was sweetened with honey and not too strong. She thought it an odd thing for a man to drink in the privacy of his study, but perhaps he kept the bottle on hand for visiting women. The founding of St. Hugh's College at Oxford meant that he must entertain them regularly now, she supposed.

James set his glass on the carpet beside his chair. "I must apologize for the surroundings," he said. "I'm sure they aren't what you expected when I invited you to visit the office of an Oxford professor." She opened her mouth to reply, but he continued over her. "To be honest, they aren't what I expected when my associates offered me the position. One typically doesn't associate the world of Oxford University with closet-sized offices in rundown buildings, but here we are." He laughed at that. "I do sometimes wonder if I've moved up in station at all since leaving Lord Harcourt's employ. He did always say I was lacking in wit.

"But I digress," he said, straightening up and looking at her. "Perhaps I should apologize for my indiscretions instead of my surroundings. Here I am blathering on about myself when you have such a weight of your own to bear."

"It's quite all right," Victoria said. In truth, she didn't mind his prattling; it saved her from having to bring up an awkward topic. "You are aware of my reasons for coming to see you?"

"I gathered some of it from your letters. You wish to discuss the circumstances surrounding the death of your parents and feel that my particular expertise may be of some use." When Victoria nodded, the scholar sighed. "I'm not sure how much assistance I can provide, you understand, but I will do what I can."

"I appreciate your time." Taking a deep breath, Victoria made herself look him in the eye. "I believe my parents were killed by supernatural forces."

To his credit, James Townsend did not laugh or raise a skeptical brow. Instead, he merely cocked his head to one side and studied her through his spectacles. "What gave rise to this belief?"

"My own eyes," she replied. She recounted the events of that night, everything she could remember. The story sounded absurd even as she told it, but

James listened with rapt attention. When she finished, he leaned back in his chair and stroked his chin.

After a few minutes of silence, Victoria said, "I've not gone mad."

"No indeed," James replied. "I'd not even considered it, in fact."

"So you believe my story?"

He nodded. "It is a fantastic one, I must admit. In that, at least, it is fortunate you found my name among your father's letters. Had you approached any of my colleagues regarding this matter, I daresay you would have found them far more skeptical. Worthy men, all of them, but perhaps a bit too cloistered in their thinking. Such matters are more academic than pragmatic for them, you see."

"But not for you?"

"Oh, no. You see, I alone of them – to my knowledge, at least – have practical experience with these sorts of things."

Victoria leaned forward. "You have experience with the creatures that attacked my family?"

"No, not them per se," James admitted, "although I am familiar with the stories regarding such creatures." Standing up, he moved to one of the cluttered shelves and began scanning the titles. "One hears reports of them all over England, though their exact nature and behavior, even their names, vary from place to place. Generally, however, they are referred to as Black Dogs, and they are regarded as signs of ill omen when they appear."

"If only it ended there," Victoria said.

James nodded. "Yes, omens are much more easily dismissed, and from what I remember, these creatures will not usually venture beyond the harassment of travelers."

"In the strictest sense, I suppose they didn't go beyond that in my case, either," Victoria said. Part of her couldn't believe she was discussing her parents' death in such a detached, factual manner. Had her heart died somewhere in the weeks since? Perhaps so, but if that was the price she had to pay, she would pay it.

James grunted his agreement and pulled a book from a pile. The movement caused several others to begin sliding off the shelf. He put out a hand to halt the impending disaster. Pushing them back onto the shelf, he tentatively removed his hand. They remained where they were, and he returned to his chair. He began leafing through the book even before he sat down, the pages crackling softly.

"Yes, here we are," he said after a few moments. "This phenomenon has been reported throughout the Isle of Britain for hundreds of years. As I said, they typically don't attack directly, seeming to prefer inducing fear and panic rather than harm. Still, as you so recently discovered, sometimes even that behavior can lead to tragic ends." Turning the page, he continued. "There are accounts of such creatures behaving benevolently, specifically in Somerset, where it is known as Gurt Dog. Not a terribly imaginative name, but only some of these are interesting. Black Shuck and Padfoot seem to be rather prevalent, though not in this area. Still, I suppose they're as good as any listed here and better than most. Shall we refer to these creatures as such?"

"I suppose so, yes," Victoria said, dreading the continuation of what had become a lengthy lecture.

"Far more intriguing a name than, say, Hairy Jack. Now then, you said the creatures that attacked you had yellow eyes?"

"Yes," Victoria said with a nod. Goosebumps rose on her arms and legs at the thought of them. "They looked like storm lanterns or windows in distant houses."

"That does seem to be an oddity, then," James said, adjusting his glasses. "Most accounts report bright red eyes, although they share the luminous quality with your sighting. Always seen at night, too. Some seem to think they are related to storms or other atmospheric phenomena, although sightings are also associated with crossroads, ancient 'spirit' paths, and places of execution. I don't suppose you were near any of those things that night?"

"Not a crossroads, certainly," Victoria replied. "I don't know about spirit paths or places of execution."

"No, of course not. Why would you?" James offered her a rueful smile. "After all, only old oafs like me go in for these sorts of tales. Pretty young ladies such as yourself have more pressing issues to attend."

"My parents no doubt wish I'd paid such matters more heed. They would have liked to see me married off before their deaths, but I would have no part of it."

"No need to torture yourself over it," James said, patting her hand. "What's past is past."

"Had I just listened to them, we may never have gone on that drive." The words tumbled unbidden out of her mouth. "All they talked about was the offer of marriage I had received earlier that week. I intended to refuse it, more out of spite than anything else, I suppose, but they kept trying to persuade me otherwise. I don't suppose it would have been all that bad, really. He wasn't a bad sort, I'd certainly been propositioned by worse men, but I still felt hesitant. I've never liked the thought of marriage, but I should have tried harder."

Realizing what she was saying, Victoria clapped her hand over her mouth. She felt herself turning crimson and looked away. Tears crept into the corners of her eyes, and she brushed them away. She'd gone and made a fool of herself, showing that she still was just a feeble-minded woman after all. James would never help her now.

"I'm sorry," she managed, her voice quiet. She started to stand when she felt a hand on her arm.

"No need to apologize," James said. "Please, sit."

She settled back into the chair with all the dignity she could gather. "I didn't mean to say all that."

"I don't imagine you did," he said, "but sometimes our emotions do get the better of us." He pulled his hand back into his lap, where it began worrying a corner of the open page. "I do think you're being dreadfully hard on yourself. It wasn't your fault, you know."

Victoria nodded, managing a small smile. She knew it was, but it would be best not to argue with the only man who could help her.

"Right. Now, then." His voice slid back into a lecture tone. "As I was saying...ah yes, these creatures appear along roads most frequently, so that in itself would explain your encounter well enough. From your account, I assume they made no noise? No howling or snarling or such?" Victoria shook her head. "Right, so then we know it wasn't a skriker. They're supposed to make a dreadful din, hence the name."

"Would that have made any difference?"

"Not in the long run, I suppose, but it's always a good idea to place these sorts of encounters in as accurate a context as possible. Generalizations can be dangerous, you see. It wouldn't do to mix up a black shuck with, say, a werewolf. Quite different creatures with quite different methods for handling them, and mistaking one for the other could very well be deadly."

"So these black shucks can be killed, then?" Victoria asked, hoping to redirect his focus back to the purpose of her visit.

"This text is unclear in that regard, I'm afraid," James said. "Quite informative on the nature of their appearance and behavior, even bits on how to ward against them, but not a word on their mortality. Being spirit creatures, I suppose it's rather a moot point. It isn't as though they have physical bodies."

Victoria's shoulders slumped. "So they're invincible?"

"I wouldn't go that far." James looked at her over his glasses. "Why? Are you hoping to hunt them for sport?"

"Not sport," she said. "Vengeance. I said as much in my letter."

"Did you?" James asked absently, returning to his book. "Perhaps you did. In any case, one thing I've found in this line of study is that very few creatures on this earth are truly indestructible."

"But you just said the black shuck is immortal because it hasn't a body."

"Mortality works differently on the spiritual plane, my dear. I almost hesitate to even use the word. It's sort of like asking how the color green would taste, if you follow me. It isn't really applicable in such cases, but we must use what limited mortal language can provide to discuss these higher matters."

Victoria bit back her reply. She wished he would simply get to answering her question, but she couldn't just say it. After a moment's consideration, she settled on a more acceptable response. "What word might be more appropriate in this case?"

The scholar's eyes explored the ceiling as he considered his answer. "Banishment, perhaps?" he said at length. "Sealing? It really depends on what your aim is. Spirit creatures may be influenced by humans, as we are part spirit ourselves. Indeed, the more unlucky ones – humans, I mean – end up as spirit creatures in many cases. Surely you've heard of ghosts and hauntings?"

"Of course," Victoria said, "but how does one deal with such encounters?"

"Via spiritual medium, most frequently," James replied. "A medium establishes contact with the spirit of the deceased and discovers why it chose to linger on the earth instead of departing for the afterlife. Should the spirit prove hostile or dangerous, a medium can work with a member of the clergy to consecrate the building against further intrusion."

"But the spirit doesn't actually die?" Victoria felt hope slipping through her fingers.

"Not in the strictest sense, perhaps, but really, what is death? Simply a change in state. If you'll pardon the example, consider your parents. When they perished in that horrible accident, their spirits were not snuffed out. They merely transitioned beyond the physical plane into a spirit realm, which most refer to as Heaven or paradise. The precise nature of that plane is not clear, though many hypothesize that it embodies an entire range of dwellings – for lack of a better term – rather than a binary system of paradise or punishment.

"When interacting with the spirit plane, therefore, it is entirely possible to prevent entities from crossing over back into this world. Just as a physical death typically signifies the cessation of exchange with the physical plane, so too does this banishment act as a sort of 'death' in that it prevents an entity from interacting with one tier of existence."

"So it would be possible to kill these creatures, then?" Victoria asked, leaning forward again.

"As much as one is able to, yes," James replied, "although you would need someone highly skilled in such things, especially in your case. This padfoot creature isn't your run-of-the-mill ghost."

Victoria's brow creased in confusion. "Can't you help me?"

"Oh, my word, no," James replied, flustered. He gestured at the mountains of books surrounding them. "As you can see, my interest is primarily scholarly."

"But I thought you said–"

"That I had practical experience in these matters, and so I do." The scholar's face distorted, unable to settle on a look of pride or sheepishness. "First-hand experience, as a matter of fact. While I was in the employ of Lord Alberick Harcourt, I had the opportunity to assist in the vanquishing of a rogue *nosferatu*, what you might call a king vampire. It was that very encounter that earned me my place at Oxford, if you want to know the truth. The other Occult scholars here felt that having one in their number who had first-hand knowledge of the *nosferatu* would be invaluable to their studies."

"Could one of them help me, then?"

James took a breath and looked down at the book in his lap. "I'm afraid that is highly unlikely."

"Why?"

The scholar didn't answer for a moment. His fingers toyed with the book's pages. "Frankly, my dear," he finally said, looking up at her, "because you are a woman."

Victoria's cheeks colored. "I don't see what that has to do with it."

James shifted in his chair, clearly uncomfortable.

"Yes, well, these are traditional sorts of men. Their scholarship is excellent, but their views are very conservative. They were among the opposition when the founding of St. Hugh's College was first proposed, and I daresay they refuse even now to acknowledge it as an institution."

"And because of my sex, they would refuse to assist me?"

"In essence," James said, looking unhappy.

For the second time since she entered the office, Victoria felt tears burning in her eyes. This time, however, they made her want to scream at the man sitting across from her, to take his precious books and throw them into the fireplace, to shatter his ridiculous bottle of cider across his desk. Her revenge was so close, and James Townsend's colleagues could help her realize it, but they wouldn't. Not because she was too young, too stupid, or too poor, but simply because she hadn't been born a man. Her fingers clutched helplessly at the folds of her dress. Was she really to just give up and return to her home, awaiting the day when she would marry some witless buffoon more interested in her estate than in her person? Could she live with herself after that, having failed her parents in the promise made over their bodies?

James was still looking at her.

"I'm sorry," she said, unable to meet his eyes. "I appreciate your hospitality and your assistance. That just wasn't the answer I was hoping to hear." James opened his mouth, but she held up her hand. "No, really, it's all right. I will figure out a way to avenge my parents on my own. Your information about spirit mediums will be very useful, I'm sure. There must be someone in this country that isn't opposed to working with a woman."

Standing, she dropped James a perfunctory curtsey and turned to leave. Her hand was on the doorknob when his voice stopped her.

"I may know someone."

She paused, not turning. "Another of your scholars?"

"Quite the opposite, in fact."

Did she hear a hint of laughter in his voice? It was enough to make her turn and look at him. "Who, then?"

Instead of replying, James stood and crossed over to his desk. Refilling his glass from the bottle, he raised a silent toast in the direction of the afternoon sun. The golden liquid disappeared down his throat, and he turned back to her. "Another woman."

THREE

The young girl looked up in confusion. Her mother stood over her, gently shaking her awake. The girl blinked sleep from her eyes. She smiled sleepily, but the hard look on her mother's face did not soften. Her mother's hair fell in black waves over her shoulders, its glossy sheen catching the soft light peeking through the door.

The girl sat up, confused and frightened. Her mother should be smiling. She always smiled in the morning while they were still warm, before they had to go out into the cold. She would always wake the girl with a smile and a piece of corn-meal bread. That day, her mother had no bread and no smile. She was serious and sad, and that made the girl afraid.

Sunlight filled the small room as the blanket covering the door was pulled to one side. The girl's father stepped up beside her mother and looked down. The girl held her breath, clutching at her blanket with small, strong fingers. She knew something was different. The faces her parents wore told her. But what could upset them? They were the biggest and smartest people she knew. Her father was a singer, a man of the spirits; he knew a lot and told her about things when she asked. Her mother was strong and kind and pretty, a source of comfort when the boys in the village told stories of monsters to scare her. Her mother didn't fear the witches they spoke of, so why was she afraid now?

"Come," her father said. "We must go."

"Where?" the girl asked.

"I do not know," her father said. Beside him, her mother was making a face like she was trying not to cry. It was enough to bring out the young girl's tears.

"Hush," her mother said. "No need for that. Be brave for us."

The girl sniffed back her tears and bit her lip. She could be brave like her mother. To show it, she lifted her arms, and her mother picked her up. The girl's father bent to retrieve the blanket, and the girl grabbed at it greedily. He smiled then, but he didn't look happy.

Stepping over to the entrance, he pulled the blanket aside and walked through. The girl's mother followed, carrying her securely. The girl kept one arm curled around her mother's neck and the other around her blanket as they left the warmth of their home and stepped into the cold winter air.

There were a lot of men outside. Some of them she knew, men from her tribe, but most of them were strangers. They wore funny clothes and had skin the color of the soft fur on a rabbit's belly. They carried metal sticks that they pointed at the people from her village. She saw her friend's mother throwing some corn cakes into a basket. Other women were wrapping clothes in blankets. Men loaded bundles onto fuzzy grey donkeys.

One of the new men came riding up on a horse. He yelled something that the girl didn't understand, and the other pale men began moving toward the villagers.

The girl felt her mother's arms squeeze her tightly. "He says we must leave now," her father said.

Victoria clasped her handbag in front of her, gloved fingers absently working their way back and forth over the top. Behind her, the city of Denver carried on its daily life with fervor. Horses clipped and clopped along the cobblestone streets, carrying riders or drawing carriages and buggies behind them. Around their massive hooves, dogs barked and scurried in motley packs. Mothers hung out of second-story windows, calling to their children in the streets to wash up and be careful and don't forget to pick up an extra loaf of bread for their visiting cousins. In the distance, the harsh call of a locomotive echoed into the blue sky. Underscoring the other sounds was the steady patter of feet in shoes and feet in boots and feet in nothing at all.

The city had taken her by surprise when she'd first arrived. Arranging the train from New York had been a simple enough affair, and the coach had been comfortable despite James Townsend's warnings. She changed trains twice, once in Cincinnati and once in Kansas City, her luggage cared for by pairs of young bag boys who kept stealing glances at her as they worked. She gave them each a smile and a tip when they finished, their faces telling her that they would have just as easily taken a kiss in place of her money.

When the locomotive had finally pulled into Denver, she had stepped out of the train car and sucked in her breath. In the distance, marching beyond the quaint city skyline like an army of blue giants, a line of mountains glowered at her. Beneath their proud peaks, curving slopes of green and brown ended abruptly in jagged cliffs, sheared and cauterized like an amputee's limbs. They sprawled across the western horizon from end to end, fading into the haze hundreds of miles away. She had never seen anything so frightening or magnificent in her life.

Now the city hid them from sight, but she could feel them lurking somewhere beyond the quaint buildings. She imagined the ground beneath her feet suddenly losing its balance and tilting upward, sending her tumbling toward the mountains like a pebble on a drawbridge. The entire city would slide downward, the screams and crashes drowned out by the horrible rumbling of the earth as it came undone.

Victoria shook her head. She had to get a grip on herself. No use adding to her real worries with imagined ones. Taking a breath, she focused her gaze on the golden cross that crowned the church in front of her. It was modest, perhaps three yards tall, but had its own understated appeal. The gold shone brightly in the morning sun, throwing shafts of light on the buildings across the street. Beneath it, saints watched the world with solemn eyes, their windows set into walls of brown stone. Such a modest church might have suited a small town in England, but it seemed at home among the crude buildings that surrounded it.

She walked up to the front door and pulled. The slab of wood, richly stained, refused to budge. Planting her feet, she wrapped both hands around the handle and leaned back. A breath of incense swirled around her as the door finally opened.

Once inside, the darkness of the foyer blinded her for a moment. She stood still, breathing in the scents of tallow and incense and candle smoke while her eyes adjusted. Carpet the color of wine spread out beneath her feet. Ahead of her, an arch opened into the small sanctuary. She took a few tentative steps through it, careful not to let her feet make any noise on the carpet. The room beyond was still and dark, but the saints still watched her from their windows. Candles flickered like stars along the rows of pews and around the altar. At the far end, a crucifix hung from the ceiling, the savior watching over this house of saints. A purple sash hung down from his arms, adding an air of royalty to the man carved in eternal agony.

"Welcome, child," came a voice near the altar. "Please, come in."

A nun robed in black and white stepped down from the dais and stood at the end of the aisle, her hands clasped in front of her. Victoria crept toward her, a sudden shyness slowing her steps. Having been raised Protestant, she felt out of place in this church, as though her mere presence angered the faces in the windows. The nun's face was kind and wrinkled, and she focused on that. She even offered the older woman a smile as she came nearer.

"I am Sister Alice," the nun said.

"Victoria Dawes," Victoria replied, dropping a curtsey.

"You're from England?" Sister Alice asked.

Victoria nodded. "I've only just arrived in Denver. I'm from Oxford, originally."

"What brings you to the house of God?"

How to answer that? Victoria looked down at her hands for a moment, biting back the first answer that appeared on her tongue. Catholics and their pride. She swallowed before looking back up. "Well, I'm looking for someone, and I was instructed to begin my search here."

Confusion deepened Sister Alice's wrinkles. "A member of the clergy?"

"Not exactly," Victoria said, "although I believe this person has worked closely with the priesthood in years past. Her name is Cora Oglesby."

"Can't say I've heard of her," Sister Alice replied. "What work did she do?"

Doubt began creeping into Victoria's thoughts. Had James Townsend been mistaken? "Well," she said, "as I understand it, she is a sort of bounty hunter. One of those rough-and-tumble gunfighters that populate the American frontier."

"That's strange. I don't know what need the Church would have of a bounty hunter. You said she worked for our parish?"

"To be honest, I'm not sure." Victoria watched the nun's confusion with a sinking feeling. "I'm working on information I received from an Oxford scholar who claims to have worked with this woman in the past. I have very urgent business with her, and he advised me to ask the Catholic clergy to help me find her."

Sister Alice gave her an apologetic smile. "I'm sorry, child. Can't say I've ever heard of any bounty hunter working for the Church, especially not one who's a woman."

"Is there anyone you might ask?" Victoria said.

"Father Baez may know," Sister Alice said, "but he's probably still asleep."

"I know it's terribly rude to ask, but could you see if he would speak with me?" Victoria unconsciously twisted her fingers together. "It really is dreadfully important."

Sister Alice looked off to her right for a moment. Victoria could almost see the scales balancing in the nun's head as she weighed the request. If Sister Alice refused to help her, Victoria would chain herself to one of the pews until this Father Baez appeared. If he couldn't help her, she would just have to move on to the next city.

"Well," Sister Alice said, turning back to her, "I don't normally like to bother him, but since you've come all this way, I suppose I can go check on him. Don't expect much, though."

"Thank you so much," Victoria said.

The nun nodded. "Have yourself a seat," she said, pointing to a pew. "I'll be back soon."

Victoria sat, the wood creaking slightly under her. Sister Alice disappeared through a door on one

side of the altar, her habit vanishing into the shadows beyond.

Leaning back into the pew, Victoria folded her
hands in her lap. She tried to imagine what her father
or mother would say if they found her in such a
place, waiting to hear whether or not a Catholic priest
knew where to find an American bounty hunter. She
shook her head and smiled. It really did sound absurd, and that she was traveling alone made it all the
more so.

Still, she had reason to believe she could follow
through with what she'd started. After all, she'd
managed the trip across the Atlantic with little difficulty. It had taken the *Jewel of Scotland* just over two
weeks to make the passage. Victoria spent much of
her time aboard in her cabin, searching histories
from her father's collection for any references to
black shucks. When her eyes grew tired, she would
venture above deck to watch the ocean swell beneath the ship. Spring storms blossomed on the
horizon, dark and menacing, but the *Jewel* slid by
them without incident.

When she'd made port in New York City, she gave
the immigrations office slight pause. They were unused to a woman traveling alone, but in the end
they'd waved her through. One of their officers had
pointed her in the direction of the rail station, and
she'd easily found a coach to take her through the
maze of streets. Grand Central Station had been
grand indeed, and the endless press of bodies took
her breath away. Once she'd regained her head, she

found a train bound for Denver and bought herself a ticket. Indeed, the hardest part of her journey had been adjusting to the coarse way Americans had of speaking.

Echoing footsteps pulled her back into the present. Looking up, she saw Sister Alice emerge from the doorway. A man entered with her, clutching her arm in one hand and the head of a cane in the other. Victoria rose to her feet as they approached.

"Victoria Dawes," Sister Alice said, "may I present Father Emmanuel Baez."

"The honor is mine," Victoria said, extending her hand.

The priest released his hold on Sister Alice's arm and kissed the young woman's hand. Drawing himself up as straight as he could, he looked at her and smiled. "A pleasure, my dear."

Sister Alice guided him to the pew and helped him to sit. Victoria took a seat nearby, careful to maintain what she considered a respectful distance. The priest leaned back against the pew, his white hair and beard seeming to shine above his robes. He looked at her again, and she could see a spark in his dark eyes. "Now, then," he said, "Sister Alice tells me you have some business with me."

"Yes," Victoria said. "I don't want to waste your time, so I'll come straight to it. I'm looking for a woman named Cora Oglesby."

Father Baez's eyes went wide, and he drew in a deep breath. "There's a name I haven't heard in years." He smiled then, a thin line beneath his beard.

"So you know of her?"

"Of course." The priest cleared his throat and sat upright. "She and I have a history. Not a very happy one, but a good one."

"Do you know where I might find her?" Victoria asked.

Father Baez started to answer, then paused. "Might I ask why you want to find her?"

"I have urgent business with her," Victoria answered, trying to sound as harmless as she could.

The priest considered that, then turned to Sister Alice. "Would you excuse us for a moment, sister?" Taken aback, the nun stood to her feet, nodded, and stalked across the dais. Once she disappeared through the side door, Father Baez turned back to Victoria. "Cora Oglesby deals in some very dark business, young lady. I pray you'll forgive my reluctance, but not everyone who knows about her has benevolent intentions."

"I understand," Victoria said. "It's precisely her dealings in those dark matters that caused me to seek her out. I need her help, you see."

The white eyebrows twitched. "Oh?" Victoria nodded and looked down, unsure if she should elaborate. Father Baez gently touched her hand. "You don't need to worry about telling me, child. We priests are used to keeping secrets," he said, eyes twinkling.

Victoria smiled. Her tale was outlandish, she knew, but if this priest really did know this Cora Oglesby, perhaps he wouldn't be a stranger to outlandish tales. She recounted her encounter with the black shucks on the road, the death of her parents, and her meeting with James Townsend. A tremor crept into her voice as she spoke. She'd only told the story in its entirety once before, and hearing herself say it aloud again drove the reality and horror of it that much closer to her heart.

When she finished, Father Baez nodded, stroking his beard with one age-spotted hand. Victoria watched him, keeping her hands still with no small effort. "Well," he said at length, "it does certainly sound like Cora's kind of job."

Victoria's breath left her lungs in a rush. "So you'll help me, then?"

He nodded. "I'll tell you what I know, but I'm afraid I haven't heard from her in a good while. Nearly four years, I think."

"Any information at all would be wonderful," she said, her eyes alight.

"Cora can be a difficult woman to find," Father Baez said, "so remember that as you search for her. When I knew her, she was never content to stay in one place for long, but certain events may have calmed her spirit a little."

"What events?"

"I'm afraid I can't tell you that," he replied. "A shepherd must keep the secrets of his sheep." When she nodded, he continued. "Before she left Denver, Cora told me that she planned to use her most recent bounty prize to open a printer's shop."

Victoria was dumbfounded. "A print shop? What would a woman like her want with a print shop?"

"Maybe age has slowed her down like it has me," Father Baez said. "You should count yourself lucky if it has."

"Why? Is she dangerous?"

"The Cora I remember could shoot the ears off a squirrel from fifty feet away, but she never turned her guns on anyone without reason as far as I know. She may be wild, but she's not a murderer or a train robber. Still," he added, looking at her with the same twinkle in his eye, "I wouldn't suggest making her angry."

The earth shimmered beneath the desert sun, submerging the horizon in pulsing, hazy waves. Victoria smiled to herself as she watched the miles roll by outside the window. She had come prepared to face the legendary heat of the American West. Reaching down beneath her seat, she patted her parasol with a gloved hand, reassuring herself that it was ready for her. One could never be too cautious when entering such extreme climates, after all.

Much like the mountains of Denver, the vast emptiness of the desert was alien to her eyes. Minute upon minute, hour upon hour, the trained sped across the sun-baked land, and still it did not end. She had been surprised to see anything at all growing out of the ground here, yet plant life carpeted much of the surrounding land. True, the shrubs seemed barely able to cling to life, their leaves a mottled yellow-brown or missing altogether, but still they persisted. Friendly cacti reared their heads above the scrub brush to wave at her with one or two arms as they kept watch over the endless miles.

The door at the front of her passenger car opened, drawing her attention from the window. A man in a dark blue uniform and matching hat stepped through the doorway.

"Next stop, Albuquerque. Albuquerque, next stop," he announced. "Tickets will be checked at the station for those continuing on to San Francisco." Task complete, he marched down the aisle toward the next car.

Victoria stretched her arms skyward and groaned. She wasn't used to this much travel at one time, and her muscles ached from the uncomfortable seats. Around her, the other passengers stirred themselves out of the stupor that had blanketed them for the last two hundred miles. Hushed conversations sprang up like whispers of wind in withered branches, murmuring about luggage and next steps. Victoria pulled her own small valise out from beneath her seat, wrapping her fingers around the handle of her parasol. When she disembarked, the luggage boys would help her carry the larger trunks to a nearby hotel.

Her fingers trembled with anticipation. She had very nearly reached the end of her westward journey. Father Baez's advice led her south, to the wilderness of Santa Fe. When she arrived, the priest there, a Father Perez, had told her to board a train for Albuquerque as soon as he heard her say the name Cora Oglesby. The huntress had set off for the frontier town not long after arriving in Santa Fe four years before, and Father Perez seemed certain that she was still there.

The car trembled as the train pulled into the Albuquerque station. Through the windows, she could hear the shrill voice of the train's whistle crying out that they had arrived. Conversations in the car grew louder as the passengers began moving toward the exit. A few remained in their seats, staring out the windows or watching the others shuffle past. Victoria waited for the gaggle to pass before standing. Valise in hand, she made for the door, eyes fixed on the glowing swath of sunlight spilling through it.

A blast of hot air greeted her as she stepped out of the car and onto the station platform. The glare was blinding. She quickly unfolded her parasol, blinking as it rose to block out the sun. Groups of passengers stood on the platform, talking among themselves while waiting for their luggage. Next to her, three men in pressed suits discussed the possibilities for expanding their business into this wild, untamed land. Their voices clipped along excitedly as ideas flew between them. She knew the language well enough; it brought back memories of her father and his many meetings. A lump swelled in her throat at the thought. Despite her sorrow, Victoria's lips curled upward in a small smile. Were it not for his ambition, she would not be standing where she was. His fortune had enabled her to cross oceans and continents.

The platform shook beneath her. Luggage boys were unloading the freight car, tossing bags and suitcases out into the sun. Already the crowd of passengers pressed in around the growing pile, searching through it for their belongings. Victoria watched them from beneath her parasol. Once the bustle subsided, she would ask one of the bag boys to help her along to the nearest hotel, promising a smile and a tip for his efforts. As she watched the crowd thin, she wondered idly just what sort of accommodations a town like this had to offer. A glance over the haphazard group of buildings standing nearest the station seemed to promise that they wouldn't be much. No matter. She wouldn't be here long. If all went well, she and the Oglesby woman would be leaving on the next day's train.

The sun drifted lazily toward the western horizon, drawing shades of deep blue and violet into the sky. Drops of sweat stood out on Victoria's forehead as she stood in front of the sand-blasted building. The streets of Albuquerque had not yet relinquished the afternoon heat, and the people wandering them moved like plague sufferers and smelled worse. She had seldom been surrounded by such an overpowering cloud of human stink. Even in the street, the stench of sweat, spit, and animals pressed up against her. It put her on edge; she could almost feel it crawling up her legs and under the neckline of her dress. How any woman, even one as uncouth as Cora Oglesby, could stand living in such a miasma confounded her.

More confusing, however, were the words painted on the sign that hung above the door in front of her.

In bold black letters, it proclaimed the name of the establishment: BEN'S PRINT SHOP. Although Victoria had never seen a printing press, she knew right away that this particular building had never set ink to a page. The men passing through the batwing doors couldn't possibly be literate. They peered at the world from beneath wide-brimmed hats, their eyes bleary from sun and liquor. Many wore guns in low-slung holsters that dangled from their belts, the leather cracked and faded. She had never seen so many guns in one place, and that men such as these carried them made her uneasy. What if they decided to turn them on her? As a young girl, she'd heard stories of hold-ups and shoot-outs in the American West, but she'd only half-believed them. Now, in the presence of men who looked as though they might re-enact such stories at the prompting of a single booze-soaked thought, she suddenly felt very alone. The memory of James Townsend's round, kindly face sprang to her mind's eye, and she fervently wished she had taken his advice and brought along an escort.

No, she told herself. She could handle herself. Cora Oglesby made a home for herself among such men. Surely Victoria could brave them for a day or two.

As if on cue, a scraggly-looking man tumbled through the batwing doors and into the street. Victoria backed up a few paces, startled. Before the man could pull himself together, an empty bottle sailed through the door, shattering on the packed earth only a few feet from his head. A voice from inside cracked like an old whip as it shouted curses at the man. Victoria could only watch as the man picked himself up and shambled off down the street. As he disappeared into the general bustle in the street, a grim satisfaction welled up inside her. Although the voice from the door sounded as old and tough as a rusted iron cog, there was no mistaking that it belonged to a woman.

The other passersby didn't give the commotion a second glance, but Victoria could feel them gawking at her when she turned her back. Worse, she couldn't exactly blame them. Choosing from among her finer traveling dresses to wear in such a rustic place practically begged for unwanted attention. The sight of the blue ruffles and bright white collar must have seemed the height of silliness to those walking about in such drab colors, but she would feel even sillier if she went back to her room to change. Better to see this through before she lost her nerve.

Squaring her shoulders, Victoria stepped up onto the wooden sidewalk and through the batwing doors. Inside, a cloud of blue smoke drifted along the ceiling, constantly fed by the cigars, cigarettes, and pipes of the men gathered around card games. A bar ran the length of the wall to her left. Bottles of liquor gleamed under the light of the kerosene lamps lining the walls. Against the far corner, a man in a bowler hat and suspenders plinked at an upright piano, occasionally stumbling upon something that resembled a melody.

A hush fell over the room as the doors swung shut behind her. Heads turned and chairs scraped along the floor as the men took in the sight of her. Their eyes were cold and probing. She could feel them exploring every inch of her body, lingering on the swells of her hips and chest. Her tongue darted across her lips. "Good day, gentlemen."

"Wrong door, sweetheart," came a voice.

"Brothel's across the way," said another, getting a laugh from the rest.

"If you're taking customers, there's a storeroom in the back."

Victoria's cheeks flushed a deep red. Her eyes dropped to the floorboards.

"Aw, see, you all went and made her color up." The voice was the one she'd heard out in the street. "That ain't no way to treat a lady of the night, now is it?"

Another laugh rolled around the room. Indignation began to boil beneath Victoria's humiliation. It rose inside her until she found the courage to look toward the speaker, blue eyes sparking with anger.

The object of her rage sat at one of the tables, surrounded by four men. Unlike her companions, she hadn't turned her chair to face the young woman when she entered. Her attention was focused on the cards sprouting from her right hand like a greasy bouquet. The woman's other hand held an empty shot glass in a loose fist, her index finger toying with the rim.

The silence in the room showed no sign of ending, so Victoria took a step toward the woman. "I beg your pardon," she said.

"You don't look like you need to beg for anything," the woman replied, turning to face her. Age and sun had folded the skin of her face into itself like sheets on a well-made bed. Her hair was the color of a photograph: black and white and grey. A single streak of white ran from the edge of her hairline into the long braid that ended halfway down her back. Dark eyes glimmered at her as the woman broke into a grin. "I reckon every man here could beg you for a year's pay and you'd still have enough to buy us all a round."

"I am not a prostitute."

The woman snorted. "Sure you ain't. Just because you only spread your legs for one rich feller don't make you any less a bawd. How many times you rut with him afore he bought you that fancy dress?"

Victoria's blue eyes narrowed, her cheeks fading from red to white. "None. Not that it's any of your concern, but I am not and have never been married, so I am no man's whore."

"Well, you ain't wearing that fancy getup for nothing. I'm more than a mite curious what would bring such a proper lady into the Print Shop if she ain't looking to ply her trade. You just get a hankering for some of my famous whiskey, or is you here on other business?"

"As a matter of fact, I am," Victoria said, her back as straight as a flagpole. "I happen to be looking for someone."

"Among this lot?" The woman's laugh was as coarse as the stubble on the men's faces. "I don't

reckon we got anything you'd be after, young missie.
Now, you got something some of these boys here'd
be after, though, so I'd watch your back if I was you."

Victoria refused to let their eyes bother her. "I was
instructed to come here. By a priest."

Another laugh. "Sounds like you got yourself
mixed in with the wrong church. Ain't no priest in
his right mind would tell a pretty thing like you to
come down where pretty things wither and rot if
they ain't trampled on first. Maybe he was aiming to
make a warning out of your tale when it's through."

"His name," Victoria said after a pause, "was Father Baez."

For the first time, the woman's face grew still. In
the silence that followed, Victoria smiled to herself.
This woman was Cora Oglesby; no doubt about it.
What's more, she'd taken the huntress off-guard.

Cora swallowed. "Well, ain't that interesting."

"It is," Victoria replied.

"Who might you be looking for?"

The young woman leaned forward slightly. "A
woman he once knew. Something of a bounty
hunter, I understand."

A few of the men around her laughed, but Cora's
face was stone. "What makes him think she's here?"

"Such a woman would truly be a rarity," Victoria
said. "There aren't too many like her, even here in
the American West. Really, I might have just as easily
found my way here without his help."

"It would have gone better for you if you had,"
Cora said. "I don't expect your woman takes kindly

to being hunted. If she's got that big a reputation, mayhap she'd set on you just for having the gall to track her down."

Victoria tried to snuff out the spark of fear that Cora's words had ignited. "That would be quite impolite of her. It isn't as though I've come this far just for a chance to kill her."

Cora nodded. "There's a smart girl." She set her cards face down on the table. "I'm out this round, boys. Gonna have me a chat with our new friend. Just holler at Eli if your throats start getting dry."

Her chair skidded backward as she stood to her feet. Cora Oglesby was not tall, perhaps only an inch or two taller than Victoria. Buckskin trousers and a faded flannel shirt hung from her frame, accented by a bandana tied around her neck. Her boots thumped across the floor, and she motioned for Victoria to follow her. Steeling her nerves, Victoria trailed Cora through a door in the rear wall of the saloon.

"Hold the door a minute," Cora said. The old huntress pulled a book of matches from her shirt pocket. Striking one against the wall, she lit a lamp hanging from the ceiling. Yellow light filled the room, illuminating stacks of wooden crates and barrels. Turning back to her visitor, Cora nodded. Victoria pulled the door closed, muffling the voices of the saloon's patrons.

"Now, then." Cora folded her arms and leaned against a stack of crates. This close, Victoria could see a line of thin white scars on the other woman's cheek. "I ain't the type to toss around words when they don't need tossing. You mind telling me why you saw fit to pester poor old Father Baez just so you could get your mitts on me?"

"I have a favor to ask of you," Victoria said. She paused, waiting for the woman's harsh laugh, but it never came.

"You going to come out with it, or can I get back to my game?"

The young woman took a deep breath. "I need your help hunting a group of creatures."

"Awful long way to come just to find a big game hunter," Cora said. "Ain't you English folk got enough of your own hunters? Why bother me about it?"

"Big game hunters couldn't help me with these sorts of creatures," Victoria replied.

Cora raised an eyebrow. "What are you getting at?"

"I'm told you are skilled at killing beasts of a...supernatural nature."

"Father Baez tell you that?"

"No," Victoria said. "I first heard your name from a friend of my father's. He is a scholar at Oxford–"

Before she could finish, Cora's lips pulled back in a grin. Unlike her earlier laughter, this smile seemed born of fondness. "Well, I'll be damned. Your daddy was a friend of old King George?"

"King George?" Victoria's brow furrowed. "I'm afraid I don't follow."

"That's what I called him," Cora said. "Easier on the tongue and all. Ain't nobody got the time to spit out all of James Townsend. Besides, he sure carried himself like he was royalty, so I thought it fit."

Despite her apprehension, Victoria felt herself smile. "I suppose he could give that impression. I don't know him well, but he is a very well-educated man. He identified the creatures I spoke of and suggested I seek you out to assist me in subduing them."

"Did he, now?" Cora leaned back. "We did have ourselves a time back in Leadville. Shot up a whole mess of vampires and a wendigo besides. Even old King George stuck himself a few suckers with that cross of his. Never did kill a one of them, though."

"He didn't?" Victoria asked. "He told me he had first-hand experience in such dealings."

"In a way, I guess that's true," Cora said. "Like I said, he was there for a lot of the scrapes we got into, both in town and up at the mine, but I had to do most of the work my own self. You Brits ain't worth half a shake when doing needs done."

Victoria squared her shoulders at the older woman. "I'll thank you not to judge all of my countrymen by the actions of one."

"You're welcome, then," Cora said, "but that don't change the facts none."

Victoria pinched the bridge of her nose between her thumb and forefinger. She wasn't sure if this woman was being deliberately obtuse or if she just wasn't that bright. Most likely both. It was time to try a different approach. "I'm not disputing the fact that you are more than capable. Had I thought James could have helped me himself, I wouldn't have traveled these long miles to seek you out." Only half a lie.

"Good to know George ain't taken leave of his sense." Cora shifted her weight toward the door. "We done now?"

"Will you help me?"

Cora's smile exposed the gap between her front teeth. "And here I thought Brits was at least good for their brains. Ain't you figured it out yet?"

Victoria hesitated. She heard the answer in Cora's tone, but she had to ask. "What?"

"My hunting days are over."

For a moment, Victoria could only stand there blinking. Cora watched her, the smile never leaving her face. Victoria knew she had to say something, something that would change this old woman's mind before it was too late. The silence hung between them as the sounds of the saloon filtered through the door, voices and laughter and the meandering melody of the piano. Victoria's mouth felt full of cotton.

Cora's boots thumped against the floorboards. She stepped over to the door and reached out her hand to open it. Victoria moved without thinking, grabbing her wrist. "Wait."

The hunter's brown eyes snapped up. "Take your pretty little hands off me," Cora said, her tone flat.

Victoria's grip tightened. "Help me."

Cora's other hand cracked across her face. The force of the blow knocked her backward into a crate. Cradling her stinging cheek, Victoria blinked back tears. She turned her head and looked at the other woman, accusation in her blue eyes.

Cora matched her gaze evenly. "I mean what I say," she said. "Don't you ever touch me, and I ain't helping you with no monster hunt. My hunting days is through."

"So you're a coward, then?" Victoria asked, rage overwhelming her sense. "You're just a drunken old fool who strikes other women who come to her begging for help." She stood to her full height, removing her hand from her face. Her cheek blazed bright red. "I came to you across countless miles, crossing an ocean and half a continent because I heard the stories of you. I heard the legends of your bravery and your heroism, and I believed them. I believed that I would find a holy warrior when I reached this place, a heroine who would help me avenge the deaths of my parents." Victoria's voice grew quieter as she spoke, her words sliding a stone lid over her hopes as her father's brothers had slid stone lids over her parents. "I suppose I was the fool, a naïve girl still believing in fairy tales. If nothing else, I gained wisdom on this journey. A poor consolation, but with only cowards and old men left to me, I should be grateful to have learned it while I am still young."

The hunter listened to her tirade, her face blank. When Victoria finished, Cora took a deep breath and looked down at her boots. The white streak in her hair shone softly in the light. Victoria stood still, surprised at herself for what she had just said. Father Baez's warnings popped back into her head, and she swallowed. Her speech may very well get her shot by this woman. To die in the storeroom of an American saloon wasn't how she pictured her end, but maybe she should have seen it coming when she stepped off the train in this miserable little town.

"What's your name, girl?" Cora's voice was quiet.

"Victoria Dawes."

"Well, Victoria Dawes," she said, eyes glinting, "consider yourself lucky. Ain't nobody in this town gets to call me a coward to my face without getting themselves a right fine licking. What I gave you was a tender little kiss compared to what I've given some." Cora shifted her weight, leaning toward the young woman to drive her point home. "You try it again, it ain't going to matter none that you is a woman, fancy or otherwise. You ain't the first woman I've whipped, and you ain't going to be the last.

"Now, you're as green as any grease-licked city sprout could be, so that's why I'm letting you off so easy like. Not so easy as some would have, maybe, but a lot more easier than most others. This here is rough country, and the sooner you skedaddle on back to England, the better. You came out here looking for heroes. Well, there ain't no heroes. Not here, not anywhere. I reckon I'm the nicest old coot you're like to meet out here. Half the men in the other room would have taken your womanly charms without a second thought had they come across you in some back alley. The other half maybe ain't that bad, but they sure ain't above taking a fine lady's finery, neither. I'm plumb amazed you ain't had yourself a run-in with such folk yet."

"Father always said I was lucky," Victoria said with a small smile.

Cora nodded. "Your daddy sounds like he left the second part out, the part where he says you ain't all that bright. Ain't you fancy people got bodyguards and such to keep you from doing fool things? What got it into your head that you could just march on out here with nothing but your own self?"

Victoria raised her chin. "I am not a coward. My parents are dead, and I am the only one who cares to see them avenged."

"Revenge's a right fine thing," Cora said, "but all you're like to find out here is your own death. You got anyone cares enough back home to come hunt down the bastard that does you in?" Victoria shook her head. "Well, then, all the more reason to call off before that happens."

"Where am I to go?" Victoria asked. "Where can I turn now?"

"Turn back home," Cora said. "Surely there's somebody in that big fancy country of yours as could help you out."

"No," Victoria replied, her hands curling into fists. "Your friend's colleagues refuse to associate with women in such matters, and I don't know of anyone else who might help. Most wouldn't even believe the story if I told it to them."

Cora brushed her hands on her trousers. "Sounds to me like you is out of luck, then. Best get on with your life and make your parents happy that way."

"I can't. I refuse. I swore to them over their graves

that I would avenge them. I can't very well return empty-handed."

"Well, you ain't returning no other way unless you find yourself a hero someplace else."

Tears sprang again to Victoria's eyes, and she hated herself for them. "It would seem to be an empty hope, wouldn't it? If all American heroes are like you, I might have simply checked the corner pub in Oxford and spared myself the trouble."

"I reckon," Cora said, nodding. "Like I said, ain't no heroes nowhere. Just folk like you and folk like me."

"Why would James send me to you, then?" Victoria asked. "He certainly believes you to be a hero of sorts."

"George ain't too keen on certain things," Cora said. "Knows a fair bit about some such, but couldn't find his sense if somebody nailed it to his boot. Spent too much time with his nose in a book, like another sorry lump I could name." Her eyes softened for a moment, seeming to stare through the wall. Before Victoria could speak, Cora stirred herself, her eyes refocusing on her visitor. "You want heroes, young missie, you'd best stop by the local boneyard. The only heroes is the ones who don't make it back."

"What does that make you, then?"

"Just an old drunk," Cora said.

"And your combat prowess?"

"Luck and a quick draw."

Desperate, Victoria reached for her last option. "Surely even an old lucky drunk understands and respects the value of money."

Cora barked a laugh. "I reckon I do. Why else would I gotten myself such a fine establishment?"

"You're the proprietor?"

"You bet your pretty little parasol," Cora said. "The Print Shop keeps me well enough to drink away half her profits. The boys out there couldn't bluff to save their own mommas, so they give me some extra whether they plan to or not."

"I'm not talking about poker winnings," Victoria said. "My parents left me a great estate. All you need do is name your price, and it's yours."

Cora shook her head. "You just ain't getting me. I ain't interested in your money or your vengeance. My hunting days is done, and I aim to keep my bones sitting in this saloon until the good Lord sees fit to take me on up to kingdom come. My price is peace and quiet."

With that, Cora opened the door and walked back into the saloon. Victoria heard her chair scrape against the floor as she reclaimed her seat at the table. The young woman leaned against a crate, her legs suddenly unable to hold her up. What was she going to do now? Her last hope was gone, crushed beneath Cora Oglesby's boot like a withered rose. She could gather the remains and continue on, but what good would it do? She had failed her parents again, a final debacle so spectacular it had dragged her halfway around the world. If her relatives ever discovered the true purpose of her trip to America, her humiliation would never end. She might at least continue on to San Francisco so she could say she simply wished to see the great American cities.

Victoria swallowed against the lump in her throat, but it continued to float there, threatening to choke her with her own despair. She fought for composure. Showing any weakness to the ruffians in the next room would be an open invitation for them to attack her. They may not do it here in the open, but they would mark her as an easy target. Cora Oglesby wouldn't protect her. The police, if there were any here, might not be able to save her. England and the Oxford constables were a very long way away.

She had to get out of Albuquerque. Coming here had been a mistake, but hopefully it wouldn't be her last. Trains ran regularly from the station, so she might be able to catch one in the morning. To San Francisco, or perhaps back to Santa Fe. Maybe she could stop by Denver to speak with Father Baez again. If he knew of Cora Oglesby, he might know of other hunters as well. Cora couldn't have been the only one the Catholic churches of America relied on to hunt down demons and monsters when they had need. If that failed, she could return to Oxford and demand that James Townsend's fraternity of scholars hear her plea. They might refuse to help her, but surely there was a decent man or two among them that might point her in the direction of another mercenary.

Her despair subdued for the moment, she took a deep breath to steady herself. Extinguishing the lamp, she crept out of the storeroom. The men largely ignored her, any memory of the earlier scene erased by the endless flow of cards and whiskey. A few saw her emerge and tossed a wink or a lech her way as they shuffled plastic chips around their tables. Victoria managed to catch Cora Oglesby's eye. The old hunter lifted her fingers to her brow as if tipping a hat that was no longer there. Victoria responded with a single, silent nod before slipping out through the batwing doors.

Standing on the sidewalk, Victoria took a moment to fill her lungs. The air was hot, dry, and dusty, but at least it didn't smell of whiskey and smoke. Behind her, she heard Cora's rasping shout as she called somebody out for cheating. It was almost sad, Victoria mused as she began walking back to her hotel. Here was a woman who could still do some good in the world, a veteran of wars few even knew existed, letting herself waste away in a small desert town. That both James Townsend and Father Baez thought so highly of her spoke of her skill and tenacity in the work she did for them. Why, then, would she suddenly decide to stop? Not age, surely. Cora Oglesby's days as a young woman were long past, but she still had some power in her; the dull ache in Victoria's cheek was proof enough of that.

A hot wind kicked up, sending dust flying in swirling clouds through the streets. Victoria winced against the grit blowing into her face. Peering through one half-open eye, she watched the other people on the street pulling down hats and pulling up bandanas. Unrefined though they were, the citizens of Albuquerque were well-suited to life here, much more so than she was. All she could do was flinch and duck, her eyes watering as bits of sand slid through her defenses. Grains nuzzled into her bodice and whipped around her ankles, itching more fiercely with every step she took. She picked up her pace, thinking only of a hot bath and a warm bed.

Victoria stared out the window, seeing more of her reflection than the town below. A few lights lay at anchor in the sea of darkness outside, lamps and lanterns lit by the townsfolk against the night. Moonlight filled the street with its bluish light. She marveled at the power of it. Even a town as rough and rustic as this could be beautiful at night, bathed in soft luminescence and blanketed by an endless field of stars.

A sudden impulse to immerse herself in such beauty took hold of her, and she picked up her overcoat from where it lay on the bed. Wrapping it around herself, she eased the door open and stepped out into the hall. Her bare feet padded down the hotel's rear steps. She stepped out into the night through a side door, the planks rough beneath her feet. Cool air kissed her face and ran its fingers through her hair, making her shiver. At night, the smells of the city faded, and the air beneath them was almost sweet. Her blue eyes glittered as she stared up at the stars. She never knew there could be so many.

Victoria smiled to herself, half in wonder at the night and half in wonder at herself. How could she feel so peaceful and safe here, in the middle of a lawless frontier town? Why did she decide to leave the safety of her room in only her dressing gown and overcoat? Maybe some of the wildness of this place was creeping into her blood, making her do things that seemed outright mad.

Somewhere in the distance, a dog began barking. Victoria turned her head toward the sound, peering down the empty street after it. Once or twice, she heard the cries of another animal, high-pitched and wild. They echoed in the night air like the cries of witches gleefully planning mischief. She shivered again and pulled her overcoat closed.

A shadow darted across the road in front of her, and she started. It paused, turning its head to look at her. Pointed ears stood erect above dark, intelligent eyes. A bushy tail sloped downward from its back, hovering just above the street. It looked like the foxes her father loved to hunt on holidays, but its coat was the same greyish hue as the ground beneath it rather than the fiery red of her father's game. The animal regarded her for a moment before losing interest and padding around the hotel's side and out of sight.

Rubbing her hands on her arms, she took a deep breath and blinked. Time to head back up to her room. She needed a good night's sleep if she was to begin her journey again in the morning. A twinge of sadness and anger twisted inside her. If only Cora had been willing to help her, she could be returning in triumph instead of defeat. Traveling with the woman would have been tiresome, though, so perhaps it wasn't entirely a shame. She smiled to herself and turned back toward the door.

The dark figure of a man blocked her way.

Victoria cried out and stumbled backward. The figure's hand shot out like a striking snake, grabbing her wrist. It jerked her back to her feet and pulled her against the man's chest. Blue eyes burned like molten sapphires in a face obscured by shadow. Victoria could see a feral hunger in their depths. Her mind dissolved, evaporating in an explosion of primal terror. She struck at those eyes with clawed fingers, raking cold flesh above and below them, but they never blinked. Their icy glow remained fixed on her as she beat against the figure's head and chest. She could feel the flesh and bone beneath the man's clothing, but her blows did not so much as knock him off-balance.

The grip on her wrist tightened as cold fingers twisted. She cried out again, contorting in pain and falling to her knees. Her assailant's strength was incredible. Pinning her arm behind her, he forced her downward with a knee planted between her shoulder blades. Splinters scraped against her cheeks, and she squeezed her eyes shut. Tears seeped around her eyelids. She could feel the man above her, his weight holding her to the ground, and she prepared herself for the filthy, probing touch of his fingers on her legs.

It never came.

She forced one eye open, rolling it this way and that, trying to see the figure. He loomed beyond her sight, the bogeyman from her childhood fears made flesh. Her eye looked up and down the street, hoping to see something, another person she might cry out to for help. Instead, her gaze fell on a small lupine shape in the street. The fox watched her with the same intelligent curiosity, its head cocked slightly to the side. Its grey coat seemed to swell and grow as she looked at it, filling her vision until she was drowning in a silvery sea. Then it faded to black.

FOUR

Victoria wrinkled her nose. The scent of animals, of hay and dung and leather, surrounded her. Opening her eyes, she searched for the source of the offensive odors. Wooden walls rose around her on three sides, vanishing into the darkness above. Where a fourth wall might have stood was only shadows. Something scratchy poked her in the cheek as she turned her head. Her hand explored the ground beneath her. Straw and, beneath it, wood.

Victoria pushed herself into a sitting position. Her wrist protested, sending sharp pains shooting up her arm. All at once, she remembered the dark figure and the events that must have led her here. Instinct pulled her legs up to her chest. Eyes probing every shadow for a sign of her attacker, she began trying to piece together where she might be. Three walls around her and straw beneath her. A stall. Yes, she had to be in a livestock stall in a barn. It would explain the overpowering smell of animals. The darkness suggested that it was still night outside. If she could just find the entrance to this barn, she might be able to figure out where she was.

A rustling.

She froze. Her pulse pounded in her ears. Every nerve, every muscle tense, ready for God alone knew what. Time passed, marked only by her shallow breaths. The darkness seemed to swim around her in streaks of blue and purple and brown. She tried to blink them away, but they remained, flitting in and out of sight like fey spirits.

After what seemed like hours, Victoria let her muscles relax slightly. Whatever made that noise hadn't moved again. Perhaps it had only been a rabbit or mouse outside the barn. Slowly, she pulled her legs under her. The straw seemed to screech as she moved, and she paused every few inches to listen for any response. Silence. She stood. Her feet were cold and stiff, and she allowed herself a brief moment of self-reproach for leaving the hotel room without her shoes.

Moonlight fell in long, blue shafts through gaps in the walls. It gave her enough light to take a tentative step toward the stall door. The straw crackled beneath her weight, and she winced at the sound. Two more steps, and she was close enough to reach the edge of the wall to her left. Her fingers clamped on to the wood, heedless of splinters. Wrapping her arms around the post, she nearly wept in relief. She was making it. Her kidnapper, confident in his speed and strength, must have left her alone. Perhaps he had gone to find another victim, or simply gone in search of rope to tie her up. Whatever the reason, she fully intended to be gone when he returned. Smiling at the thought, she poked her head out of the stall and looked around.

Two pale points of red light hung in the darkness.

Victoria sucked in a breath. The lights did not move or change. They weren't lanterns or any sort of electric light, yet they seemed familiar somehow. Wracking her memory for a moment, she realized she had seen the same red glow in the eyes of her father's hounds at night as she passed the kennels. Relief washed over her, and she nearly laughed out loud. Those lights were just the eyes of some animal, most likely a raccoon or mouse, watching her. It was probably more frightened of her than she was of it. The thought gave her courage. She may be alone in a strange country, but she still had her wits and the use of her limbs. Breathing a small sigh, she turned away from them and started searching for the barn's exit.

A rustling.

Her heart leapt into her throat. Turning toward the sound, she was again greeted by those two points of light floating like will-o'-the-wisps in the sea of shadows. Only now they were moving. Terror anchored her feet in place. She willed them to move, drawing on every bit of strength she had left, but they remained welded to the barn floor. Helpless, she watched the eyes advance. Straw rustled. Somewhere in the night, an animal screamed.

A figure stepped into a shaft of moonlight. Shadows of a head and long hair appeared around the floating lights. She could make out shapes like arms and legs moving in slow strides, each step bringing the thing closer. It passed in and out of the moonlight as it came, making it seem to grow closer in sudden leaps. The haunting lights remained fixed on her. Her mind screamed at her body to run, to fight, to move, but it only responded with a racing heart and shallow, ragged breaths.

Moonlight passed over the shadow's face, revealing a woman's features. It stopped as if to let her take in the sight. Skin creased in thin shadows around the glowing eyes, smoothing out over a broad nose and high cheekbones. The woman's lips pressed together, forming a line of darkness like a scar beneath her nose.

"Who are you?"

Victoria's own voice startled her. It quavered, thin and reedy.

The woman's head cocked to one side. Red eyes glimmered.

"Who."

The word was clear, oddly accented, but the voice was human.

"Where am I?"

"Who," the woman repeated in the same calm voice.

Victoria's tongue ran over her lips. "Can you understand me?"

"Who."

The strange conversation only fueled Victoria's fear. Was this woman simple-minded? Was she mad? Who or what was she?

"You sound like a goddamned owl," said a voice from above them. Victoria's eyes darted upward. Blue orbs burned in the darkness, regarding her with murderous intensity. A scream burst from her throat, and the new voice laughed. "And you sound like a coyote. Am I the only human here?"

There was a sliding sound, and the eyes plummeted toward the ground. Boots clapped against wood as the intruder landed. He straightened up, eyes leering at her from a shadow. A swath of moonlight fell across his torso, illuminating a belt buckle and button-up shirt. The fall would have broken any man's legs, but he seemed unharmed. "Then again, I ain't exactly human my own self."

Victoria's limbs finally responded. She slid into a half-crouch, arms splayed out, ready for the man to attack her. He responded with another laugh. "Ain't you just a regular tom cat? Never would have guessed you lady Brits was so feisty. I should've bagged me one a long time ago."

"What do you want with me?" Victoria demanded, fear lending strength to her voice.

"A man has needs, darlin," the man said, "and I ain't just any old man. I'm quite a bit more, if you take my meaning, and I got extra needs that need seeing to, too."

"Quiet, demon." The woman's voice resonated in the darkness. The man's glowing eyes snapped toward her. After a moment, he took a step backward.

The woman's gaze returned to Victoria. "You are from the east?"

Victoria nodded.

"And you visit the woman hunter?"

"Yes," Victoria said, confused.

The strange eyes blinked. "This is not pleasing."

"It's bad enough that bitch is getting herself some fancy visitors," the man said. "Who gives a shake where they're from?"

"East is dawn-child," the woman said. "East is the path of the Witchery Way."

"You saying this one here's a witch?"

"I am no witch," Victoria said.

The woman blinked again. "You say no?"

"Yes, I say no."

"Your words say both at once," the woman said. "I see your wind."

"She's British. That means she's stuffy, but it don't mean she's a witch," the man said. "Hell, look at her. She ain't bright enough to be no witch."

"You waste your wind, demon. I would not hear you speak."

The blue eyes flashed in defiance, but the man didn't reply.

"You, British," the woman said. "What is your name?"

Victoria hesitated.

"Tell me your name."

Her mouth moved against her will. "Victoria Dawes."

"What is your purpose here, Victoria Dawes?"

Again she held back, and again something pulled the words from her. "I came to see Cora Oglesby, the woman hunter."

"This you have said." The woman stepped toward Victoria. "It is not my answer. I say again: why did you come here?"

"Was it to teach that Oglesby bitch witchcraft?" the man asked.

"I told you, I'm not a witch," Victoria said. "I don't know where you're getting that idea, but you're wrong."

Neither of her captors replied. Silence enclosed the barn's interior as they continued to regard her with their inhuman eyes. Weariness began creeping into her arms and legs. It pulled at her eyelids and shoulders, drawing them downward. The straw beneath her toes suddenly felt soft and inviting, and she was so very tired. What could laying down for a minute hurt? Just a quick nap. She had a train to catch in the morning, after all, and her eyelids were so very heavy.

Victoria shook her head. No, she couldn't sleep. How could she even consider it with these two monsters so close? What was wrong with her? Gathering her strength, she stood to her full height and took a deep breath.

The red eyes floated backward slightly. Victoria looked into them, a new resolve hardening her voice. "What do you want with me?"

"To learn, Victoria Dawes," the woman replied. "I see you visit the woman hunter, and I am curious. Why should a woman from the east visit her?"

"My business is my own," Victoria replied.

"It's our business when you hop your pretty little self over to that saloon and have a nice jawing with that Cora Oglesby," the man's voice said. "We have a mighty keen interest in her our own selves, so when she gets strange visitors, we tend to take notice."

"What do you want with Cora?"

"To learn," the woman said again.

"Your methods of acquiring knowledge are rather dubious," Victoria said. "Kidnapping is generally regarded as a crime."

The woman stepped closer, eyes gleaming. "You do not know crime."

"I'm no constable, I grant you that," Victoria said.

"Your wind grows hungry," the woman said.

"My what?"

The woman stared at her without replying. Victoria challenged her eerie gaze, trying to demonstrate her strength of will. An unseen force began building against her chest, as if someone were trying to push her backward. She leaned into the pressure, fighting it with both body and mind. The woman's eyes grew brighter. The pressure increased, and Victoria struggled to breathe against its weight. At any moment, she expected her feet to slide across the floor.

The glowing points turned away from her, and the pressure vanished. Victoria sucked in a breath and nearly stumbled forward. Her head throbbed.

"Hungry, yes, but also strong," the woman said quietly.

"What?" the man asked.

"This one," she said, turning back to her prisoner, "has a great gale inside her. Perhaps she does not know how to free it, but it is there."

"What's that got to do with anything?"

"We have learned something." Moonlight glimmered on the woman's skin as she extended her hand. Victoria shied away.

"Nothing useful," the man complained.

"You are not one to speak of usefulness," she replied.

"And what do you mean by that?"

Victoria sensed the onset of an argument. She began easing away from the two, making her way backward. She didn't know if she would find a door in that direction, but at the very least she could put some more distance between herself and her quarreling captors. Each step was precise, calculated to make as little noise as possible. It was an art she'd mastered as a little girl to swipe lemon bars from the pantry after her bedtime. The danger of getting caught had seemed just as real to her then, but she knew the consequences this night would be far more deadly.

Three agonizing steps later, she felt something solid behind her. Her fingers touched wood. She stole a quick glance backward. The rear wall of the barn stood behind her. Now if she could just edge along it until she came to a door, she could make her escape.

Icy fingers clamped around her neck. Victoria felt herself lifted off her feet and pinned against the wall. Her chest heaved as her lungs worked to pull air past the powerful grip. It wouldn't come. She dug her nails under the fingers, trying to pry them away.

Blue flames burned mere inches from her face. They left streaks across her vision as her eyes rolled frantically, searching for help that would never come. Already her arms grew heavy, even as her lungs screamed in agony.

"Enough, demon."

The voice was quiet, reaching out to her across what seemed like miles of darkness. Death released its hold on her throat, and she fell. Pulling her knees up to her chest, she lay on one side and breathed in ragged gasps.

After a few minutes, her head slowed its sickening spinning. Looking up, she saw the two sets of eyes peering down at her.

"We mean you no harm," the woman said.

"What do you want?" Victoria asked. "Please, just tell me what you want."

The blue eyes moved forward, and she cowered against the wall, covering her head with her arms.

"Peace!" Steel lined the woman's voice. "You are not to move or speak until we have finished, demon. Do you understand?" Silence. "Good." Turning back to the huddled woman, the woman's voice spoke in gentler tones. "Please, do not fear. My friend is hot with anger, and it makes him act like a fool. I will not let him harm you."

As the woman spoke, Victoria's limbs slowly unwrapped themselves. She looked up at the uncanny eyes floating above her. "Please."

"I must know why you came here," the woman said. "Why did you visit the woman hunter?"

"To ask for her help," Victoria said in a small voice.

"Why do you seek help?"

"My parents. They died. Monsters killed them. I was told Cora could help me."

"What monsters?"

"I don't know." With each word, Victoria relaxed more. It felt so good to tell this woman the truth. "They were large and black, like shadows. Their eyes were yellow. They scared our horse and drove us into the river."

The woman did not speak for a moment. The silence crawled up Victoria's legs. Had she said something wrong? She was only telling this woman what she wanted to know. If she really meant what she said, she would call off her friend and let her go. Victoria just had to keep cooperating.

"I do not know your monsters," the woman said at last. "Why should the woman hunter? Is there no man in your country who knows?"

"One did. Does. A professor named James. He told me to come find Cora."

At the mention of James, the blue eyes grew bright. Tendrils of fear coiled around Victoria's chest, and her neck ached at the memory of those cruel fingers. She braced herself for another attack, but he remained where he was. Victoria looked back at the woman with new admiration.

"You see?" she said. "He will not hurt you again."

"Thank you," Victoria whispered with a grateful smile.

"So this...professor told you to come to the woman

hunter?" the woman asked. Victoria nodded. "What did he tell you of her?"

"She is strong. She kills monsters." Her vision blurred. "But he was wrong. She refused to help me. She doesn't hunt monsters anymore, so she can't help me." She wiped at tears with the back of her hand.

The woman leaned in close. "What did you say? She does not hunt?"

"Not anymore," Victoria said. "She said she stopped. She wants to live in peace. She won't help me." A small sob escaped her lips.

Silence again. Victoria looked up. The red eyes had vanished, but the woman's presence lingered nearby, strong and sinister. The man's blue gaze still floated in the shadows, though it no longer looked her way. Victoria wrapped her arms around herself. The hopelessness of her situation descended like a thick, smothering blanket. She fought against the flood of tears that would, if unleashed, dissolve her into a useless, blubbing mess. Even if she were to die in this place, she would not die weeping.

A sudden breeze swirled through the barn, sending straw fluttering every which way. Victoria's head came up, and her breath caught in her throat.

The two creatures were gone.

Confused, Victoria waited, straining her eyes in the darkness. Seconds passed. The breeze faded away, leaving her in silence. Bracing herself against the wall, she rose on shaky legs. No lights glinted at her from the shadows, no hands reached out to strangle her. Taking a step forward, she paused, listening. Nothing.

Wetting her lips with her tongue, she marshaled her courage. "Hello?" she called, half-cringing. Her voice rang against the walls before fading into the shadows. There was no answer.

Somewhere inside her, a small hope blossomed. She took one step, then another. Her legs stopped shaking. Straw rustled beneath her feet as she began walking faster, her eyes sweeping the empty stalls for any movement. The barn door loomed ahead of her, the great white X painted on it promising an escape from this nightmare.

When Victoria reached the door, she stared up at it for a moment. How had the two creatures managed to leave the barn without opening it? Not that it mattered. Hooking her fingers around an exposed corner, she pulled. The door didn't budge. She pulled again. It swayed slightly in place as the sound of creaking wood drifted down from its runners.

With a grunt of frustration, Victoria shoved in the opposite direction. Metal squealed and groaned as the door shuddered, but it moved. She pushed harder, her toes digging into the rough wood beneath her. Inch by inch, the door slid aside. Fresh air tickled her ankles through the ever-widening gap. The scent of the night sent thrills through her body as the door's momentum started carrying her along. She let herself laugh then, and the stars seemed to share her mirth as they glittered down from their places in the endless sky.

The door reached the end of its rail and jerked to a halt, sending Victoria sprawling. Righting herself, she pulled her dressing gown back down to cover her legs. A patch of moonlight illuminated the straw covering the floor, making the barn's interior far less frightening. Where once had been an abyss of confusion and fear now stood just an old building. Giddy with her newfound freedom, Victoria gave it a quick curtsey before stepping out into the night.

Outside, a scene of quiet desolation awaited her. Wooden fences extended from the walls of the barn to frame a large yard. A wind pump stood at the far end of the enclosure, groaning at the occasional breath of wind. Some distance away, a large house sat on top of a small rise. Victoria's hopes rose when she saw it, and she began walking.

The ground was rough, covered with rocks and short, scrubby plants that poked and scratched at her bare feet. She picked her way across the yard, doing her best to avoid the worst of them. The moonlight helped, but she still put her weight down a few times only to wince and pull her foot back. Her feet ached worse with every misstep. By the time she reached the house, she fully understood why all the locals wore thick leather boots.

The house's windows were dark, but she stepped up to the door and knocked anyway. No answer. She knocked again, calling out for help. The house remained dark, wrapped in a brooding silence.

Uneasiness crept back into Victoria's stomach as she stood on the porch. She felt exposed. Her back

was to the barn and the expanse of desert beyond it.
Those people or creatures or whatever they were
could still be out there, watching her. In the barn,
they had disappeared in a gust of wind. They might
be able to return the same way. She glanced over her
shoulder. Nothing moved behind her, but that didn't
mean she was safe. With those things out there
somewhere, she was never safe.

Victoria's nerves finally overwhelmed her good
manners, and she tried the doorknob. Finding it un-
locked, she pushed the door open and stepped inside.
The air was just as cold inside even though none of
the windows were open. She called out again, her
voice ringing in the absolute stillness, but nothing
stirred. Spirits sinking, she began exploring the house.

"They are not at home."

Victoria's heart stopped. Her head snapped
around. Red eyes gleamed at her.

Without thinking, Victoria sprinted across the
room and up the narrow staircase. Darkness enveloped her. At the top, she found a hallway with
doors in both walls. Choosing the door on the right,
she slammed her body into it. Wood cracked, and the
door fell open. A bedroom. She dashed to the sole
window and tried to open it. It was sealed. She
would have to break it. Something in the room, a
chair or a lamp, could do it. She turned from the
window to search.

A face looked back at her.

Victoria screamed, jumping backward into the
wall. Something was crouched on the bed. It had a

human shape, but the face was horribly misshapen. Teeth erupted from its mouth in jagged clumps, mashing together in a tangled mass that poked through the remains of a beard. One eye was missing, torn out by whatever carved the gash that ran from the monster's right temple to its left cheek; the remaining eye regarded her with feral hunger as its teeth clicked together.

The creature placed a hand on the bedpost, edging closer to her. She pressed herself against the wall. Tearing her eyes from the horror, she glanced to her right. The door hung on its hinges at an odd angle, damaged by her violent entrance, but it was still open.

A hiss of air whistled through crooked teeth. Victoria kept the monstrosity in sight as she worked her way toward the door. Its eye watched her progress with a predator's interest, but the creature didn't lunge for her. Instead, it crawled down onto the floor, keeping pace with her. Remains of a shirt and trousers hung from its bones. Powerful legs coiled beneath it, ready to spring.

Another hiss broke Victoria's nerve, and she ran. Her bare feet carried her back into the hall and down the stairs. She could hear the thumping of the creature's limbs on the floor. Reaching the lower level, she risked a quick glance over her shoulder. A grey shape loped along only a few paces behind her. Fresh terror gave her a boost of speed, and she careened through the open front door into the night.

Rocks jabbed at her feet, but she didn't feel them.

Small cacti scratched her exposed ankles, but she
didn't care. Her lungs burned, her eyes watered, but
she kept going. All that mattered was outrunning the
thing behind her. She could see the barn ahead of
her. Maybe she could hide in there, or find something to fight with, a pitchfork or a shovel. Anything
was better than facing it down with nothing but her
dressing gown and overcoat.

The barn was close now. Victoria put all her energy
into one last sprint. Head down, she rounded the
corner and collided with the strange man.

Bouncing back from the impact, Victoria lost her
balance and fell. The man stood over her in an instant, boots planted on either side of her chest. His
blue eyes burned down at her. Moonlight lit his face,
and she saw his features for the first time. Shaggy
hair covered his ears and fell in straight locks across
his cheeks. A beard, well-trimmed, framed his lips,
brushing up beneath his nose. But for his eyes, he
looked like an ordinary man, even handsome. Denim
trousers and a roughspun, button-up shirt identified
him as a local.

"Howdy, darlin."

Victoria dug her palms into the dirt and shoved
backward. Rolling onto her stomach, she pulled her
legs under her in an effort to double back the way
she came. A glance ahead stopped her cold; the creature from the bedroom crouched on all fours,
waiting for her. She rose to her feet and turned to
face the man. Her hope of escape was gone, but she
refused to cower before him a second time.

A grin spread his lips. "You sure ain't hard on the eyes, you know that?" His blue gaze swept up and down her body. "I always do get randy at the sight of a woman in her bed clothes. Guess part of me is still a man."

His laughter made her skin crawl. "Is that why you kidnapped a helpless woman at night?"

"I reckon that had something to do with it," he said, "though hell knows it ain't the only reason. Fact is, it wasn't even my idea."

"Whose was it?"

"Hers," he said. "She ain't bad, but I never go in for no squaws. Ain't natural, if you follow me. You, now, is perfectly natural. Just the sight of you makes me wish I hadn't been turned."

Despite her resolution, Victoria felt herself shrinking away from him. "What do you mean, turned?"'

"Into what I is. I wasn't born this way, you know."

"What are you?"

"A god." He laughed at her look of disgust. "Ain't that hard to believe, is it? After all, you seen for yourself what I can do. Ain't no ordinary man has my strength and speed. I don't got to eat, I don't never get sick or cold, and I ain't never going to die. If that ain't a god, then I don't know what is."

"Enough of your waste, demon." Startled, Victoria turned. The strange woman stood a few feet away. Black hair cascaded down her shoulders in waves, framing a round, broad-nosed face. Even in the moonlight, her eyes still glimmered like an animal's. Her skin was a grey shadow, darker than Victoria's.

Simple hide trousers and a tunic covered her body but left her arms bare.

"Who are you?" Victoria asked.

"What matters, Victoria Dawes, is who I am not." Her face betrayed no hint of emotion as she spoke. "I am not your friend, and I am not your enemy. Return to your country with the woman hunter."

"I already told you," Victoria said, "she won't come with me."

"You must force her, then," the woman said, "for your own good. If you do, I will be your friend. If you do not, I will become your enemy."

Victoria swallowed. She hadn't expected this. "Why do you want me to take her with me?"

"You do not need to know. Know only that you must."

"Just like that?" the man said. "No funning or nothing?"

"Yes," the woman replied. "She can be useful."

A glimmer of hope sparked to life somewhere deep in Victoria's being. "So as long as I take Cora Oglesby with me when I depart, you'll let me go free?"

"What if I says no?" the man asked.

The woman regarded him placidly. "You have no word in this, demon. You will do as I say."

Blue eyes blazing, the man stepped forward. "I ain't about to let no squaw tell me what to do."

"You will," she replied. "You will also take Victoria Dawes back to the white town, and you will not harm her in any way."

They glared at one another, inhuman eyes locked

in a battle of will. Victoria could almost see the tension stretching from eye to eye, flickering and flashing in the moonlight. She gave brief thought to the idea of using the opportunity to flee, but a hiss from the creature behind her made her reconsider. Another glance at it made her stomach lurch, and she looked down at her bare toes instead.

The man was the first to break, his eyes blinking as he drew in a breath. His gaze dropped to his boots and he gave a single nod. The Indian woman showed no outward sign of triumph or relief as she turned back to Victoria. "He will take you back to the white town."

"Might he…just point me in the right direction?" Victoria asked. "I'm sure I can make it on my own."

"You cannot," the woman said. "We are far from the white town, more than you could walk in a day and a night. This demon can run like the deer without stopping for rest. Be sure you do not slow him down, as the sun will soon rise."

"Why does that matter?"

She didn't reply. Victoria looked at the man, bracing herself for the journey ahead. Her skin crawled at the thought of touching him, but if they were really that far from Albuquerque, she would need his help getting back. A dressing gown, an overcoat, and bare feet were hardly well-suited to traveling through the desert, and she had no supplies at all. As much as she hated the thought, she really was at his mercy.

"You must start soon." This was directed at the man. "If you do not, you will not be safe by sunrise."

The man nodded, turning his blue gaze at Victoria. "You ready, darlin?"

"Yes," Victoria said, "but I will not be carried like a babe in arms. You will carry me on your back."

"Well, ain't you little miss queenie all of a sudden-like," the man said.

"Do as she says, demon," the woman said, "and send your creature away. I do not like to look at it."

Shocked, Victoria looked at the ghoul. Its lips pulled back from its teeth in a hideous grin as it turned and ambled back toward the house. Once it disappeared through the door, she turned her look of confusion on the man.

He scowled back. "Let's get this over with."

Crouching down, he presented his back to her. She gingerly bent over him, clasping her arms around his neck. His skin was icy to the touch. Wrapping a hand around each of her legs, he stood to his feet and shrugged his shoulders. "You ain't nothing, darling."

Before she could reply, he sprang away. His legs became a blur beneath them as he picked up speed, each stride taking them yards at a time. She tightened her grip around his neck. Despite his appearance, the man didn't stink. In fact, he barely had any smell at all. The barren landscape slid past them with alarming speed, the brush becoming a smooth stream of colors punctuated every so often by large dark shapes. Wind whistled past her ears and stung her eyes. She squinted against it, blinking back the tears so she could still see where they were going. Even if she couldn't change the man's direction or speed, being able to see the desert ahead of them gave her some feeling of control.

Soon, Victoria found herself settling into the journey. For all his lecherousness and arrogance, the man's stride didn't jostle her around nearly as much as she thought it would. She almost felt as though she were back on the train, riding through the night on her way home. But for the wind, she might have dozed off.

After a while, she could see a large shadow ahead, crouched against the horizon. As it grew, the man began slowing his pace. Indistinct shapes became houses and buildings. Soon, she could make out the main avenue, along which stood Cora's saloon. She even thought she recognized the train station, a squat building to the left of the biggest cluster.

Her courier stopped before they reached the buildings and dumped her on the ground. Holding out her arms to break her fall, she scraped one of her palms bloody. She picked herself up and turned to face him, cradling her injured hand. His blue eyes simmered with an inflamed hunger.

"You ain't making this easy, darlin," he said.

"What do you mean?" she asked, drawing away from him.

He just shook his head. "There's others. Don't get it in your head that I ain't fixing for you, though. That squaw ain't the boss of me, and I reckon I'll have my way with you soon enough. Maybe I'll even make you my wife. How'd you like that?"

Victoria's back stiffened. Another betrothal she wanted no part of. "Thank you for bringing me back," she said. "Now, if you'll excuse me, I could do with a good sleep."

"One more thing." He leaned in close, his breath brushing her cheek. "Tell that Oglesby bitch that I'm gunning for her."

The reply left her mouth before she could think twice. "What shall I say? 'Oh, Madam Oglesby, a gentleman said he wants you dead'? Hardly a credible threat."

His eyes flashed. "I ain't got to take your lip, missie."

"It isn't cheek, my good man," Victoria said. "I'm just not certain Cora will take an anonymous threat seriously. She's not exactly a timid woman."

"Oh, she'll listen to me," he said. A smirk came to his lips then. "Tell her that Fodor Glava is aiming to finish what he started."

FIVE

Victoria chose a more demure dress to call on Cora Oglesby the next day: cream-colored with brown trim about the neck and cuffs. She woke just before noon and took her time preparing herself, rehearsing what she might say to the old hunter to change her mind. Nothing sounded right. It didn't help that she had used her strongest pleas the day before, and Cora probably wouldn't be swayed by tales of desert-dwelling demons. Whatever else the old woman was, she wasn't tractable.

Her anxiety mounted as she stepped out of the hotel's front door and began walking toward the saloon. If she couldn't convince Cora to come with her, what would the red-eyed woman do in retaliation? Her control over the other man, while not absolute, was certainly frightening. If he had other enslaved creatures like the bearded nightmare, he should be easily able to overwhelm the Indian woman, yet he bowed to her will. If she could command him, a man she openly acknowledged as a demon, what could she do to a mere human? Victoria tried not to think about it, but the thought nagged at her as she walked through the dusty street.

All too quickly, she found herself standing in front of Ben's Print Shop once more. Around her, the un-washed denizens of Albuquerque went about their daily business. Horses pounded up clouds of dust beneath their hooves as they plodded along, heads bowed beneath the sun's glare. She squinted up at it from beneath her parasol. The woman had spoken of the man-demon needing to avoid sunlight. Hot as it was, at least she should be safe during the day. Feeling a bit better at the thought, Victoria returned her gaze to the saloon's batwing doors. Her fist clenched in determination, and she marched onto the wooden sidewalk and into the Print Shop.

The same sickly smells waited for her inside, along with the same haze of smoke. Cora had fewer patrons at this hour, it seemed. Only two of the tables were occupied, and both groups were far less energetic about their games than they had been the day before. Cora herself stood behind the bar, caught up in an ar-gument with one of her patrons. Victoria stepped up to the bar a short distance from them and waited.

"Ain't possible," Cora said.

"I'm telling you, it's true," the man replied. He was somewhat better dressed than the other patrons, and his squawking accent – similar to the ones she'd heard in New York City – set him apart from the drawling locals. "Some fellow in Germany has done it, or so I hear."

"What's it look like?"

"It has three wheels, and a bench on top for two people. The thing that makes it all work is behind the bench."

"Where he can stuff himself a midget or some such to make his foolery look real," Cora said. "Ain't nothing but a big old trick of the eye, and you're a damn fool for letting it take you in, Booker." She caught sight of Victoria then. Her eyes lit up, and she motioned for her to join them. "This here's a right fancy lady from England. She'll know if you're telling true or not."

"Victoria Dawes," Victoria said, offering her hand.

"Robert Booker," the man replied. "I take it you've met our lovely Cora?" Victoria nodded. "Well, I'm her business partner here at the saloon. She pours the drinks and tames the drunks, and I make sure her finances are in order."

"I also provide the color," Cora said. "Folks keep coming in because they like my jawing. Only interesting things you can ever say is outlandish yarns like the one you was just telling."

"It isn't a yarn," Robert insisted.

"We'll ask Miss Fancy here." Cora grabbed Victoria's hand. "Is there any such thing as a horseless carriage?"

"A what?"

"A carriage what moves with no horses or nothing pulling it."

Victoria blinked. "Not to my knowledge, no."

"Ha!" Cora shoved Robert with her other hand.

"See there? If Vicky here ain't seen one, they doesn't exist."

"My name," Victoria replied, "is Victoria."

"Whatever. You proved my point."

"I don't think the opinion of one young woman, however refined, proves your point," Robert said. "No offense, ma'am," he quickly added.

"None taken."

"Enough of your manners and your yarns," Cora said. "I ain't going to stand here and watch you make moony eyes at pretty ladies. I got a business to run."

Robert blushed. "Yes, well, see that you do. I don't want to lose out on this venture, not with new devices rolling out every day. Think of all the opportunities!"

"I got your opportunity right here," Cora said, lifting up a bottle without a label. She pulled out the stopper and took a drink.

"That's a day's profit right there."

Cora laughed. "I only drink the stuff the rest of the boys ain't man enough to stomach." She offered the bottle to Victoria, who shook her head earnestly. "More for me, then."

"Well," Robert said with a sigh, "no use correcting an old dog. I'll leave you two ladies to your whiskey. Don't forget our meeting on Friday, Cora. We still need to decide how best to invest this month's surplus."

"Long as it ain't magic carriages," Cora said. Robert rolled his eyes, nodded to Victoria, and left. Cora took another swig from the bottle, eyeing the young woman. "So, Miss Fancy, what brings you back here? I thought I was nice and plain in our talk yesterday."

"You were," Victoria said. "I understood you quite clearly."

"So? You get a sudden hankering for my rotgut?"

Victoria shook her head again. "Not at all."

"Well, I'm out of notions."

"Yes," Victoria said. She took a moment to steady herself. "I had a rather interesting encounter last night."

"Is that right?" Cora asked. "Was it your idea or his?"

A furious flush bloomed on Victoria's cheeks. "Nothing of the sort, I assure you. No, my encounter was much more unusual. Unusual in a way someone of your talents might understand." Leaning in close, she lowered her voice. "I was abducted by a pair of supernatural beings."

Cora nodded. "Ain't surprising."

"What do you mean?"

"This town ain't exactly free of critters, if you take my meaning." Cora leaned against the back wall behind the bar. "No surprise, really, seeing how close we are to all them old Indian things. Burial grounds and dead cities what have you. Them things is bound to stir up nasty critters now and again. Why, we got ourselves a mess of old ruins just outside of town somewhere. Local Indians say the whole place is plumb silly with spooks."

"And you just let them be?"

The old hunter shrugged. "They don't bother me,

so I don't bother them. Ain't going to get yourself nowhere if you go poking your nose into every little thing."

"You did once," Victoria said. "You survived then."

"Maybe so. Then again, I was paid to survive. Gives a body a bit of incentive."

"I offered you that same incentive."

Cora nodded again. "So you did. Had you run me down ten years ago, might have been I'd have gone with you, but not no more."

"And nothing I can say will change your mind?"

"You British folk do catch on," Cora said, "even if it is a tad slow. Now then, unless you're aiming to buy yourself a drink, I suggest you make yourself scarce. The boys here ain't changed since yesterday, and you're still far too fancy a girl to be running about by your lonesome."

"My captors seemed to take an interest in you," Victoria said, hoping to pique her interest.

"Most folk do," Cora said with a smirk. "After all, I ain't exactly a run-of-the-mill lady. Not many women seen what I seen and live to tell about it. Plus, I can drink any of these fellers under the table, and I play a mean game of cards. Find me another gal like that, and I'll eat my own boot and thank you after every bite."

"They wanted you to come with me back to England."

Cora laughed, a dry, rolling sound that turned a few heads at the tables. Victoria's impatience grew as the sound went on. The old woman was really enjoying herself, and Victoria did not appreciate being the source of her amusement.

Finally, Cora's laughter faded away, returning in a few chuckles as she spoke. "That's a fresh one, I'll grant you that. Ain't never heard no story quite that hare-brained."

"It's the truth."

"I reckon it ain't," Cora said. "Too convenient by half."

"Precisely," Victoria replied, seizing on a new tactic. "Do you really think I think you're stupid enough to fall for it? Why would I say it unless it were true?"

A frown deepened Cora's wrinkles. "That is odd, now that you say it like that. Then again, maybe you think I'm stupid enough to fall for what you just said. Ain't the first time somebody tried to pull the saddle over my eyes."

"I promise you, I'm not."

"Say what you like," Cora said. "I ain't coming." She set the bottle down behind the bar and walked away. Victoria watched her go, the Indian woman's eyes burning like blood moons in her mind. The worn-out old gunfighter would be the death of her. Without Cora beside her on the train, the strange woman would find her and kill her. She might even send the blue-eyed demon to do the work once night fell. Maybe if she could get far enough away, catch a fast-moving train to San Francisco or back to Santa Fe, they wouldn't be able to follow her.

"There was one more thing," Victoria said.

Down at the end of the bar, Cora turned. "Make it quick."

"One of my captors wanted me to give you a message."

"If it's 'get on the train', you can save your breath," Cora said.

Victoria shook her head. "No, nothing of the sort. It was a threat."

"Well, that's a bit better," Cora said. "Go on."

"He told me to tell you that he was gunning for you."

"That it?" Cora asked. She let out a short laugh. "Don't sound like nothing to me. Hell, I got me a few boys here who spout that at me whenever I take a hand." Shaking her head, she turned her back to Victoria.

"He said his name was Fodor Glava."

Cora went rigid. Victoria held her breath.

"What?"

It was just one word, quiet and short, but Victoria heard it. She also heard the ocean of ice beneath it.

"Yes," Victoria replied. "He said that he was Fodor Glava, and that he was aiming to finish what he started."

The old hunter's braid slid across her back as her head turned. One brown eye fixed Victoria in a gaze of steel. "You're sure you heard that right?"

"Absolutely." Cora's reaction surprised her, but Victoria kept her composure. "I made sure to remember his name. It wasn't that difficult, really; it's quite remarkable."

"Yes, I suppose it is." The hunter's words were soft.

Her voice trembled slightly. She turned toward the young woman, but her eyes no longer looked her way. They wandered over the bar, taking in every inch of it like she was seeing it for the first time. Her fingers glided over the top, lingered on the edge. She didn't blink.

Then, without a word, Cora turned away. Her boots thumped across the saloon's floor, carrying her toward the stairs in the back. Victoria watched her go, her mind locked up in confusion. Nobody else in the room even noticed Cora's departure. They continued to bicker and banter, tossing chips and cards on the tables. The old piano stood forlorn behind them. A shout from out in the street drifted through the saloon's door. Minutes passed, marked only by the shuffling of cards and muttering of curses, yet still she stood rooted to the floor, one elbow resting on the bar.

Her mind finally shook free, and the questions began rolling through it. Should she go up after her? The message had clearly shaken the old hunter, shaken worse than Victoria would have thought possible. Seeing Cora's entire demeanor change, her devil-may-care attitude vanish in an instant, had confused and frightened her. Whoever this Fodor Glava was, he clearly held a great power over her. If the red-eyed woman could control him, she might be more than a match even for the great Cora Oglesby. The thought chilled Victoria's blood. She couldn't begin to guess what Cora would do with the message she had delivered, but the Indian woman's threat now loomed large and menacing.

Victoria glanced over her shoulder. A few men sauntered through the door, each looking her up and down before heading over to one of the occupied tables. Chairs grated against the floor as the others raised their fingers in greeting.

"Hey, sweetheart," one of the newcomers called, "ain't you working a bit early?"

Victoria ignored the comment and the laughter that followed.

"You ought to come over and sit on my lap," another said. She shot him a cool look. He grinned back as the other men at the table whistled and jeered.

"Looks like you got yourself a bed bunny for tonight, Wilson."

"She keep you real warm, I bet."

"Hardly," Victoria said.

Hoots echoed around the table. "Well, if you ain't going to look after my pecker, you might at least see about wetting my whistle," the man named Wilson said.

"I am not your barmaid."

"You ain't a barmaid and you ain't a whore," Wilson said. "What good are you, then?"

Victoria stared at him. "Too good for you."

The front legs of Wilson's chair thudded to the floor. "What'd you say?"

"You heard me," she replied, looking away.

"I don't let no bitch mouth off to me like that," Wilson said, "especially not one so high and mighty as you. Now, I'm a gentlemen, so I's let you say you're sorry and let it go at that."

"An apology?" Victoria tossed her hair back over her shoulder, refusing to meet his eyes lest she lose her nerve. "I don't believe one's in order."

"Too bad for you." The floor creaked as Wilson stood to his feet. "I done my best to be civil, but now I got to teach you your proper place. Won't do to have the whores getting all uppity in this town." The planks beneath her feet trembled as he walked toward her, but she continued to feign disinterest. Her pulse quickened with each step.

"Now then, missie." His breath, sour and wet, poured into her ear, "you going to bend over nicely, or do I got to get mean?"

Victoria turned toward the door, but he grabbed her arm before she could take a step. Instinct took over, and she brought her other hand around, smacking him across the face. Laughter filled the room. Wilson's eyes blazed as he whirled back on her. Victoria's spine popped as he leaned into her, pushing her down onto the bar.

Twisting against him, Victoria tried to get enough leverage to kick him in the shins, but her legs wouldn't cooperate. The smell of sweat clung to him like a second skin, smothering her. She screamed, but the men at the tables just sat and watched. Wilson's face loomed only inches above her, yellow teeth bared in a grin. All of Cora's warnings exploded in her mind. If only she had listened. She could feel his crotch pressing into the folds of her dress.

"Enough!" The hunter's voice cracked like thunder across the saloon. Wilson turned his face toward the sound, and his grip loosened. Victoria cried out as she shoved him away. He stumbled backward, nearly tripping over a chair. Pulling herself upright, Victoria blinked back her tears and looked up at her savior.

Cora stood on the staircase. Silver metal gleamed in her right hand, the long barrel pointed at the man named Wilson. The hunter's eyes glinted as she descended, planting each boot deliberately. When she reached the bottom, she continued her advance, the gun's barrel never wavering. The room rang with her footsteps. They came to rest in front of Wilson, silver pressed firmly into his chest.

Nobody breathed.

"Leave her be," Cora said. "I need her." Wilson's mouth opened to reply. Cora twisted the gun. "No lip from you. Now get."

Wilson stared at her a moment, then nodded. Keeping his eyes on her, he slowly backed toward the saloon's door. The batwings creaked as he stepped through, disappearing into the glow of the daylight. Only when his shadow faded did Victoria dare to breathe again.

Cora cocked her head toward the young Englishwoman as she slid the revolver into a low-slung holster on her belt. Victoria's blue eyes were rimmed with white as she blinked back.

"Didn't I warn you about them, Miss Fancy?" Before Victoria could respond, she turned to the flabbergasted men at the tables. "What're you all gawking at? Ain't you never seen a gun before?"

She spat on the floor. "Fine lot you are, watching a lady get roughed up and not lifting a finger. I ought to shoot the bunch of you for yellow cowards." A few of the men grumbled in protest, but they fell silent when Cora's hand returned to the butt of her gun. "Go on now, all of you. The Print Shop is closed for today."

They rose to their feet and shuffled past the two women, some with a glare at Victoria. When the batwings creaked shut behind the last man, Cora heaved a sigh. Crossing her arms, she leaned against the bar and looked at Victoria. "Can't leave you alone for five minutes, can I?"

Victoria's tongue darted across her lips. She tried to speak, but the words caught in her throat.

"You're welcome," Cora said, "but don't go thinking I did that because I like you. Fact is, I ain't all that fond of you. I reckon that little display with Wilson showed you that this ain't no place fit for prancing ponies and the like. You prance too much out here, you get yourself hurt. Hard places make hard men, and you got to be just as hard if you aim to keep all your parts and pieces."

"I'll remember that," Victoria said.

Cora nodded. "See that you do, because I ain't going to jump in next time." She fell silent, seeming to ponder that for a second. Victoria did not want to dwell on it any longer, but she could think of nothing else to say. Even now, she could still feel Wilson's fingers on her arms, dirty nails digging into her skin.

"But," Cora said, "that ain't the real reason we're still talking." Her face grew grave, a look of determination and cold fury that made Victoria slightly uneasy. "I reckon you figured that me and that Fodor Glava got us some history."

"Yes," Victoria said, unsure if she should explain further.

Cora didn't give her the option. "We've crossed paths a time or two, and it never was a happy time when we did. Thing is, I'm right sure our last meeting ended with my stabbing him and shooting him and cutting off his head."

Victoria covered her mouth with her hand. "What did you say?"

"That I killed the dirty son of a bitch like the dog he was," Cora said. "Don't go all fluttery on me. Ain't no man living or dead deserved it more, except maybe the feller who made him. What's the term King George used? Sired, I think. I reckon Glava's sire was a nasty bit of work himself. Maybe he's still off somewhere killing folk, maybe not. Ain't my concern. What is my concern is that I know I killed that Glava dead."

"So you think I'm lying to you again."

"Well, I'd be lying my own self if I said that thought ain't crossed my mind," Cora said. "More I thought it over, though, the more I figured that there ain't no way you could have known to say that name to me. We ain't never met before, you clearly ain't been out west before, and you ain't in the business your own self. Then I thought, well, maybe old King George or

Father Baez gave you the tip-off." Victoria was about
to deny it, but Cora held up her hand. "No need to
say a word. Sure, both of them was there four years
ago and saw enough to tell, but ain't neither one
going to just up and spout out secrets like that. Father
Baez ain't the sort, and I wouldn't bet a nickel on
George being able to pull a single name out of that
pudding bowl he calls a head."

Victoria smiled at that. "Yes, he is a singularly scat-
tered man, isn't he?"

"Back in Leadville, I figured we'd ride up to that
big house of his one day and find him outside in his
bloomers and nothing else."

"We?" Victoria asked.

"I meant me."

The sudden edge in Cora's voice took Victoria by
surprise. "I'm sorry," she said, although she wasn't
sure why she was apologizing.

Cora waved her hand dismissively. "It ain't important. What been eating at me is how this feller of
yours knew that name. Even more, I want to know
why he knew to tell you to tell me." She looked at
Victoria for a long moment. The younger woman
shifted her weight. She laced her fingers together
and rested her hands on the bar. She tried meeting
Cora's gaze but soon began studying the bottles lining the wall. There was something about the old
hunter's eyes that unsettled her. They sparked with
intelligence, but there was something else lurking in
them. Something darker, hidden in the shadow cast
by that intelligence.

"Well, I guess it don't matter none, anyhow," Cora finally said. "Only a few people in the world as would know that name, and I just named all of them. Puts me in a right fine puzzlement, and I ain't going to sleep proper till I get an answer."

"What will you do, then?" Victoria asked.

"Hunt that bastard down and make him sing for me," Cora replied. "Can't be Glava himself, but whoever he is, he knows about him. Worse, he's making himself out to be him. Anyone who'd take that monster's name is looking to be one in his own right, and I won't stand for it."

Victoria nodded. She wasn't sure why Cora was telling her all of this. Disappointment and fear still churned inside her, and hearing Cora talk only intensified the vortex. Instead of boarding an east-bound train with her, the old hunter wanted to ride off into the desert after the blue-eyed man. Even if Cora somehow managed to find the man calling himself Fodor Glava, she probably wouldn't do it in time to save Victoria from the red-eyed woman's wrath. The young woman tried to swallow her fear, eyes downcast as she wracked her brain for some way out of the trap she'd stumbled into.

"Seems right two-faced of me, I know," Cora said. "Here I am telling you I'm setting out to hunt me down a monster in the self-same morning I said I ain't helping you with yours."

Victoria looked at the old hunter in surprise. She hadn't expected her to just come out and say what Victoria herself had already considered. Holding her tongue, she hoped Cora would next admit that such hypocrisy didn't sit well with her or something of that nature.

"Fact is, I ain't any more inclined to trot on out to England to do your job than I was yesterday. I still prefer poker and whiskey to travel, even in a fancy train car, and I ain't got no interest at all in prancing about with the likes of you and George all day. If the good Lord wanted me to be fancy, he'd have made me out of silk and pearls or some such."

Cora paused, running a hand over her chin as if what she was going to say next wouldn't come out without encouragement. "You understand," she said, "that I ain't the sort to rely on nobody. Ain't but a few folks in this wide world that I trust, and I've had to kill some of them, too. I don't want to be adding to either list right now, but it seems I have to if I'm to get my answers. You're the only one who can take me to this feller, meaning I have to ask you for help to find him. I don't like it none, but there it is.

"So here's the deal." Her fist slammed down onto the bar, making Victoria jump. "You take me to this feller of yours so I can have my answers from him. Once he's had his say and I've put him in the ground, I'll follow you back to wherever you want and settle your spooks. Deal?"

Victoria couldn't believe her sudden change of fortune. "You would really do that?" she asked.

"If I hadn't said it, you would have," Cora said. "I need your help, you need mine. I reckon my helping you will be a sight more work than you helping me, but I guess I'm just generous like that. So we got a deal?"

"Yes! Yes, absolutely," Victoria said, trying unsuccessfully to keep the excitement out of her voice. She shook Cora's offered hand. "When do we start?"

SIX

Her stomach rolled and pinched, begging to be fed. The girl ignored it as best she could. It would do no good to go to her father for help. He could not feed her any more than he could feed himself. His legs were thin like a bird's legs now, and his face had sharp edges. She didn't like the way he looked.

They had been living in the new area for a long time. She could barely remember her old home, the one with the big blanket over the entrance. It seemed like something she dreamed at night to forget what it was like to be awake. She was always hungry, but she didn't like waiting in line for food from the soldiers. All of the people looked sad when they stood in that line. They talked of times when they could plant their own food, when they were safe from the Apaches, when they lived in the land their ancestors had given them. They did not belong here, in the place they called Hwéeldi.

The girl did not understand everything they said. She didn't remember the life she had before Hwéeldi. To hear the other people speak of it, it had been a happy life, and it made her sad to think she didn't remember it.

She did remember her mother, though, and the memory made her sadder than anything else. Her mother had been brave and strong and good. How could she have died? When she closed her eyes, the girl could sometimes see the blood covering her mother's feet as she shivered from the cold. Other women had ridden in the cart with the girl, but her mother would not sit next to them, even when her feet began leaving red footprints in the dirt.

When she thought about it, it made the girl angry. If her mother had ridden in the cart with them, she might not have died and left her alone with her father. The girl didn't like being angry at her mother. Still, she would sometimes think of that memory before she went to sleep at night. If she did, she might dream of her mother again. The dreams weren't always nice, but her mother was alive in them, and that was enough.

One night, she dreamed that her mother came to her as she stood in the line for food. She was as pretty as ever, the sun shining in her hair. In the strange way of dreams, the girl didn't remember that her mother was dead; she just smiled at her. Her mother wrapped the girl's hand in one of her own and led her away from the line into one of the stone buildings used by the soldiers. The girl was frightened to be in this room, but she only held on to her mother's hand and said nothing. Her mother was wise; if she was in this room, it was allowed.

Soldiers suddenly appeared in the room with their blue clothes and long weapons. The girl knew now that those weapons were loud and dangerous. She had seen the soldiers kill men with them. Hiding behind her mother, the girl cringed as they yelled and pointed their weapons. Her *mother tried to speak to them, but they did not understand her. The girl knew some of the white man's tongue and looked up, hoping to speak for her mother.*

The weapons roared, and the girl woke with tears on her cheeks.

Victoria itched. Her arms itched, her legs itched, her head itched, her feet itched, her hands itched, even her face itched. She blamed her new clothes for much of the problem, but the sun and the desert wind were also at fault. The sun beat down on her, making sweat bead on her forehead beneath the brim of her hat. Stirred up by the wind, dust and sand clung to the sweat, forming a film that covered her from eyebrow to collarbone. Denim trousers – the first trousers she'd ever worn – rode up behind her knees and chaffed her thighs. Her new shirt was slightly too large, billowing out around her chest, and yet it still bunched up under her armpits and stuck to her back. Blisters were already starting to form on her feet, drawn up by the rubbing of her new boots. The horse's constant motion beneath her, up and down, back and forth, twisted her hips and back until the joints creaked with every step.

She was miserable.

"You sure we're riding the right way?" Cora asked from beside her.

Victoria squinted at the horizon. "As long as we don't change direction, yes. It was dark, though, so I can't be certain." Truth be told, she wasn't at all sure they were going the right way. They'd started from where the blue-eyed man had left her just outside of town and ridden back along his path. None of the landscape looked familiar because it all looked the same: scrub brush the color of aged cheese and taller bushes standing like sentinels at irregular intervals. Mesas loomed on the horizon, distant and serene, attended by rolling hills.

The sight was enough to make her dizzy, and she dropped her gaze to the saddle horn. What made her most uncomfortable about her predicament, even more than the blisters swelling on her heels or the vast expanse surrounding her, was the weight resting on her left leg. She glanced nervously at the smooth wooden grip sticking out of the holster like a thick, hooked finger. The guns her father used to hunt game had always frightened her; to carry one on her person, even a small one, made her more than a little uneasy. She kept expecting the heat or the motion of the horse to somehow make it fire and blow her leg off. When dismounting to make water or eat a quick meal of salted beef, she made sure to carefully remove the revolver from its holster and hand it to a smirking Cora.

"How far was it, again?" Cora interrupted her thoughts.

"I'm not sure, exactly," Victoria said. "The woman with him said it was farther than I could walk in a day and a night."

"So two day's walk, then? I'd say that's about a day's ride if we push it some." Cora tapped her heels into her horse, an aging chestnut mare she called Our

Lady of Virginia. The mare responded by breaking into a brisk trot. Victoria urged her own horse forward to match Cora's pace. She hadn't bothered coming up with a name for her new mount, a silver-grey gelding whose coat seemed to shimmer in the sunlight. Cora had picked it out. No horse would be more reliable than a good old Confederate grey, she said.

Aside from her own mare, anyway. Victoria's stomach had turned slightly when she saw how comfortable and indeed friendly Cora was with her horse. The old hunter not only spoke to it as if it could understand her, she even fed it handfuls of oats from time to time. Victoria shuddered at the thought of a horse's wide, slobbering lips covering her hands. Even if she did bother to name her new beast, she would never go that far.

"Quick!" Cora's voice cracked like rawhide strips.

Victoria's head snapped up, but she couldn't see anything. "What is it?"

Cora punched Our Lady's sides, and the mare sprang away. Startled, Victoria tried to follow her, but the gelding didn't heed her kicks or her voice. It tossed its head at her and kept its trotting pace, forcing Victoria to watch Cora thunder off into the desert. The old hunter pulled a rifle out of her back scabbard as she rode. Somehow, she managed to hold it level as the horse ran beneath her, aiming at something Victoria couldn't see. Even at this distance, the gunshot clapped her ears like thunder. She flinched along with her horse, cowering slightly in the saddle. A second shot.

When the ringing in her ears died away, she could hear Cora whooping at her. She looked in the direction of the hollers and saw the old hunter pointing at the ground.

"What is it?" Victoria asked.

"Supper," Cora replied. "Now go on and fetch it up."

"I beg your pardon?"

"Them's the rules, Vicky. One shoots, the other roots."

"My name is Victoria."

"Sure is." Cora slid the rifle back into the scabbard. "If you don't pick up that hare, I'll make sure they carve it up real pretty on your tombstone."

Victoria couldn't tell how serious Cora was, but she figured it was safer not to take chances. Father Baez's warning came back into her mind, bringing with it a slight chill despite the afternoon sun. The old hunter was more than just her hope for vengeance now. Out here, she was also her best hope for survival. While she probably wouldn't shoot her outright, Cora could easily make this trip and the trip to England miserable if she chose.

Sighing, Victoria turned her horse toward her companion. Keeping her hand on her new gun, she climbed down from the saddle and walked to where Cora was pointing. Her boots rubbed against her blisters, but at least her feet were safe from the rocks and spines covering the ground. She smiled at the thought. She might be traveling with a woman of questionable sanity toward a rendezvous with two not-quite-human creatures in the middle of the

American desert, but at least she wasn't wearing her dressing gown this time. Indeed, before she'd discovered just how uncomfortable they could be, she'd quite liked the sight of herself dressed in such a roguish manner.

Her smile vanished when she caught sight of a small, bloody mass lying among the brambles. She glanced back at Cora, but the hunter merely waved her on. Steadying herself, Victoria stepped toward the remains. Tan fur streaked with brown covered a small, round body. The rabbit's head was gone, its neck ending in a red, oozing stump. Victoria held one hand over her mouth and nose as she reached toward the animal. She wrapped her fingers around one long, furry leg and lifted. The rabbit was heavier than she expected. Its front legs hung at awkward angles, one foot pointing accusingly back at her.

Holding the carcass at arm's length, Victoria turned back to Cora and held it out.

"Ain't you going to tie it up?" Cora said.

"What?"

"Well, I reckon you could carry it in your lap the rest of the way if you're so inclined, but most folk like to tie up their kills."

"It isn't my kill, it's yours," Victoria said.

"You'll change your tune come nightfall," Cora said. "Won't be nothing better in all the world than half a roast hare. We can't roast it if we don't have it, and I ain't carrying it." She turned Our Lady around and nudged her forward.

"Wait!" Victoria said, running after her. "How am I supposed to tie it up?"

Reaching into one of her saddlebags, Cora produced a spool of twine and tossed it to her. "Don't tell me you can't tie a knot, or I might just give up on you right here."

Victoria replied with a huff of indignation. Setting the carcass down, she recovered the spool from where it had fallen and walked back to her horse. She wasn't a frontier explorer or fur trapper, but she could at least tie a knot. Aristocratic society in England came with its own set of dangers and trappings. Without a rudimentary knowledge of knots and bows, she'd have embarrassed herself at more than one social.

Tying a headless rabbit to a horse in the middle of the desert was a new application of that knowledge, however. She figured the saddle horn was as good a place as any to loop the first knot. Holding the twine in place with one hand, she balanced the spool on the saddle seat. Pulling a long, horrid knife – yet another piece of her new outfit – from her belt, she sawed at the bit of twine joining her loop to the spool. After it snapped, she quickly put the knife back in her belt and proceeded to tie the first knot.

Now for the unpleasant part. Picking up the rabbit by its hind legs, she hurried back and set to work. The rabbit's blood smelled faintly of old coinage, and she wrinkled her nose. After a few unsuccessful attempts, she managed to loop the twine around the joints in the hind legs. The rabbit almost seemed to twitch and dance as she tied the knot around its ankles. Despite herself, she pictured the March Hare from Mr. Carroll's story dancing headless in her hands, waving his tea kettle about in one bloody paw. The image made her shudder, and she nearly let the knot slip as she looped it around a second time.

Finally, the ordeal was done. Wiping her hands on her trousers, she stepped back to evaluate. The hare hung upside down, blood still dripping from its neck. Swallowing back a sudden impulse to vomit, she tucked the twine into one of her own saddlebags. By the time she pulled herself up into the saddle, Cora was already several hundred yards ahead. The carcass bumped into her leg as she spurred her horse into a trot.

"Get it sorted?" Cora asked as she rode up.

"I believe so," Victoria said. She lifted the twine for Cora's inspection.

Cora barely glanced at the hare. "Why, you're a regular grizzly trapper."

"I don't appreciate your sarcasm."

"Weren't sarcasm, neither," Cora said.

Victoria opened her mouth to reply, but the smirk on Cora's lips made her think twice. The old hunter was baiting her. Victoria dropped the conversation and the hare, turning her attention to the landscape before them. Nothing had changed except the length of their shadows, which had started to grow as the sun climbed downward from its noonday spot.

Hours later, as the sun approached the horizon, Cora pulled her mare up short. Lost in the haze,

Victoria didn't notice. She kept plodding toward the setting sun until the hunter's voice brought her around.

"Hold up a second," Cora said.

Victoria started, jerking the reins back. Her horse snorted in protest. "What is it?"

Cora held up a hand to block the sun's glare. Crow's feet deepened around her eyes as she squinted into the distance. "Looks like we might be getting some weather up ahead."

"What do you mean?" Victoria asked, turning to look for herself.

"That line on the horizon there," Cora said. "That looks like more than a little trouble."

Victoria could barely make out the dark grey smudge in the distance. "Are you sure? It can't be more than a light shower."

Cora's laughter rolled back at them from a nearby hill. "I don't reckon we've ever seen one of those around these parts. Here, it's either parched or flooding, and nothing in between."

"Really?" Victoria asked, looking at the withered plants surrounding them. "It doesn't look to me as though these plants have ever seen so much as a sprinkle, much less a flood."

"Just you wait," Cora said. "You're about to see the sky boil up all angry and menacing in half the time it takes you to blink. When it does, we'd best be close to this ranch of yours, or the going will get a good sight harder."

Victoria squinted into the sunlight. They stood on

a small hill that spilled down into a wide plain before them. In the distance, she could see rust-colored cliffs rising from the desert floor to form the sides of a small mesa. The shape of it looked vaguely familiar, but she couldn't be sure if she'd actually seen it before or if it just looked like one of the countless others they'd ridden past. "I do think we're getting closer."

Another laugh. "We'd best be, Vicky. If you've been playing me for a fool, we'll find out just how good you are with that shiny new gun of yours."

"A fine test that would be," Victoria answered. "You know I've never fired a gun in my life."

"Time to change that, I reckon," Cora said. She pulled her own revolver from its holster. The sun glinted on the nickel finish. "Go on, draw."

Victoria gently wrapped her fingers around the wood grip of her gun. Taking a breath, she slid it from its leather cradle. Cora had picked it out specifically for her back in Albuquerque, saying it was best suited for a fine lady. Except for its new, unused polish and shine, it looked exactly like Cora's revolver, which she called a Colt .38. Victoria knew the number had something to do with the bullets, but she wasn't sure what.

"Glad to see you can do that much," Cora said, "though I'd try to do it without wincing next time if I was you."

"I don't want it to go off before I'm ready is all," Victoria said.

"No worry about that unless you get your fine lady

fingers on the trigger," Cora replied. "These here guns are good quality. So long as you treat them right, they ain't never going to let you down." She urged her mare forward, beckoning for Victoria to follow. "Come on, now. Ain't no reason you can't learn to ride and shoot at the same time."

Reluctantly, Victoria gave her gelding a punch with her heels. Her stomach twisted inside her, feeling like it was going to jump out of her mouth at any moment. She swallowed. No need to worry. If this rustic, uneducated woman could master the use of guns, so could she. One of her grandfathers had served in the Royal Navy, hunting pirates far and wide. She had the blood of a soldier in her veins; firing a gun would soon become second nature.

"Now, then," Cora said, "I reckon even a fine lady is familiar with the simple idea of a gun, right? You just point it at something and pull the trigger?"

"Yes."

"Good. Means we can go on to the finer bits of it. First off, you got to pick something you think would be better with a few more holes in it." Cora pointed at a large bush ahead of them on her right. "There, now, that looks like it might be trouble if we don't see to it first, don't it?"

"I suppose, yes," Victoria replied.

"Once you've got your target, all you got to do is point the gun, pull back the hammer, and squeeze the trigger. It's best if you try to aim a bit first, though. No good wasting bullets if you ain't got to, especially the ones we shoot." Cora leveled her arm at the bush. "Aiming's best if you close one eye and line up the sight over your varmint. Once you got your shot lined up, pull back the hammer." She demonstrated. "This is about as far as you get when aiming at most folk. Even them as call themselves outlaws will go all watery in the legs when you got a bead on them. Real outlaws and monsters, well, they're a different story."

"Have you ever shot another human?" Victoria asked.

"You bet your bonnet I has," Cora said. "Back in my younger days, me and Ben would fall afoul with bandits every now and again. Some we knew, some we didn't, but it don't matter none when the other feller's sending lead your way. So we shot back, killed a handful, and the rest tucked tail."

"Who's Ben?"

Cora's gun arm drooped. She looked down at Our Lady of Virginia without replying. Victoria watched her, suddenly anxious, the revolver in her hand forgotten. The silence stretched out like the desert around them. In the distance, some animal let out a high-pitched cry, and Victoria's gelding tossed his head.

"My late husband," Cora finally said.

Victoria felt a tug of pity for the old gunfighter. "I'm sorry. How did he die?"

"Ain't none of your business is how," Cora said. Without warning, she brought her Colt back up and fired. The gunshot jolted Victoria from head to toe and stuffed her ears with cotton. The gelding whinnied in alarm.

Cora spurred Our Lady into a trot, putting several yards between them. "There now," she called over her shoulder, "you give it a try."

Victoria remembered the revolver in her hand. She squeezed the grip against her palm and lifted it. It wasn't as big as some of the ones she'd seen the men in Albuquerque carry, but it was still heavy for its size. Holding it out at arm's length made it difficult to keep the barrel raised. Gritting her teeth, she closed one eye and looked down the gun at the bush Cora had picked out. The metal nub at the end of the barrel wavered in her hand. She forced it to hold still while she pulled the hammer back. The cylinder rotated with a soft click.

Now for the moment of reckoning.

Closing her eyes, she pulled the trigger. The Colt stung her fingers as it jolted in her hand, but she kept her hold on it. Her horse broke into a run, nearly throwing her backward out of the saddle. Her free hand wrapped around the saddle horn before she could open her eyes. Instinct took over, and she crouched low in the saddle, bending low over the gelding's grey mane. Her balance restored, she gripped the animal between her knees and released her hold on the saddle horn. The reins bounced along the horse's neck. She grabbed them with her free hand and began pulling backward, easing the gelding out of his frightened run.

As they slowed to a trot, the thunder of the gelding's hooves was replaced by rasping echoes of laughter. Turning her grey back toward the hunter,

Victoria frowned. "I hardly see what's so amusing," she called to her companion.

"Just been a good long while since I rode with a greenhorn is all," Cora replied. "I plumb forget how funny you lot can be."

"I think I performed rather well, all things considered," Victoria said, sitting up straight. "After all, I completed the lesson and managed to keep my seat."

"You ain't no stranger to riding, I'll give you that," Cora said, suppressing another chuckle. "Still, a display like that ain't going to do you any favors in a firefight. Can't go spooking your horse with every shot."

"What do you suggest I do, then?" Victoria asked. "Tell the dumb beast I'm about to fire a gun and that it might want to brace itself?"

"Might work. Might also try making friends with him." Cora patted her mare's neck. "Me and Our Lady been riding together for well over ten years now. I trust her more than any other creature on God's green earth, animal and human both. We've pulled each other out of more scrapes than I can recollect. She knows I wouldn't never do a thing to put her in danger unless it was necessary, so she don't bat an eye when she feels me setting up to shoot."

Victoria grimaced. "You expect me to befriend an animal?"

Cora urged Our Lady forward until the two women were no more than three feet apart. "What, that don't sit well with you?" Reading Victoria's expression, she shook her head. "You ain't going to last out here, kid."

"I am not a child."

"No, you ain't," Cora said. "Even kids know how much rides on the backs of horses in these parts, and it ain't just your pretty little rump. Horses are the difference between life and death out here. You got a good one under you, you got a good chance of surviving most everything this desert can throw at you. Sun, coyotes, thirst…all of them's easier to deal with if you're mounted right. That's why they ain't cheap. That pretty grey cost you a bundle, didn't he?"

"Yes," Victoria admitted. "A full one hundred and fifty of your dollars."

"One hundred fifty," Cora repeated. "That's more than a schoolteacher would see in two years of teaching. Maybe them as own a railroad or two wouldn't bat an eye at that, but most folk can't buy a horse all easy-like the way you done."

"I'll spend my money how I see fit," Victoria said.

"Ain't my point. Point is, you'd best make friends with that critter under you. He's apt to save your life if you do. If you don't, he'll throw you sooner or later."

"I never bothered to befriend any of the horses I rode as a girl, and they didn't throw me off."

"But was you shooting guns at other folk shooting back?" Victoria shook her head. "There you go, then. Them horses you rode before didn't need to trust you none."

"But this one does?"

Cora nodded emphatically. "Now you're catching on. Put it another way: how do you reckon you'd get back to town if you didn't have a horse?"

"If I didn't have a horse," Victoria said, "I wouldn't have left town in the first place."

"Well, ain't you the clever one," Cora said. "Silly me trying to teach a fancy lady anything, seeing as how I ain't book-learned."

Before Victoria could reply, Cora put her heels to her horse. Our Lady eased into a healthy gallop in the space of a few seconds. Soon, both horse and rider disappeared into the dust clouds they stirred up, leaving Victoria alone on the hillside.

Turning her own horse to follow, Victoria urged him into a trot. The headless hare bounced against her leg. Overhead, the shape of a bird circled, black against the blue sky.

How could she befriend a horse? Even if she felt so inclined, it wasn't as though she'd brought apples or sugar along in her saddlebags. Cora's list of supplies included salted beef, a flavorless sort of biscuit she called hardtack, and sacks of oats for the horses. Tough food for a tough land, she'd said in the general store. Tough food wouldn't win a horse's love, though; even Victoria knew that. She'd seen her father's grooms tending to the horses, watched how they'd slip the animals apple slices while brushing them down at night. A silly thing to do, or so she'd thought then.

Did she really need to bother with such things, even now? She was familiar enough with the animals to know that this one wasn't scared of her. When she'd fired her gun, the horse had spooked and bolted, but it hadn't thrown her. Besides, she planned on keeping the animal just long enough to help Cora hunt down the blue-eyed man, the one calling himself Fodor Glava. Once they were done, she would sell it back to the Albuquerque livery and leave this God-forsaken desert behind her. She would return to Oxford with its proper laws, proper dress, and proper baths.

The thought made her smile. Punching her heels into the gelding, she bent low over his neck and galloped down the hill after Cora.

SEVEN

"This it, then?"

Victoria nodded. Thunder growled overhead. The line of clouds that had seemed so distant from the ridge had grown into an angry wall that blocked out the setting sun. No rain fell yet, but Victoria could see it was only a matter of time. In that premature twilight, they had finally come upon the ranch. The buildings were dwarfed by the cliffs rising toward the sky behind them. Victoria felt a strange sense of vertigo, but whether it was from the towering mesa or returning to the site of her harrowing ordeal two nights prior, she didn't know.

"You got yourself a head for directions, Vicky. I'll give you that."

Victoria took the compliment in silence. All she had done was strike out in the same direction she'd seen the blue-eyed man leave in when he deposited her outside of Albuquerque. Such a simple task didn't seem worthy of praise, but she wouldn't deny it, either.

"Well, at least it ain't one of them Indian ruins. Nasty places if half the yarns about them are true."

"Haven't you visited them yourself?" Victoria asked. "I would think that sort of thing would be of great interest to you."

"Just never got around to it is all," Cora said.

The two women nudged their mounts into a slow walk. In the veiled sunlight, the ranch didn't look half as terrifying. The barn was missing a few shingles from its roof and could have done with a fresh coat of paint. Rust stains ran along the wind pump's legs like gangrenous veins, and the house looked as though nobody had gone in or out since her encounter. It was more a scene of sorrow over failed ambition, left behind by the homesteaders whose bid for a new life had come up short. She had difficulty imagining it as a monster's lair, but even so, she examined every corner and every shadow as they approached.

Beside her, Cora was just as watchful, her alertness underscored by the rifle in her hands. She didn't have it propped against her shoulder, ready to fire at the slightest hint of movement, but its presence gave Victoria a measure of comfort.

Victoria explained the details of her encounter to the old hunter as they approached. Cora listened attentively, even as her eyes remained on the silent buildings before them. She asked a few questions, mostly about the man. How tall was he? What did he look like? How did he speak? Victoria answered as best she could, but she grew more uneasy as the line of questions continued. That Cora's attention was centered on the man worried her. The woman was the more dangerous of the two, she felt, but Cora seemed uninterested in her. Even the savage ghoul provoked more questions than the Indian woman did.

Another rumbling of thunder, this one louder. Cora glanced skyward. "Ain't got much time," she said. Reaching into her satchel, she pulled out a rosary and slid it around her left wrist. "Let's check the barn first."

Victoria nodded. She considered pulling her own gun, then thought better of it. Dismounting with it in one hand would probably be dangerous. Best to wait until they were on foot.

No sooner had she decided this than Cora cradled her rifle in the crook of one arm and climbed out of the saddle. Tying the reins to a fence post, she looked up at Victoria expectantly. The younger woman took her time dismounting. Her eyes began searching the area in earnest. Being mounted had given her a feeling of security; if things went wrong, she felt sure her horse could outrun the threat. Without that assurance, she felt exposed and vulnerable.

"Don't dally, now," Cora said, tying the gelding's reins off for her. "Rain ain't going to wait for you to fluff your skirts. Draw your gun and let's get on."

Victoria adjusted her hat to hide her blush and drew her revolver. "What's the plan?"

"Well, from what you said, I reckon we're looking at a vampire nest," Cora replied. "Ain't sure how many suckers there are, though there's bound to be at least two. One of them's the feller what calls himself Glava. He's the more dangerous of them, so don't you go getting it in your head that you can whip him by your lonesome." Cora snapped her fingers as a thought hit her. "Plumb forgot. Here, hold this and give me your gun."

Cora shoved her rifle at Victoria with one hand and held out her other palm. Victoria handed over her revolver. Taking the rifle from the hunter, she marveled at its weight. The barrel must have been ten pounds at least. She had to hold it with both hands, and she wasn't sure if she could shoot it even if she had to. Curious, she pressed the butt up against her shoulder like she'd seen Cora do. Her arm shook under the barrel's weight as she aimed at a fence post across the yard, and she had to lower it after only a few seconds.

"Careful there," Cora said. "You might go and blow your own foot off."

Victoria let out a nervous laugh. "Not much chance of that," she said.

"You an expert on guns now, too?"

"Hardly." Victoria held the rifle in both hands again, her fingers well away from the trigger.

"Well, here's another lesson, then," Cora said, handing the revolver back. Victoria gladly traded weapons. "I've put some of my silver bullets in your gun. They're the only kind that can kill vampires, you follow?"

"Not really, but I believe you."

Cora nodded in satisfaction. "Good to know you ain't a complete fool. Now, even with the silver rounds, you ain't going to kill a sucker if you just shoot it in the arm or somewhere like that. You got to hit them in the head or the heart. I know you ain't big on aiming yet, but try your best. You might get lucky, and luck's half of survival in this business."

"That isn't very reassuring."

"Well, these ain't normal critters," Cora said. "Don't fret about it too much. Just shoot at them if they pop their ugly faces out. Even if you only nick one, it still might slow it down some. Enough for me to get a bead on it anyway. Oh, and use this." She produced a small wooden crucifix from her satchel. "This here will make them go all watery and buy you some time for shooting or running or hollering."

Victoria ran her thumb over the carved image. "Why do they fear crucifixes?"

"Ain't rightly sure, myself," Cora said. "I always figured it was just that crucifixes are holy and suckers ain't. Don't need to know much more than that, really."

"Even after all of your experience?"

Cora pumped the action of her Winchester. "Ain't just vampires I hunted. They popped up every now and again, but they ain't really all that common. Had more run-ins with hellhounds during my time."

"Hellhounds?" Victoria asked, her curiosity suddenly piqued. Maybe that was the name of the black shuck in America. "What are those?"

"Some other time," Cora said.

"But–"

The hunter put a finger to her lips and frowned as she approached the barn. Crouching by the door, Cora waved Victoria over. The young woman hunkered down next to her, careful to keep her revolver pointed away.

"Right," Cora said in a low voice. "This is where you said they had you?" Victoria nodded. "Good. Now, if they're around here still, they probably know we're here. Hard to creep up on critters with sharp ears."

"What will we do, then?" Victoria asked.

"Surprise ain't an option, so we go for storm."

Victoria glanced skyward. "Storm?"

"Not that kind," Cora said. "We'd best be done with this business when them clouds decides to dump on us. What I mean is, we go in sudden-like, try to shake them up."

Victoria swallowed. The man who called himself Fodor Glava didn't seem like the kind to startle easily, and she wasn't sure that slavering man-creature could even feel fear. Still, neither of those were her biggest concern. "What about the Indian woman?"

"She ain't a worry," Cora said.

"Are you sure?" Victoria asked. "She seemed to have a power over the other man."

Cora shook her head. "Ain't likely. You probably just didn't know what was going on. This Fodor Glava feller is one of them king vampires George knows about. Nossy-something. Anyhow, they got control over the other kind of vampires, so I'll warrant he's master of that squaw you saw, too."

The old hunter's reasoning didn't sit well with Victoria. She knew what she had seen: the man had submitted to the woman's will, and more than once. Still, Cora knew more about these matters than she did, so maybe there was something else at work. Victoria tried to set aside her misgivings.

"I'll charge in first, and you follow," Cora was saying. "Keep an eye on our rear in case the bastard has an ace in his palm."

Victoria nodded. Cora offered her a lopsided grin as she rose to her feet. The hunter's brown eyes scanned the yard once more before she turned toward the barn door.

A yell burst forth from Cora's lungs. She ran into the barn's interior and halted a few steps inside, rifle raised. The rosary hung from her left wrist, whipping back and forth as she swept the Winchester's barrel over the grey shadows. Nothing jumped out at her.

Victoria stood, her blisters throbbing in protest. The yard remained empty. Wind kicked through the tall grass growing along the fence. Crucifix and gun pointed outward, she slowly backed through the open doorway. The daylight became a blue square surrounded by darkness. Fear began working crawling up her sides, making its way toward her throat. The terror and confusion of that night still lingered in the barn. Phantom eyes of red and blue drifted through her peripheral vision only to vanish when she turned her head. In her mounting panic, she nearly pulled the trigger half a dozen times.

She shook her head. No, she was stronger than this. If the woman at her back, rustic and uneducated, could barge into a nest of monsters without hesitation, so could she. After all, she was her father's daughter and descended from Navy sailors. Her grandfather had faced down pirate ships; she could handle one old barn.

Behind her, she heard Cora's steadily advancing footsteps. Victoria clung to that sound, a spire of rock in the rising ocean of her fears. With every step, every tinkling of the old hunter's spurs, Victoria's panic subsided.

"Hey!" Cora's shout shattered Victoria's nerves. "You in here, you bastard?"

"By God," Victoria said, "you scared the life out of me."

The hunter lowered her rifle. "You're the only one, I reckon. Ain't nothing here."

"Are you sure?"

"Sure as I can be," Cora replied. "If that feller is here, he's keen on keeping to himself." She looked above them. "Could be he's up there somewhere sleeping."

"Sleeping?" Victoria asked. "Who could sleep through a shout like that?"

"A sucker," Cora said. "They like to sleep during the day. Why don't you shimmy on up that ladder over there and have a look?"

Victoria's eyes went wide. "What?"

"You heard me. I'll keep an eye out down here."

"And what should I do if I find something?"

Cora shrugged. "I say shoot it. If you come up with something better, go with that."

"You can't be serious," Victoria said. "You could very well be sending me to my death."

"Not much chance of that," Cora said. "I don't reckon much of anything is up there except hay, and these old bones ain't up to climbing a ladder unless they got a damn good reason. If you do happen across a sleeping monster, I reckon even you couldn't miss. Now go on and get yourself up there."

The hunter turned toward the door, rifle at the ready. Victoria almost tapped her on the shoulder to refuse, then thought better of it. Cora obviously didn't think there was any danger, or she would have gone up herself. Victoria wasn't foolish enough to believe that it would have been because of any motherly protectiveness. The old hunter held Victoria and her abilities in contempt, so in her mind, sending her to investigate a real threat would have been useless.

Time to prove her wrong, then. Victoria strode toward the ladder Cora had pointed out. Holding the crucifix lightly between her teeth, she gripped a rung with her free hand and began climbing.

It was slow going. She had never climbed a ladder one-handed before, and she was already tired from the day's ride. Maybe something was up there after all, and Cora really hadn't wanted to make the climb. With each rung, that possibility seemed more and more likely, but Victoria would not be outdone. Grumbling to herself, she continued to move up toward the barn loft.

Near the top, she paused when a thought struck her. Suppose there really was a vampire in the loft? Would Cora be able to climb up quickly enough to help? Would she even bother? She already had everything she needed: the location of the man called Fodor Glava. Maybe she would just abandon Victoria to her fate now to save herself the trip to England. Victoria stole a quick glance toward the ground. The old hunter still stood guard in front of the door, but for how long?

Still, Victoria had no choice: it was either check the loft or climb back down and accuse Cora of treachery to her face. She had better odds of surviving a vampire.

The ladder brought her through the hole in the loft floor. Victoria paused when she reached it, taking a look around. A single window admitted a stream of grey light into the interior, illuminating bales of hay that were strewn about in no apparent order. In the semi-dark, they looked like a herd of squarish beasts sleeping away the day.

After a few moments passed with no visible movement, Victoria finished the climb and cautiously stepped off the ladder. Her footsteps sounded hollow on the boards, and she forced herself not to think about the expanse of nothing beneath her. It would only make her giddy, and she needed all of her wits if there was anything up here. Taking the crucifix back into her left hand, she began exploring the loft.

Near the ladder lay a coil of rope she mistook at first for a snake. Rolling her eyes at herself, she walked over to the nearest hay bale. It seemed ordinary, and nothing hid behind it. The same was true of the others she inspected. With each non-discovery, her fears wilted a little more.

Coming around the last of the bales, she paused. There was something lying in the far corner. It was probably just a pile of rags, but it looked wrong somehow. Long and thin, like a person hiding beneath a blanket. It was too small to be either the blue-eyed man or his enslaved ghoul. Still, it was in the corner farthest from the window. It made her uneasy, but curiosity soon overcame her caution, and she moved to investigate.

The closer she came to it, the more the object resembled a sleeping person. Pausing a few feet away from it, she reassured herself that it was probably just a bundle of hay or farm tools wrapped in a burlap sheet. If it was a vampire, surely it would have attacked her by now. Nothing to fear.

Stepping up to the lump, she prodded it with the toe of her boot. It didn't move. More confident now, Victoria slid the crucifix into her belt and reached down. The burlap was rough on her fingers as she pulled it back.

The face of a young girl emerged.

Victoria cried out in surprise, jumping backward. She tripped over her own boots and fell onto the floorboards, her gun sliding off into the shadows.

Scrambling on to her hands and knees, she turned for another look at the bundle, a mixture of terror and revulsion twisting her face.

"What is it?" Cora's voice drifted up from below, but Victoria barely heard. Her mouth had gone dry, like someone had stuffed her throat full of cotton. Shallow breaths escaped her lungs as she stared, transfixed by the creature under the burlap.

She had thought it was the face of a young girl, perhaps ten or eleven years old. Some parts still retained the girl's features: soft brown hair, delicate eyebrows, and a thin nose. The similarities ended there, however. A snarl of sharp teeth clustered like broken twigs in the girl's mouth. Some of them had skewered her lips as they grown, punching through her skin like knives through fabric. The skin itself was waxy and bloodless. The girl's eyes were closed, and her chest did not rise and fall with her breathing, yet Victoria was certain that the creature wasn't dead.

"Dammit, girl, what's happening up there?" Cora called.

The girl's eyes snapped open.

Victoria's breath caught in her throat as it looked at her. She could see the same need, the same feral hunger that the other ghoul had shown. Whatever that creature was, this was the same kind.

The girl let out a hiss as she rolled over onto her hands and knees. She mimicked Victoria's posture, crouched, ready to spring. At that moment, Victoria realized her hands were empty. She didn't dare take her eyes off the girl to search for her lost revolver.

For all she knew, holding still was the only thing keeping the monster from attacking. Her mind raced. Cora was still hollering at her from the bottom of the ladder, but she didn't answer. She couldn't. If the creature sprang at her, she would be defenseless.

In a flash, she remembered the crucifix in her belt. Cora had said something about the creatures fearing it. Mustering her courage, she began moving her hand toward her waist. If she could just reach it, she might have a chance.

The girl hissed again, and Victoria froze. She waited for the spring, for the impact of that small body against hers and the scraping of those teeth on her flesh. Child-sized hands curled into claws, but the girl remained crouched. Victoria steeled her nerves and moved her hand again. She didn't have much time.

As her fingers curled around the wooden figure, a gunshot rolled up through the floorboards. Victoria flinched, and the girl lunged at her. Tiny fingers gouged her arms as the two rolled over in the dust. The creature came out on top, teeth snapping, eyes dark with hunger. Victoria squeezed the crucifix in a death grip and brought it up. The wood pressed into the cold skin on the girl's neck. Smoke billowed as the flesh sizzled, and the girl rolled away with a choked cry.

Victoria scrambled to her feet, eyes probing the swirling clouds for her foe. There, on the far side. The girl was crouched again, a wild cat in human form, filled with need. Victoria extended the cross toward her. Hissing in anger, the creature shied away, retreating into the shadows.

Cross held out, Victoria began moving toward where she remembered her gun had fallen. It was slow going. She paused after each step, squinting after the girl. The savage form still lurked in the darkness, moving opposite the raised crucifix. At times, it seemed to meld with the shadows, slipping out of her sight only to reappear seconds later.

Another gunshot from below. Victoria could hear the hunter's voice yelling something, but she couldn't make out the words. No matter. At least Cora was still alive. Once she took care of whatever she was fighting down there, she would come up to the loft and make short work of this abomination.

As if reading her thoughts, the girl suddenly leaped to one side, vanishing behind a bale of hay. Victoria froze. Her gaze jumped from one end of the bale to the other, watching, waiting for that thing to emerge. The shadows played tricks with her eyesight. They swam and swirled in clouds of purple and black. She tried to blink them away, but they persisted, invading her sight even when her eyes were closed.

"Vicky!"

Victoria glanced at the ladder. "Get up here!" she called.

"No time," Cora yelled back. "Got me a critter down here somewhere."

"I have one up here, too."

"Well, sort it out. I got my hands full."

Victoria growled in frustration, turning her attention

back to the hay bale. If Cora couldn't help her, she would just have to help herself. Stealing a quick glance behind her, she thought she saw a faint gleam on the floor. Her gun. It was close.

The sound of scrambling hands on the boards brought her head back around. In the corner of her eye, she caught a dark shape charging toward her. She whirled the crucifix to face it, but the girl was already airborne. They collided and went down. A blast of cold breath poured over her face. It had no smell. Small hands grabbed her neck, squeezing until she thought her eyes would pop out of their sockets. She punched at the girl's torso with an empty fist, trying to knock her away. The crucifix was gone.

Victoria could feel herself slipping away. Her lungs screamed for air. Her vision swam. With one last burst of energy, she flailed her arms out in both directions, praying, hoping the crucifix was still within reach.

Her fingers bumped into something cold. She grabbed for it. Metal. Her gun. Thank God, it was her gun.

Wrapping her hand around the barrel, she shoved to one side with all her might. The girl was incredibly strong, but she still only weighed as much as a child. Her cold fingers remained clamped round Victoria's throat as they rolled over.

Now lying face-to-face on the floor like lovers, Victoria looked into the girl's eyes. They were alive with lust, even through the thin white film covering them. The girl's fingers moved, one hand slipping from Victoria's neck. Fangs parted. Victoria sucked in a desperate breath. Pain exploded through her neck as the girl's teeth sliced into her. She heard a faint slurping sound, and she knew she was dying.

Gritting her teeth, not knowing what would happen, she shoved the revolver's barrel into the girl's side and pulled the trigger.

The recoil threw the gun out of her grasp. At once blind and deaf, Victoria lay stunned. She could breathe again, but that was all she knew. Seconds passed. Her vision began to clear, the bright purple streak left by the barrel's flash fading into the shadows. Another breath, choked with gun smoke.

A fit of coughing took her, and she curled into a fetal position while her body expelled the smoke and the panic and the feeling of cold fingers around her throat. She tried to pull herself up. A hand, a knee, a push against the rough wood. Soon she was kneeling, leaning against a bale. Hay tickled her ear. A final spasm shook her small frame before releasing her.

As the ringing in her ears subsided, she could hear a faint, gurgling moan. Her eyes went wide, searching the loft for its source. Catching sight of her gun lying on the floor, she crawled toward it, her boots making hollow thumps against the boards.

With the revolver again in her hand, she rose to her feet. Her pulse pounded in her temples. She could feel a warm trickle of blood flowing down her neck. Dabbing at it with her hand made it sting, and her fingers came away sticky. She would need to tie it off, but not now. She had to find the source of the sound and silence it once and for all.

Following the moans, she soon came upon a ruined heap of flesh. The girl lay on her side, rocking back and forth. A dark liquid dripped from her teeth, blood mixed with something thicker. The bullet had torn a hole in her dress and into her chest. Smoke poured out of the wound, as if the girl's soul were leaking out of her and drifting up among the rafters. The eyes rolled toward Victoria, still full of hunger and rage.

Looking down on her broken foe, a sudden wave of pity washed over her. Despite its grotesque features, it still looked more like a young girl than a monster. The revolver shook in Victoria's hand. For a moment, she didn't see the girl's' fangs or her filmy eyes. Instead, she saw a dying child, weeping with what strength she had left, her body ripped apart by Victoria's gun.

Dropping the revolver, Victoria turned her head and retched.

When the feeling passed, she wiped her mouth and retrieved her gun. The girl reached for her, fingers like claws. A moan of rage bubbled out between jagged teeth. Victoria's mouth was a thin line, and her blue eyes were dark with purpose. She centered the revolver's barrel between the girl's milky eyes and pulled the hammer back. When the gun kicked, she was expecting it. The flash from the barrel lit the loft like a bolt of lightning, and the thunder shook dust down from the rafters. As her vision cleared, she saw the girl's lifeless eyes staring back at her.

Air left her lungs in a deep sigh. Victoria holstered her gun and tried to shake the sting from her hand. Turning from the dead girl at her feet, she made her way back to the ladder. The daylight had all but disappeared from the window. Peering outside, Victoria could see an angry mass of clouds churning overhead. Cora's words echoed in her mind; if they were going to finish their business before it rained, they needed to hurry.

"Cora," she called out when she reached the ladder. "Are you there?"

No answer. Victoria crouched by the opening and looked through. The barn appeared to be empty. "Cora?"

Silence.

Placing a boot on the ladder, Victoria began her descent. She glanced over her shoulders as she climbed, searching for any sign of the hunter or another one of those creatures. Aside from the rumbling of thunder above her head, the barn was still. All sorts of horrid thoughts flooded her mind. Cora had been killed by whatever she was fighting. The blue-eyed man had reappeared and killed her. Victoria would find nothing but the hunter's corpse. Still, she couldn't very well stay in the hayloft, waiting for the nightmares to find their way up to her.

As soon as Victoria reached the bottom of the ladder, she remembered the crucifix, still laying somewhere on the loft floor. Her shoulders slumped at her own stupidity. She gave the ladder a rueful look, not eager to make the climb again. It was necessary, though. The crucifix had saved her from the girl-creature, buying her enough time to reach her gun. For whatever reason, the little carving had power over these things. Sighing, she reached for the ladder again.

A shout from outside stopped her cold. It was Cora's voice. Victoria turned her head, listening intently. Another shout, followed by a gunshot. Something was wrong.

Before she could think, Victoria was already running. Her revolver appeared in her hand. A blast of warm wind welcomed her as she charged through the barn door. Skidding to a stop, she frantically searched the yard for the old hunter.

A shout rose up over the wind. It came from the direction of the house. Gun at the ready, Victoria ran toward the sound. As she approached, she could see the door hanging open, blowing this way and that in the wind. Her blisters rubbed painfully against her boots, but she kept running. Somewhere in her mind, the thought that this run across the yard was easier than her last brought a grim smile to her face. She'd nearly been eaten alive by a child, her crucifix was lost, and her companion may or may not still be alive, but at least she was appropriately dressed.

"Cora!" she yelled as she ran onto the porch. "Can you hear me?"

"That you, Vicky?"

"Yes! Where are you?"

"Upstairs. Get your skinny rump up here double quick!"

Victoria thundered into the house, guided by her blurry memories from before. Her mind was so focused on what she would do, what she might see when she made it up the stairs that she nearly tripped over a corpse in the living room.

Catching herself on a chair, she gave the body a quick glance over. It was a woman, her flower-print dress rolled back to her knees. The corpse lay face down on the floor. Keeping her gun trained on the woman's head, she pushed against the shoulder with the toe of her boot.

A wretched face rolled into view. The woman had once been pretty, perhaps, before her teeth grew too large for her mouth. Thick black fluid oozed across her face from a hole above her right eye.

Keeping her gun aimed at the corpse, Victoria carefully stepped over it. Her muscles were taut, ready to spring into action should the body so much as twitch, but the dead woman didn't move. She took another step. Nothing. Lowering the gun, she let herself relax.

A crash from the second floor made her jump. Cora had taken care of the woman-creature, but the man from the other night was still unaccounted for. The old hunter was most likely fighting him at that moment, and she needed help.

Making a dash for the stairs, Victoria felt her boot strike something on the floor, sending it skittering to one side. Cora's rifle. She stared at it, the implications exploding in her mind like cannon fire. The creatures had managed to disarm Cora. She was facing one of them unarmed. If the blue-eyed man or the Indian woman arrived, she would be defenseless. Victoria hesitated, unsure if she should pick up the rifle and take it up to its owner.

"Vicky!" Cora's shout was strained. Victoria's boots pounded up the stairs. She could hear thumping and grunting coming from the door on the left. It stood slightly ajar, and she pushed it open with her free hand, revolver raised.

Cora stood against one wall, rosary dangling from her outstretched fist. Her other hand was empty. Across the room from her, the man-creature crouched on the floor. The hunter's struggle had punched a few gouges into the wallpaper. Clothing and broken glass littered the floor from a toppled dresser.

"Goddamn it, girl, where you been?" Cora asked.

"I–"

"Don't matter none. Toss me your gun."

Without her gun, Victoria would be defenseless. "But–"

"Do it!" Cora yelled, holding out her hand. Victoria tossed the weapon into the room. It fell short of the hunter by a few feet. Cursing, Cora made a grab for it.

The ghoul seized the opportunity and lunged. It crashed into Cora, knocking her backward into the wall. Hunter and monster grappled on the floor, Cora's hands clamped around her enemy's throat. She pushed against it with all her might, barely able to keep the hungry jaws from her own neck. More curses burst from her lips.

Victoria stood still, transfixed by the mortal struggle. After all of the legends and stories she'd heard of Cora Oglesby, seeing her fight was remarkably underwhelming. She had expected the old hunter to dominate her foes with ease and finesse, making killing monsters appear no harder than taking tea after a game of lawn darts. Watching her now, she seemed no more than a common barroom brawler wrestling another drunkard over some slight.

Cora managed to land a punch to the creature's jaw with the fist holding the rosary. Smoke exploded outward in a ring. The creature hissed in pain, but it kept its hold on the hunter. Cora struck it again, keeping the rosary pressed into its smoking flesh. The hiss became a wail. Writhing in agony, the vampire twisted away from her.

Rolling into a crouching position, Cora's eyes darted around the floor. "Where'd it go?"

"Where did what go?" Victoria asked.

Spying the gun a few feet behind her, Cora dove for it.

Victoria saw the monster pull itself to its feet. "Watch out!" she cried as the creature lunged at Cora. The hunter spun around, dropping onto her back as she did so. Reaching out with her free hand, Cora grabbed the ghoul by the wrist and yanked. It sailed over her as she rolled beneath it. When it reached the apex of the throw, a flash erupted from the hunter's other hand. Thunder shook the windows. The creature crashed into the far wall and crumpled to the floor.

Cora didn't spare it a glance. She pulled herself onto her hands and knees and crawled toward the large bed in the corner. Thrusting her arm into the darkness beneath it, she began groping for something. Perplexed, Victoria watched her search until she heard the monster stirring. Her gaze snapped to the place where it fell, and her body went rigid.

The dead eye was fixed on her.

With a croaking moan, the monster began crawling toward her. Speechless with terror, Victoria backed into the hallway, bumping up against the far wall. The creature's teeth gnashed together. Victoria's breathing quickened as it approached, inch by inch, hand over pale hand. Her eyes were small islands of blue in a sea of white. Desperate, she drew the broad-bladed knife with a shaking hand. It was probably useless against this living corpse, but she wouldn't let it kill her without a fight. She braced herself, knife hand drawn back, for the final struggle.

Cora appeared in the doorway behind the monster. Her boot came down on its ankle with a dry snap. Pinned, it curled around like an injured worm, arms reaching for the hunter's leg. Metal gleamed as Cora swung a curved sword. The creature recoiled from the blow, hands clutching at the fresh gash in its ruined face.

The hunter stepped up next to the wretched creature, driving the toe of her boot into its ribcage. It hissed like a broken steam pipe, its eye nearly bursting out of its head as it glared at her. Grasping the hilt with both hands, Cora drove the sword through the monster's head.

In the silence that followed, Victoria realized how loudly she was breathing and forced herself to calm down. Fingers trembling, she slid the knife back into her belt.

"You okay?" Cora asked.

Victoria's throat was dry, but she managed a nod.

"Good," Cora said. She placed a boot on the corpse's neck. The sword slid out of the skull with a slick wet sound. Still holding the saber, Cora turned and went back into the bedroom. A few seconds later, a revolver slid through the doorway. Victoria stepped around the body, careful not to touch the splayed limbs, and picked it up. For the first time, the gun's weight on her belt comforted her.

Cora popped up from behind the fallen dresser. "I ain't sure whether I should thank you or crack you over the head." She stepped around the dresser, and Victoria's arms came up defensively.

"I'd prefer the former," Victoria said.

"I reckon you might," Cora said, "and I reckon I'd have been in a tight spot if you hadn't showed up when you did. What I can't puzzle out is why you thought it best to just stand there and gape at me instead of lending a hand."

Victoria's face burned. "I'm sorry. I don't know what came over me."

"Well, ain't too much of a loss. Vampire's dead, and you probably would have wound up shooting me."

"I resent that," Victoria said. "I'll have you know that I defeated one of these creatures on my own after you left me in the barn. It very nearly killed me in the process."

Cora snorted. "You're making that up."

"I will prove it to you," Victoria said. "The corpse is still up in the barn loft along with my crucifix."

"You dropped my crucifix?" When Victoria nodded, Cora shook her head. "You're like to kill us both, you know that? What kind of vampire hunter goes around dropping their weapons like they was cow dung?"

Victoria straightened her back. "It wasn't intentional. Besides, I don't call myself a vampire hunter, so I don't really see how that applies to me."

"You're one now whether you call yourself it or not," Cora said, "though calling yourself one might make explaining what happened to your throat a bit easier."

Victoria touched her neck, suddenly remembering the bite wound. Pulling a red bandana from her trouser pocket, she tied it around her throat. Cora smirked at her before she stepped out of the bedroom and started down the stairs.

The jingling of the hunter's spurs rang in Victoria's ears. A vampire hunter? Her? The title sounded ominous, something to carve on her tombstone after her untimely death. She shook her head. Whatever else she may be, she certainly wasn't a vampire hunter. Killing one vampire didn't make her one any more than killing a squirrel with a stone made her a squirrel hunter. Cora was just trying to rattle her.

"Get on down here, Vicky." Cora's voice echoed in the hallway. "We got us work to do."

Victoria laid a palm on the butt of her gun and made her way down the stairs. Cora stood in the living room, wiping her saber on the dead woman's dress. Gore streaked the floral pattern. She slid the blade back into the sheath at her side and turned to Victoria "Bastards got all my guns off me."

"What?"

"Ain't rightly sure how it happened. This one jumped out at me in the barn, and I followed it into the house," she said, shoving the corpse with her boot. "Had it in my sights when the other feller got me from behind. Lost my rifle when I went down."

"Yes, I saw it over there," Victoria said, pointing.

Cora nodded. "I managed to get that one off me before the lady had her a chance to join in. Got my Colt out and blew her away, and the other one lit out up the stairs. I chased it on up and saw that both doors was open. I checked the left one first, not thinking straight, and the damn thing got me from behind again. My gun went flying out my hand again, and I didn't get my sword out long before that got knocked away, too. We went around a few times, dancing about each other like tom cats in a spat, and that's about when you showed up."

"Was this encounter unusual, then?" Victoria asked. "It seems that they were able to sneak up on you a number of times."

"Well, I ain't no spring chicken no more," Cora said. "In case you forgot, been a good while since I've done this sort of thing. My old bones got some rust on them now, and they take to creaking a good deal more."

Victoria nodded, feeling slightly guilty for having asked. Cora had to be at least twenty years her senior, and her years had been hard-won in this unforgiving frontier. Looking at the hunter's leathery, sun-browned face, Victoria became aware of her own pale skin. Her hands were soft and unwrinkled, not wiry and gnarled from use. In that moment, she felt more out of place than she had standing on the streets of Albuquerque in her finery. She may have bought boots and denim trousers, a horse and a gun, but she wasn't of this world and never would be.

"Well, we should get them horses put away," Cora said. "Mind fetching my rifle for me?"

Without looking up, Victoria picked up the weapon and handed it to her.

"Much obliged." Cora slid the rifle into place on her back. "Now then, let's have us a look at your kill."

EIGHT

A peal of thunder shook Victoria out of a deep sleep. She sat bolt upright, eyes wide, heart pounding. Nothing around her looked familiar. Where was she? What had that noise been? After a few seconds, her thoughts caught up to her fear, and she relaxed.

The fire had burned itself low, leaving a few embers still glowing in the fireplace. Victoria shivered. Outside, rain beat against the roof and swept across the yard in great sheets, driven by bursts of wind. Lightning lit the night in fits. It illuminated the yard, the barn, the wind pump, and even the cliffs. Victoria stood and crossed over to a window, holding her arms around herself. What would have happened to them if they hadn't reached the ranch before the tempest hit? They might not have survived the night, and if they had, it would have been without any rest at all.

"Mighty fine sight, ain't it?" Cora's voice came from a chair facing the door.

Victoria turned toward her. The hunter was

nothing but a silhouette. "Indeed. It's quite fright-ening, truth be told. I was just imagining what it would be like to be caught outside in such a storm."

The silhouette nodded. "Ain't fun, I can tell you that."

"You've been in one?"

"Several," Cora said. "Can't go too long riding around the west without getting caught by weather sooner or later. Ain't regular out here, see. A body can ride from Denver to Santa Fe and have the front half of his horse sunburnt and the back half frozen by a blizzard."

"Surely not," Victoria said.

"Can't trust a cowpuncher's stories none," Cora said, "but all the same, sure seems like it was possi-ble sometimes. Why, I seen a storm settle in over one half of a town and leave the other half all sunny and nice. You'll get to where you don't trust the weather, neither, you stay out here long enough. Best one can do is take along what he can and shoot what he can to keep his stores full. After that, it's just luck of the draw."

"Yes, shooting and dressing game," Victoria said. "Such an enjoyable way to pass the time."

Cora laughed. "Stew's awful good for all the blood and guts, though, ain't it?"

Despite herself, Victoria had to nod in agreement. Once she'd gotten past the horror of eating an ani-mal she had just skinned and gutted herself, the taste was surprisingly pleasant. No steak and kidney pie, but not bad. When soaked in the broth, even the hardtack was far less abhorrent. The generous amount of salt Cora had added to the stew had no doubt helped the flavor along, though.

"You feel up to sitting for a spell?" Cora asked, stretching her arms. "All that excitement earlier done wore me out."

"Yes, I could have a turn at the watch," Victoria said. "How long was I asleep?"

"No more than a few hours," Cora said. "You was snoring like a mountain cat, though. Kept making me think one of them vampires was coming back to life."

"Very funny." Victoria walked over to the chair, and Cora got up. "I don't imagine your slumber is without the slightest noise."

"Oh, I ain't claiming nothing of the sort. I reckon you'll be ready to stuff your hat down my throat just to keep me quiet before too long. Don't go trying it, though, or you'll be the one with a mouthful of something unpleasant." Cora moved over to the remains of the fire, stretched out, and put her hat over her face. After a moment, she picked it up again. "Oh, my rifle is there by the chair if you need it."

"I hope it won't be necessary," Victoria said, but the hunter had already resumed her sleeping position. Victoria thought about stoking the fire for her but decided against it. If Cora had wanted the fire built up, she would have done it herself. She probably had some tactical reason for not doing so, some unwritten rule of vampire hunter code. Victoria herself couldn't be less interested in any code such individuals may hold to. Cora was a competent fighter, true, and she could almost be a pleasant companion at times, but Victoria held no more illusions about the wild romance of such a lifestyle. If the old hunter was any indication, hunting vampires for hire made one uncouth and brazen, neither of which were qualities Victoria desired to foster in herself.

Another flash of lightning lit the yard, making the three bundles lying just beyond the porch visible for an instant. Cora had insisted on dragging the corpses outside so they could be exposed to sunlight as soon as possible, and for once Victoria hadn't argued. The bodies would turn into dust when the sun rose, the hunter said, so they simply lined them up in the yard and headed back into the house to see about starting a fire and preparing the stew.

When the next flash came, Victoria blinked. Had she seen a shadow? Leaning forward, she peered out through the window, but she couldn't see anything. The clouds covered the moon, leaving the intermittent flickers of lightning the only source of light. Victoria drew her revolver, curling her fingers around the grip for reassurance.

When the next burst of light came, Victoria was certain. A figure was standing in the yard near the barn. A shiver ran up her spine. It had been nothing more than a shadow, but she knew it all the same: her captors had returned.

Keeping her eyes fixed on the yard, Victoria turned her head slightly. "Cora." No answer. "Cora," she said again, louder.

There was a snort from the fireplace. "What? What's wrong?"

"I think something's out there," Victoria said.

"Is that right?" A rustling sound as she rolled over. "Go on and sort it out, then."

"What?"

"Get your pretty little rear out there and go chase your spook."

"I'll do no such thing," Victoria said.

"Then what's the point of putting you on the watch?" Cora asked. "Sentry ain't no good if they don't go have a look at what they spot, now is they?"

"Perhaps not, but you're the expert here. I wouldn't know the first thing to do–"

"You already done it earlier."

"–if it ends up being something other than one of the creatures we previously fought," Victoria finished. "I believe it is one of the beings that captured me two nights ago."

"You should be itching for the payback, then." Before Victoria could reply, Cora groaned and sat up. "But if you got sand in your bloomers about it, I reckon I can go have a look."

"Thank you."

"For what?"

Victoria blinked. "Going in my stead."

"Who says you ain't going?" Cora's boots thumped across the floor. She picked up her rifle from where it stood propped up against the chair, then turned to Victoria. "I sure don't."

"But surely we need someone to remain behind?"

"And do what?" Cora asked. "Ain't like we got a big old crate of gold or some such needs guarding. Always take more if more's available, whether you're talking bullets, biscuits, or back-watchers. Either you're coming with or we both sit tight here."

"But–"

"Put it this way: if I run myself on out there chasing your spook and it decides to stop by the house for a bite of fancy girl, what are you going to do about it?"

Victoria paused. The thought made her blood run cold. Even with her new weapons, she knew she wouldn't stand much of a chance against Fodor Glava or the Indian woman without Cora. If either one of them appeared while the hunter was away, Victoria might not be able to escape. The Indian woman's threat still lingered in the back of her mind. If she discovered that Victoria had not only disobeyed her command but brought the hunter straight to her, she was not likely to be forgiving.

Still, she had handled herself well when she'd fought with the vampire in the barn. Cora hadn't been around to help her then, and she had not only survived but killed her foe. Maybe there wasn't as much to killing monsters as she thought. Moreover, it seemed highly unlikely that Cora had received any kind of formal training in the business. If she could master the art through self-tutelage, so could Victoria.

"Do what you will," Victoria said, "but I am staying here."

Cora regarded her in silence. Although the hunter's eyes were invisible in the near-total darkness, Victoria could feel them boring into her. Raising her chin, the young woman leaned back in the chair with a look that she hoped was as powerful.

"Suit yourself." A flash of lightning outlined the creases in Cora's face. "Do me a favor, though: if they get their fangs in you while I'm away, go on and shoot yourself before you turn."

Turning away from Victoria, she slid the rifle into the scabbard on her back and pulled her hat down low. The door opened with a loud creak, and the cold smell of rain filled the room. A gust of wind swirled through the doorway only to be cut off as Cora shut the door behind her.

Victoria watched the old hunter disappear into the downpour, anger churning inside her like the clouds overhead. No matter what she said or did, Cora seemed to have little regard for her. Even killing the vampire hadn't pried a word of praise out of her. Now, Victoria had managed to fall even further in her companion's esteem by choosing what seemed like a perfectly sensible option. Besides, her part of the bargain with Cora said nothing about helping her kill anything, vampire or otherwise. All she had agreed to do was lead the hunter to the spot where the man called Fodor Glava had been, and she had done so. What sort of person rewarded a favor with contempt?

Victoria shook her head. She was letting herself think on the subject far more than she should. A gust of wind slammed into the walls, making them creak and crack. Standing to her feet, she walked over to the dying fire and set about rekindling it. Cora may have had some unspoken law against warmth and light, but she was off on her own business. Rebuilding the fire with fresh kindling took a bit more effort, but she soon had a small pile ready on the stone hearth.

Victoria had purchased a small book of matches on Cora's insistence, and she pulled them out of her satchel with a brief sense of gratitude. The small flame danced down the match, but it refused to jump to the kindling. Muttering under her breath, Victoria blew it out and struck another.

"Is a bit chilly in here, ain't it?"

Victoria let out a short scream and spun around, the match falling from her fingers. Blue eyes flashed at her from the doorway.

"Of course, I can't tell the difference no how," the man said. He swaggered toward her, planting his boots deliberately with each step. "Rain, snow, or stars is all the same to me. Just one more perk to being what I is."

As he spoke, Victoria rose to her feet. Trying to calm her pounding heart, she worked her fingers around the crucifix in her belt. The wooden carving pulled free, and she pointed it at those wicked blue flames.

The man called Fodor Glava halted his advance. "Hey, now, that ain't no kind of way to treat an old friend, now is it? Here I was expecting hugs and kisses, but you got to get all mean about things. How do you reckon that makes a body feel?"

"Afraid," Victoria said, pulling her revolver free of its holster.

"Well, ain't you a regular bobcat all of a sudden like?" The shadow raised its arms. "Don't shoot me, missie, I ain't done nothing wrong."

Victoria squeezed the trigger. Flame belched out of the gun's barrel as man-made thunder crashed around her. The man called Fodor Glava vanished from sight. For one brief moment, elation swept through her: she had killed the man Cora Oglesby was hunting, proving herself worthy of the hunter's respect.

Laughter filled the room. "Don't go fooling yourself, sweetheart. You ain't nothing but a housecat, and I'm one big old grizzly bear."

"Are you certain of that?" Victoria asked. "From what I'm told of them, grizzly bears don't hide from little girls."

"Oh, we is a sly bunch," came the reply. "Ain't all muscle and fur and teeth, you know. Some of us has the wits of a fox and the speed to match."

"We hunt foxes for sport in England," she said. No matter how he boasted, he clearly feared her crucifix and her gun, or he would have already killed her. The thought gave her courage.

"You ain't never met a fox like me, honey."

Something blue flashed in the corner of her eye. She turned and fired. The gunshot lit up the room, but the man simply vanished once more.

"And here I thought proper gals knew better than to shoot guns at folk. Ain't ladylike no matter how you slice it, though I reckon it's getting me more than a mite randy. What say you and me have ourselves a poke after we get done with our dance?" Victoria shuddered at the thought and was answered by another laugh. "Well, if you is that excited about it, we may just cut the dance short."

Victoria took a step forward, sweeping the Colt's barrel around the room. "You're welcome to try."

"Don't mind if I do."

The voice came from behind her. Before she could turn to face it, something slammed into her back. She pitched forward, arms flung in front of her to break the fall. Her palms hit the floor with a dull thud, but they couldn't stop her from half-rolling, half-skidding along the boards.

When she came to a stop, Victoria pushed herself up on her hands and knees. The floor pitched and rolled like the deck of a ship. Struggling to rise, she realized her right hand was now empty. The impact must have knocked the Colt out of her grasp. She now faced this monster armed with nothing but a small carving.

As if to underline the point, the blue eyes loomed above the place where she had been standing a moment before. "This here's a pretty little gun you got," the man said. "Seems a right shame that it got itself all banged up like it did. That's what happens when a girl plays at gunfighting, I reckon."

There was a thump at her feet. Kneeling down, Victoria reached toward the sound. Her fingers touched on cold metal. Picking it up, she could immediately tell that something was wrong with the revolver. It felt different in her hand, as if the weight had shifted. She ran it along the back of her other hand, and her heart sank.

The barrel was bent back on itself.

"We gave you a chance, darlin," the man said. "We let you go easy and free, but you just had to stick in our boots like a devil's thorn." His eyes blazed as he approached her. "Ain't pretty what happens to them as stick in the devil's own boot, neither."

Victoria raised the crucifix, and the blue eyes halted. "I do not fear you," she lied.

"Then you ain't got the sense of a toad. Waving that matchstick around ain't going to get you nowhere. I ain't afraid of no kindling."

Holding her useless gun, Victoria backed away from the man. Her mind raced. Even if she had the bowie knife with her, she knew it wouldn't work against him. It was just ordinary steel, and Cora had explained to her how only blessed steel or silver weapons could harm vampires. Without a weapon, she couldn't hope to fight.

The man called Fodor Glava seemed to read her thoughts. "You ain't got a prayer, darlin. Best you just come quiet-like. Makes it easier on one of us, at least."

His laughter turned Victoria's stomach. "Then kill me," she said. Her words might be her doom, but she wouldn't die kneeling to this man. "If it really is just a piece of kindling, what's stopping you?"

"I like them alive," he said. "Ain't no fun if you just lays there like a dead fish."

"I do not fear you," she said again, trying to muster her resolve.

"Pudding-headed whore. You got every reason to be scared of me, and here you is being all uppity. Digging your own grave, or so they say." He laughed. "You ain't exactly going to need a grave when I get through with you. No, I reckon I'll keep you on as my own personal pokey-poke for all time. A fine gentleman such as myself deserves himself a fancy girl, ain't that right?"

The man's eyes vanished without warning. Startled, she looked around. Lightning lit the interior of the house, but he was nowhere to be seen. The crucifix trembled in her hand as thunder shook the air. In that instant, her nerve broke. The fear of death consumed her, overwhelming what little courage she had rallied. It took control of her body, turning her toward the door and forcing her legs into a mad dash. Dropping the ruined gun on the floor, she nearly tore the doorknob apart as she twisted it and yanked the door open.

Victoria kept just enough sense to point the crucifix behind her as she ran out into the storm. Rain splattered in cold droplets on her face. Blinking it away, she charged through the yard in the direction of the barn. Mud splashed beneath her heels, and she fought to keep her footing amid the hidden rocks and twisted scrub. She could feel the man giving chase, the hunger and lust burning brightly in his eyes, but she could not spare the time to glance backward.

Lightning flooded the yard with brilliance, allowing her a brief moment of sight. The barn loomed just ahead, its hunched shape offering her the one chance of salvation she had. Victoria brought her arms in close for a final, desperate sprint. An arm of the crucifix jabbed into her side with every stride, but she barely felt it. Her only thought was to reach the safety of the barn and the vampire hunter within.

Somehow, Victoria reached the building and ran through the open door. Not two steps inside, her legs suddenly gave out. She stumbled for a moment before falling hard. The panic that had fueled her mad dash across the yard screamed at her to get up, but her body refused to respond. Lungs burning, she fought to regain her breath as she lay in the straw. Her shirt stuck to her like a second skin, cold and itchy.

Streams of white light cut through the shadows, followed seconds later by a teeth-rattling thunder-clap. As it rolled into the distance, Victoria heard a rustling at the other end of the barn. She tried to quiet her breathing, but her racing heart made it impossible.

Drawing on the last of her strength, Victoria struggled to her feet. Her fingers squeezed the crucifix as she started walking toward the sound. The creature making it seemed restless; the rustling continued without pause. Step by step, she worked her way toward it, checking over her shoulder for any sign of the vampire. The darkness around her was absolute save for the flashes of lightning, but Victoria didn't see the telltale light from his eyes.

The rustling was very close now, hidden in the next stall. Crouching down, she ran her fingers over the savior's wooden body for reassurance. Now that she'd reached the sound, she wasn't sure what she should do next. If it was the red-eyed woman or another of the feral vampires, she couldn't very well fight them with nothing but her crucifix.

Pressing up against the post, Victoria leaned around it just enough to see into the stall. At that moment, a bolt of lightning split the shadows. It gleamed on a black eye rimmed with white. Fear shot through her limbs, but it quickly dissolved. The tension drained from her body like water through a sluice gate, leaving her legs feeling wobbly. She fell to her knees as darkness again closed in around her. Thunder shook the walls, and although she could no longer see them, she knew her horse's terrified eyes were still watching her. Her sigh of relief came out as a laugh.

"What's so funny, darlin?"

Victoria spun around so quickly she toppled over. Framed by the barn door, the man's silhouette was like a slender black candle with blue flame smoldering at its crown. She could see hunger and amusement flickering in those eyes.

Pulling herself together, Victoria rose to her feet and raised the crucifix. The man continued to watch her, apparently relishing her helplessness. Victoria knew her luck had run out. Without a real weapon, it was just a matter of time before he overwhelmed and consumed her. Cora must have run out into the storm in pursuit of her quarry, or maybe she was lying dead somewhere nearby. Either way, the hunter wouldn't be coming to her rescue. Still, Victoria wouldn't allow him to make her his mistress, no matter what happened. If need be, she would kill herself before he could take her. If only she hadn't left her knife behind.

The barn had plenty of sharp tools handy, though. Keeping the crucifix raised, she began edging over to where she remembered Cora had left the pitchfork. The tines were rusted, but they would do the job well enough if she could just get to it.

Without warning, the man's eyes vanished from the entrance. Victoria searched the shadows, hoping to see that wicked blue glow, but the barn was dark. The constant drumming of rain on the roof made it impossible to hear something sneaking up on her. She began panning the crucifix around the room as she worked her way across the barn.

Something struck her head from behind. Dazed, she fell to one knee, fighting to stay conscious. The world was spinning. She felt like she might vomit. Had she dropped the crucifix?

A cold hand clamped onto the back of her neck. Crippling pain lanced through her body. Her fingers tried to pull it off, but it was like trying to pry open a wolf's jaws. The hand lifted her mercilessly until her feet kicked at the air just above the floor.

"Now, then," came the man's voice, "what was you saying about not being scared of me?"

Victoria couldn't answer. It took all of her effort just to draw in a breath.

"What's that? Ain't got no more fancy words for me?" The hand shook her like a rag doll. Lights flashed across her vision. "Well, my pecker's got a thing or two to say to you, so you just sit still and let him have his say."

He threw her to the ground. Her head slammed into the floorboards. Stunned, she lay in the middle of a spinning vortex, struggling to remain conscious. Footsteps rustled in the straw nearby, but she couldn't remember who they belonged to.

Lucidity broke through the haze like a sunbeam. She pushed herself into a sitting position even though it felt as though someone had piled a load of bricks onto her back. The nearby shuffling continued. It had to be Fodor Glava. He was going to rape her and kill her. She needed her crucifix, but where was it? Frantic, she crawled away from the sound, hoping to find the figurine or some sort of weapon. Her time was almost up; at any moment, she would feel the grip of cold fingers somewhere on her body, and then it would be too late.

"Damn fool."

Why was he speaking to her again? Why did his voice sound strange? She turned her head.

Cora stood in the doorway, her rifle trained on Fodor Glava. A storm lantern hung from her belt, bathing her in an orange halo.

"Cora!" In that moment, Victoria could have hugged her.

"Hush up," Cora said, keeping her gaze to the man standing in the shadows. "You there. Just what do you think you're doing?"

"Cora Oglesby," he replied. "About time you showed up. Your girl here ain't much sport."

"She ain't my girl. She's just a lost lamb showed up on my doorstep."

"Awful keen on protecting her, ain't you?"

Cora stepped toward him. "Ain't nothing special. I just happen to like shooting wolves is all. You're the feller calls himself Fodor Glava, I presume?"

"Naturally," he replied with a bow. "Sure is nice to see you again."

"You can stick the act where the sun don't shine," Cora said. "I know you ain't him because I done him in four years past."

The man laughed. "You can't never kill what's dead."

"Seems to me I been doing just that for more years than I've got fingers and toes. So either I've earned my keep shamming folk all this time, or you ain't got a clue what you is." Cora closed one eye and sighted down the rifle's barrel. "Care to call my bluff?"

For once, the man didn't reply.

"That's what I thought," Cora said, "but now that we know who you ain't, I want to know who you are and why you go about calling yourself Glava."

"His blood is in me, so why shouldn't I?" he said. "I've just as much a claim to it as he did now."

Cora cocked her head to one side. "Ain't that odd?

He never so much as gave you a mention when I was running him through. Could be he had other things on his mind. Still, I reckon he might have said something about making a dimwit of a disciple."

"I was his ace in the hole, see? His backup gun if you managed to whip him. He had it all figured out."

"Except for the part where I've got you on the business end of my gun," Cora said. "How are you supposed to get your revenge now or whatever you was planning to do?"

"I got my ways," he replied.

"Ain't going to do you much good if they ain't coming by in the next few minutes." Cora glanced down at Victoria. "Get up, girl."

Victoria scrambled to her feet and hurried over to her, keeping an eye on the man. "Yes?"

"Here." Cora shoved the rifle into her hands. "Keep this on him."

The weight of the gun was almost too much for her. Hoisting it with difficulty, she pointed the barrel at the blue eyes. "What will you do?"

"Get my answer," Cora said. She untied the lantern from her belt and lifted it. "Now, let's see who you really are."

"He is a demon," said a new voice. "That is all you need to know."

Cora's head turned so quickly Victoria heard her neck bones pop. "Who in tarnation are you?" the hunter asked.

"You only need to know what I am," the woman replied.

Victoria glanced over her shoulder at the speaker, and a chill ran down her spine. The silhouette of a woman stood in the doorway, eyes gleaming red in the night.

"She's my ace," said the man.

"Don't look like much of one," Cora said.

"I am more than what I seem," the woman said, "much as you are, Cora Oglesby."

Cora laughed. "All I am is an old drunk. If that's more than I seem to be, maybe I ought to gussy myself up from time to time."

"Don't go flattering her, now," said the man. He took a step forward.

Victoria tightened her grip on the rifle. "Don't move."

"You, Victoria Dawes," said the woman. "You did not obey me."

"I tried," Victoria said, "but she insisted on coming out here before she would leave with me."

"Well, I'll be damned," Cora said, glancing at Victoria. "You wasn't joshing me after all. This squaw really did send you after me."

"Mind your words," the woman said, "or they will be your death."

"Them's some big words," Cora said. "I'd lay fifty on them being a bluff."

"You would be wise to reconsider," the woman replied. She stepped forward into the lantern's halo of light.

Victoria could not help but stare. Aside from a hide mantle around her shoulders, the woman was naked. Droplets of rain clung to her, creeping down skin the color of rust to pool at her feet. Gooseflesh covered her exposed arms and legs, but she didn't seem to feel the chill. Sodden ropes of black hair were plastered to her face, neck, and chest.

"This is my lucky day," the man said.

The woman ignored the comment. Peeling the hide mantle from her shoulders, she threw it at Cora's feet. "This is a warning."

"I seen me plenty of hides," Cora said. "Yours ain't all that special, though it could do with a good tanner. Ain't you Indians got folks that can do that?"

"Look at it closely, hunter," the woman said.

Cora rolled her eyes. Crouching down, she held the lantern over the strip of flesh. Her smirk slowly faded, and she smoothed the skin out with her free hand. The blood drained from her face. She shot a quick look at the woman before storming into the shadows.

Victoria watched the light from the hunter's lantern retreat, confused and frightened by her reaction. Left alone between the two creatures, she backed up until she could see them both without turning her head. The Indian paid her no heed, but she could feel the man's blue eyes on her. Her arms ached, but she kept the rifle raised, reminding both herself and him that she still had the power to kill him.

A roar of anger filled the barn. It was so loud and full of rage that it was barely human, and Victoria took it at first for another clap of thunder. Cora charged back into the group, revolver drawn, face red with fury. She pressed the barrel against the woman's forehead.

"What did you do?"

The woman regarded her with calm black eyes. "As I said, it is a warning."

Cora pulled the hammer back. "Where is my horse?"

"Dead."

Orange light glinted on the Colt's barrel as Cora stepped back and pulled the trigger.

Click.

Instead of a gunshot's deafening report, the revolver simply clicked.

In a blink, the woman's hand came from nowhere, knocking the gun away. It flipped end-over-end into the shadows. Cora reached for her saber, but the woman grabbed her wrist. "Be still."

Cora's other fist smashed into the woman's jaw. The woman rocked backward, but she didn't release the hunter's arm. When Cora hauled back for a second blow, the Indian caught the swinging fist in her palm. "Be still," she said again.

Cora spat in her face. "Go to hell."

"I offer you this chance, hunter," the woman said, "because we share the pain of loss."

The hunter deflated a little. "What are you talking about?"

"Do not ask idle questions. I know of your husband."

Cora lowered her arms. "How?"

"I heard you speak of him."

"When?" Cora asked, confusion bleeding into the anger on her face.

"Earlier today," the woman replied. "You told the young one of your husband as you rode toward this place."

"How do you know that?"

The woman motioned toward the hide. "I was your horse."

Cora blinked at her, then threw back her head and filled the barn with laughter. Victoria and the blue-eyed man openly stared at her, and even the Indian woman seemed confused by her reaction. True, the woman's reply made little sense, but Victoria hardly thought it merited such an uproarious guffaw.

The echoes soon died out, and Cora shook her head. "I got to hand it to you, that is the best yarn I've heard in a good while. Them boys back at the Print Shop could have a few lessons from you on spinning tales."

"I do not deceive you," the woman said. She pointed at Victoria, who shifted uneasily at the attention. "That one fired her weapon at a bush, and her horse fled at the sound. When you killed the rabbit for your supper, you made her tie it to her horse. You spoke of the importance of animals and of your husband."

As the woman went on, the smile disappeared from Cora's face. Her eyes grew stony. Victoria watched her countenance change, the rifle all but forgotten in her hands.

"Well, ain't that odd," Cora said when the woman finished. "You was dogging us all the way from town, and I never knew. You Indians got some first-rate tracking skills, you know that?"

"Believe what you will," the woman replied. "But I urge you to take this chance and escape with your lives. Return with Victoria Dawes to the east, hunter. Assist her with her demons. Leave the land of my people, and do not return."

"I ain't about to take orders from the same squaw that done killed my horse," Cora said. "We ain't settled until I take that price out of your hide."

Before the woman could respond, Cora spun toward Victoria and snatched the rifle from her hands. Victoria stepped backward, stunned, as the hunter swiveled back toward her enemy. The Winchester's barrel spouted flame, but the Indian was no longer where she had stood a moment before. Cursing, Cora chambered another round and fired at the fleeing shadow. The silver bullet sailed over the woman's head and out into the falling rain.

"Cora, behind you!" Victoria screamed.

Without missing a beat, the hunter spun in place. The rifle's barrel cracked across the blue-eyed man's face as he charged, sending him tumbling to one side. Cora followed his roll, sending a round through his leg. He bellowed in anger, but before she could put a bullet through his head, he recovered and fled into the night.

Seconds passed, marked by the pounding of Victoria's heart. The ringing in her ears faded, replaced by the hollow drumming of rain on the roof. Cora kept the rifle pointed at the open door, every muscle stretched taut, waiting for the slightest movement. None came.

A gunshot cut through the sound of falling rain as fire lit the inside of the barn. Cora worked the action, aimed at the roof, and fired again. Between shots, Victoria could hear the hunter's rage-filled screaming. Only when she had emptied the rifle's magazine did she fall silent, her back to the young Englishwoman.

"Get your things," the hunter said without turning.

"But–"

"Do it!"

Cora's voice cut the air like a whip-crack, making Victoria jump. Scrambling for the lantern, she raised it above her head and began searching for her lost crucifix. Her boot swept from side to side, pushing loose straw out of the way. Behind her, she heard a steady metallic clicking as the hunter loaded fresh bullets into her rifle. Victoria could sense Cora's impatience mounting with each one. She swept faster.

A few tense seconds later, she heard the unmistakable sound of wood tumbling on wood. Chasing it with both lantern and hand, she pulled her crucifix from a small pile of straw. It looked none the worse for the wear.

Tucking it in her belt where it belonged, she looked at Cora. "Done."

"What about your gun?"

"It's back in the house," Victoria said, letting her frustration leak into her voice. "It's useless now. That Fodor Glava person bent the barrel backward."

"Get my gun, then," Cora said. "I think it fell over there somewhere."

Victoria sighed. Lifting the lantern again, she moved to where the gun looked like it may have fallen and began her search. When she located the Colt, she slipped it into her empty holster and returned to Cora's side. "Got everything?" the hunter asked. Victoria nodded. "I'd say we're done here," Cora said. "No point spending the night out here. You ready for another wetting?"

"I suppose so. Do you want your gun back?"

"Hang on to it a spell. We can't have you running around defenseless, now can we?" Victoria blushed, but Cora had already turned toward the door. "Tie that light to your belt so you got your hands free. Never know if they're planning on jumping us out there."

Victoria did as instructed, then pulled the crucifix from her belt. "Ready."

The hunter plunged into the downpour, vanishing from sight almost instantly. Holding her breath, Victoria followed. The shock of cold water made her flinch. She resisted the urge to wrap her arms around herself, keeping the crucifix extended toward the darkness.

NINE

The sun shone down on the woman and her husband as they walked side-by-side along the road. A grey mule plodded beside them, flicking its ears at buzzing flies. New rations were strapped across the mule's strong back. The woman knew it hurt her husband's pride to beg for rations from the American soldiers, but she would not let them starve. She had known enough of hunger.

In the distance, she saw a cloud of dust slowly moving toward them. Shapes soon became clear within it. A small band of soldiers, no more than half a dozen. A patrol returning to the fort after a day roaming the desert. She had seen many such groups near the American fort. While she did not like them, neither did she fear them. They were enforcers of the American laws, but they could not interfere with the Diné. Their treaty said as much.

The woman and her husband continued walking along the road as it stretched across the land. The soldiers drew nearer, the cloud of dust billowing out behind them like a storm. Soon, she felt the thunder of the horses' hooves in the ground. They moved aside to let the soldiers *pass, leading their mule into the scrub by the side of the road.*

As they rode by, one of the soldiers pulled his horse around and rode toward the woman and her husband. He had the wide mustache favored by so many Americans, and his teeth flashed white beneath it as he smiled at them.

"Where might you be going?" he asked.

"Home," she answered. She had learned their speech while living at Hwéeldi.

"Not with our food, you aren't," the soldier said.

"This food is ours," she said, laying a hand on the mule's grey coat.

"Grew it yourselves, did you?" By now, the other soldiers had gathered around the one that spoke.

"No," her husband said.

"That's what I thought," the soldier said. "Now just hand it on over and you can be on your way."

"It is ours," her husband said, standing to his full height.

"Not anymore, it's not."

The soldier spurred his horse toward them. Her husband pulled the woman out of its way, then turned back to the man. The soldier had taken the donkey's lead rope in his hand. Her husband reached for it, and the man cracked him across the face with his other hand. "Don't you threaten me, boy."

Her husband staggered back a pace, then stood to face the man. "It is ours."

"Then come take it," the solider said, drawing a revolver.

The gunshot echoed off the nearby mesa, followed by the woman's scream.

● ● ● ●

"Well, I guess that means we're walking back to town."

Victoria could only nod in agreement. She was afraid of bringing her breakfast back up if she tried to speak.

In front of them, Victoria's horse lay in its stall. Its eyes were frozen in the same terrified look she had seen the night before, but rust-colored blood now covered the straw beneath it. Looking at its lifeless corpse, Victoria felt a stab of pity for the poor creature. It had carried her faithfully out to this place, and she had let it die.

"Why did they do this?" she finally asked.

"Just making themselves a point, I expect," Cora said. "Can't have things go too easy on us." The hunter frowned, looking around the barn. "Sure wish they'd left me some of Our Lady behind. Seems fitting I should bury her proper-like."

"Maybe she isn't here," Victoria said. Cora shot her a questioning look. "Think about it. If the Indian woman really was in the form of your horse, she must have been with us back in town when we started. That woman must have killed your horse before yesterday morning."

"I reckon so," Cora replied. "Guess that means I got to have words with them livery boys when we're done with all this. No-good fools just let squaw spooks make off with horses like that. It's a wonder they ain't got my horse killed before now."

Victoria stifled a groan as she contemplated the long day ahead of them. "Do you really think we can walk back?"

"As long as your pretty little self can keep up," Cora said. "Won't be something you're like to go doing again just for the fun of it all, but it can be done."

"Won't we die of thirst before we make it back?"

"Won't die of it, but won't be turning down a bucket of trough water by the end, neither. We've got our skins, and I reckon the folks here left us some canning bottles or some such. We ration our water out like we should, we'll do okay."

"Easy enough," Victoria said, rolling her eyes. "Shall we get on with this lovely parade, then?"

Cora nodded. "Daylight's wasting, and I sure ain't going to be caught around here come nightfall. They know this place too well, and we don't."

The two women returned to the house and set about gathering what few supplies they had. The fire had dried out their riding clothes well enough that they could be worn with only minor discomfort. Victoria had expressed her concern when they'd woke to find them still slightly damp, but Cora assured her that an hour in the desert sun would finish what the fire had started.

Filling their water skins from water pump's spigot, they shouldered their packs and set out into the rising sun. Victoria's pack weighed more than she liked, Cora having burdened her with jars of preserved vegetables they'd found in the cellar. She gritted her teeth and bore the extra weight, determined not to give Cora the satisfaction of hearing her complain. The hunter had given her the functioning revolver as well, but that was one burden Victoria no longer minded.

The rest of it grew heavier as the morning dragged on, and the blisters on her feet ached with every step. Her vision grew bleary. Above them, the sun climbed higher into the cloudless sky, making the horizon shimmer with false promises of water and shade. The water skin bounced against her side, teasing her with promises of cool relief for her parched throat.

When the sun neared its zenith, Cora called for a halt. The two women took shelter beneath an over-hang that jutted out from a nearby cliff. It wasn't much shade, but any relief from the glaring sunlight was an improvement.

"No more than a few mouthfuls," Cora said. "It's got to last us awhile yet."

"How much farther, do you think?" Victoria asked.

Cora squinted at the horizon. "We ain't made much progress today. I'd say we got us at least an-other day, maybe two."

"You mean we will need to spend the night out-doors?"

"Of course," Cora said. "Took us a full day's ride to make it out here. You wasn't thinking you could make a horse's speed all on foot, was you?"

Victoria shook her head. It seemed silly to her now, but some part of her had still hoped they would make it back to Albuquerque before nightfall. "Will we be safe from them if we sleep out?"

The old hunter sighed. "Probably not, but ain't like we got a choice. We'll trade watches and keep the fire built up."

"What good will fire do?"

"Critters of the night usually don't take to it," Cora said. "That goes for regular critters and them that ain't so regular. Fought me a monster a few years back that was right scared of no more than a candle if you waved it in its face."

"Is that how you defeated it?" Victoria asked. "With fire?"

Cora shook her head. "Ain't what finally laid it out for good, but it played its part sure enough."

The hunter's face clouded over, and Victoria thought better of any more questions. Instead, she peered up at the sky, wishing a cloud or two might appear to offer some respite from the heat. The blue expanse stretched from one horizon to the other, unmarred by even the thinnest wisp of white.

Victoria took a small sip from her water skin. It already felt dangerously light. Replacing the stopper, she sloshed the water around inside to reassure herself that it would see her through this ordeal. The sun had evaporated what rainwater had lingered in pools that morning with frightening speed. Her concern grew as the puddles shrank, but she tried to reassure herself that they had brought enough.

All too soon, Cora stood. "Best get moving," she said, taking one final sip of water. "Don't want to waste any daylight if we can help it."

Victoria made sure the stopper was firmly wedged into the neck of her own bottle before standing. Tucking her uneaten hardtack into her satchel, she took a deep breath and nodded. The hunter returned the nod, then stepped back out into the unrelenting light.

Cora muttered under her breath as she held the match to the pile of sticks and twigs. Despite the heat of the day, the wood was reluctant to catch. She waited a few moments before throwing the match aside in disgust.

"Go find some leaves or something," she said.

Victoria sighed. Her arms and legs ached from the day's long march, and she wanted nothing more than to stretch out on the ground and let them rest. She looked around their small camp and shook her head. "I don't think I'd be able to find any out here. I haven't seen a tree since I arrived."

"Either you find us some leaves, or I'll start this fire using that pretty braid of yours," Cora replied.

Clutching at her hair, Victoria took a step backward. "You wouldn't dare."

"We got to have us a fire," Cora said, "and what we got here ain't going to take. Ain't the first time I've had to use hair to keep myself from freezing to death during the night. Leaves burn better, but I'll make do with what I got. Now, you want to move your rump, or should I take out my knife?"

Victoria threw up her arms, but she moved away from the camp to search for Cora's leaves. Above her, the sky had turned a deep blue. The sun had already set, but the western horizon still burned orange where it had slipped away. One or two stars glittered in celebration of the coming night. Only a few days ago, she might have stopped to admire them before going about her task. She'd always loved the stars, but she never knew they could be as bright and clear as they were in the American desert. It almost felt as though she could gather them in her palm if she pushed up on tiptoes and reached for them.

Surprisingly, it didn't take her long to fill her satchel with dark green leaves stripped from one of the larger bushes that stood near their camp. Cora nodded in approval when Victoria presented them, and within minutes, a small fire was snapping and hissing at their feet.

Victoria sat down beside it with a groan and worked her boots off, wincing with each tug. The blisters on her heels and the bottoms of her feet glared at her like dark red eyes. A few strips of white flesh still clung to some of them like grotesque eyelids.

"Best to let those air out for the night," Cora remarked.

Victoria blushed and tucked her feet under her, ignoring the renewed screeches of pain. "They aren't so bad."

"Sure they ain't. First few days in a new pair of boots are the hardest. You'll toughen up in a week or so. If not, the sawbones back in town can take your feet off for a decent price."

Victoria knew she wasn't serious, but the thought still made her shudder. She inched closer to the fire. Feeling the hunter's dark eyes on her, she reluctantly pulled her feet back out and clasped her hands around her knees.

A silence fell between the two women. Victoria gazed skyward, watching the stars grow brighter in a sky the color of a drowned man's lips. The sight brought to mind memories of the night her parents died, and she was suddenly fighting back tears. She kept her head upturned so Cora wouldn't see them glistening in the corners of her eyes. The same stars that had watched her parents die now looked down on her in disapproval. It had been almost two months since their deaths, and she had done nothing to avenge them.

"Yet," she murmured to them. "When the time comes, you will get your justice."

"That right there is a dangerous habit," Cora said.

Startled, Victoria snapped her head toward her. "What is?"

"Talking to them that's dead," she replied. "Don't go making it a habit, or you won't be able to tell that they're dead before too long."

"I don't know what you're talking about."

"Sure, and I'm the Queen of England." The hard lines of Cora's face softened as the old hunter gazed into the fire. Her brows twitched, and her eyes flitted about the flames like moths. Confused by this change in her companion, Victoria held her tongue and watched. Somewhere in the distance, the cry of an animal echoed off the darkened cliffs. Others raised their voices in reply like a chorus of wailing banshees. Victoria hugged her knees tighter to her chest.

Across from her, Cora sighed. "I reckon I ought to let you in on what's going on here."

"What do you mean?" Victoria asked.

"Well," Cora said, "like it or not, you're caught up in this whole mess now. Before last night, I didn't figure things would get as complicated as all this. My plan was to ride out to that ranch, beat my answers out of that blue-eyed feller, and be done with it. Saw no need to tell you any more than that, neither."

The hunter paused to rummage through her satchel. Finally emerging with a piece of hardtack, she tore off a bite. Her eyes glittered in the firelight as she regarded the young woman, chewing thoughtfully. Victoria fidgeted under the hunter's gaze. Pebbles grated against the hard-packed earth as she shifted her weight. She tucked a stray strand of blond hair behind her ear. Still Cora watched and chewed.

Victoria was on the verge of speaking up when the hunter finally swallowed. She didn't speak right away, but her eyes finally left Victoria's face. The fire snapped, sending a flurry of sparks toward the stars.

"Ain't easy for me to admit," she began, "but I ain't no closer to puzzling out who that feller was. All I know for sure is who he ain't, and that's Fodor Glava."

"You're sure?" Victoria asked. "Couldn't he have come back from the dead if he was a vampire like you say?"

Cora shook her head. "No vampire could stitch his own head back on his shoulders, no matter how strong he was. I know I sent that bastard on down to hell where he belongs, and that feller last night done confirmed my thinking in that regard. No matter what he says, he ain't Glava.

"But," she continued, "he ain't just nobody, neither. He's got himself the same tricks and traps that old Glava had, what with the vryko-whatevers and all."

"The what?"

"Nasty ones," Cora said. "Them ones as couldn't speak and was all fangs and such. George had a fancy name for them, too, but it's gone right out of my head. Before I met him and Glava, I done figured them badgery ones was the only kind of vampires out there. Never knew they came in a speaking variety, and it ended up that I paid a price for not knowing."

"What price?"

"I'm getting to it," Cora said, rubbing her brow as if soothing an aching head. "Point is, not knowing what you're fighting is usually a one-way ticket to an early grave, and that's if you get lucky. Some folk ain't so lucky and get themselves turned into some nasty piece of work like them fools back at the ranch."

"I remember James Townsend saying something similar," Victoria said. "About knowing your enemy as best you can."

"King George has him a head for facts, I'll give him that. Thought he was just a big bag of wind when we first met him, but he ended up being useful. All of his book learning about vampires and such is what helped me put an end to that Glava bastard. Just came a bit too late is all."

Victoria's brow wrinkled. "Too late? What do you mean?"

The hunter paused. Her hand snaked into her

satchel as if it had a mind of its own, emerging with a small flask. Cora unscrewed the stopper and took a swig. Her eyes never left the fire as she swallowed the first mouthful, then the second.

"Well, if I'd have met old George sooner rather than later, I might have spared myself some powerful unpleasant business."

Victoria could hear the liquid in the flask sloshing as Cora took another drink. A large piece of kindling collapsed in the fire, creating a shower of sparks. The hunter bent over and tossed a stick into the flames. "Part of it was my own yellowness. Ain't nobody in this wide world likes admitting they're yellow, but there it is. If I wasn't such a coward, maybe it wouldn't have happened."

Cora seemed to be speaking more to herself than to her companion now. Victoria looked down at her toes, her brow furrowing. The silence between them was almost tangible, a weight on her chest that grew heavier with each breath. She wanted to say something, anything to break it, but nothing sounded right.

"Anyhow," Cora finally said, "take two cuts of coward and stew it with a big mix of ignorance, and you got yourself a right fine recipe for making your own tragedy."

"What tragedy?" Victoria asked, relieved to have found her voice.

Cora inhaled sharply, as if she had just then remembered to breathe. She held the breath for several seconds, her jaw working in silence.

"Fact of it is," she said, "that Fodor Glava bastard killed my Ben."

It was Victoria's turn to inhale. Her eyes went wide as her fingers covered her mouth, but Cora paid her no mind. "Killed him and turned him into one of those things. There he was, coming at me like a rabid dog. There wasn't nothing left of him inside that body no more, but it still looked just like him. The monster wearing his skin would have done in for poor old Father Baez, but I..." she swallowed. "I done it in first. I pointed my gun right at my Ben's face and pulled the trigger."

Cora threw her head back and drained the contents of the flask in one long draught. When she finished, she tossed the empty flask aside and stared into the fire. Victoria watched her, unable to speak. The tough-as-nails hunter had been replaced by an old woman, shrunken and twisted by the weight of unfathomable sorrow. A breeze drifted through the flames, making the shadows around them sway. In that moment, Victoria felt as though they were surrounded by demons on all sides, dancing and laughing in unheard glee at all the agony and suffering they brought into the world. A hollow pit opened in her stomach, black and deep. Cora's pain, carved in deep lines across her face, brought Victoria's own loss back in a suffocating rush, and she fought to contain her tears.

She might have sat there until the fire had burned itself out, overwhelmed by her own helplessness, but the scraping of the hunter's boots across the ground

cut through her stupor. Looking up, Victoria found
Cora's eyes glistening as they looked at her. "There I
was, a widow of her own making, and after Ben and
I swore to each other that we'd always watch the
other's back."

"You took a vow?"

The firelight outlined the scars running along Cora's
cheek as she shook her head. "Never was nothing formal, mind you, but it was there. We was married,
after all, and part of having and holding was keeping
each other alive, or so I figured. Then I went and
broke that promise, and I never been able to make it
right in my mind since.

"Anyhow, after I realized what I'd done, I rode
down that son of a bitch Glava and made him pay.
Shot him and stabbed him and cut his head off, so I
know he's dead. George and a whole mess of others
seen me do it, too, so I got witnesses. Whoever that
feller was back there, he ain't Glava, and that's how
I know."

Cora crossed her arms and leaned back against a
rock, her eyes studying the younger woman's face.
Tension flowed from those dark eyes, and Victoria
shifted uneasily. She wasn't sure what the hunter
expected her to do or say.

The enormity of what Cora had just told her defied
understanding, yet her mind still wrestled with it,
trying to make some sense of it. As terrible as the
death of her own parents had been, she had at least
been left with the cold comfort of knowing she
couldn't have prevented it. She had also had time to

mourn them, to make her vows of vengeance and travel to see them fulfilled. Cora had none of those comforts when her husband was killed, and she had to endure the horror of shooting him herself. Victoria couldn't fathom what that would do to a person. That the hunter could have carried on at all spoke volumes about her strength and determination.

Victoria's blue eyes finally lifted to meet the hunter's gaze. "I'm so sorry."

Cora snorted. "I don't need your sorry, missie. Didn't tell you my story for it, neither. I told you so you got a better sense of things when they come up again, as I expect they will. That blue-eyed feller and that woman both know a good deal more than they should, and that don't sit well with me."

"Why not?"

"Could be they know even more than they're letting on, for one," Cora said. "Good Lord only knows what else they learned about me, or even about you. Maybe they know what brought you out here to begin with, and they're planning on using that somehow."

Victoria dropped her gaze. "They already do know that, I'm afraid."

"How's that?"

"I told them why I journeyed here from England when they first captured me," Victoria said.

"What?" Cora asked, leaning forward. "What put it in your head to go and do a fool thing like that?"

"I'm not sure anymore," Victoria replied. "I was terribly frightened, and I don't doubt that that had a great deal to do with my confession. Even still, there were parts of that evening that felt particularly uncanny." She laughed at herself. "I mean, it was all uncanny, but some parts more than others, if you follow me."

The hunter nodded. "Things usually is in this line of work."

"It's almost like I lost myself for a while when they were speaking to me," Victoria said. The memory of it made a shiver run over her limbs. "I felt weak and sleepy, even in the face of that danger. I nearly fell asleep on my feet once, and even though I managed to keep myself awake, my head was foggy afterward. The things that woman said seemed sensible, and answering her questions seemed just as sensible."

"She ain't no ordinary squaw, that you can bet on," Cora said. "She got her some strange ways and means. Like how my gun wouldn't shoot at her last night."

"I thought it did," Victoria said. "You shot at her twice."

"With my Winchester, sure, but I was meaning my Colt." Cora pointed to the gun, still holstered around Victoria's hips. "That little shooter ain't never let me down once since I first picked her up. I keep her clean, give her lots of love and oil, and she kills what I need killed by way of repayment. Until last night, that is. I just about fell over from shock when I heard that click."

"Why do you suppose it didn't work?"

Cora shook her head. "Ain't got a clue, but I'd bet

the Print Shop on it being part of some scheme or bad medicine on her part."

"Bad medicine?" Victoria asked, cocking her head.

"Bad magic," Cora said. "You know, like witches and them do."

That sparked a memory in Victoria's mind, and her eyes lit up. "You know, now that you mention it, the Indian woman did ask me whether or not I was a witch. The issue seemed to concern her."

"You, a witch?" Cora's laugh rolled off into the shadows. "That's a yarn if I ever heard one. No witch I ever heard of would let herself get roughed up by a vampire. Shucks, even getting yourself kidnapped by them in the first place ought to have tipped them off that you ain't no witch."

Victoria's ears burned. "I hardly think my staying indoors last night was all that foolhardy."

"Think what you like," Cora said, waving a hand dismissively. "You was saying something about our squaw?"

"Yes," Victoria said, eager to steer the conversation away from her mistakes. "She inquired several times whether or not I had knowledge of witchcraft, and even though I repeatedly denied her accusations, she seemed unconvinced."

Cora wrinkled her brow. "That don't make much sense, now do it? If she's a witch – and I do think we're on the right track there – what would she be afraid of another witch for? Maybe she was hoping you would help her out with whatever she's plotting. You know, like a witch sisterhood thing."

"Perhaps," Victoria said, unconvinced. "Still, if she is a witch, how do we fight her? Do we have to burn her at the stake?"

"That's generally how a body settles a witch, if I remember right," Cora said.

"What do you mean? Have you never fought one yourself?"

"Not that I can recollect, and sure not one that can use Indian magic. Most of the monsters I've whipped in my day have been ordinary monsters, vampires and werewolves and hellhounds and the like. Ain't but once I even met another Indian monster, and that was that wendigo critter up in Leadville, what Jules turned into. Wasn't no witch, but it did take a special kind of bullet to kill."

"Your silver bullets didn't work?"

Cora shook her head. "They needed some special Indian blessing to whip it proper. Wouldn't do with my regular old Catholic blessing. Maybe we need something like that for this here new one, too."

"Where would we get something like that?"

"Well, from what I gather, it all depends on which tribe your spook is part of," Cora said. "Like that wendigo thing wasn't content with just any Indian blessing, see? It had to be from the proper sort of Indian priest. I'd reckon our squaw will take something like that." Before Victoria could ask her next question, Cora went on to answer it. "Seems like the Navajos in these parts would be a good place to start. I got me one or two come in regular to the Print Shop. Maybe I can get some tales out of them for a few drinks."

With that, the hunter rose to her feet. "All this jawing is making my old bones cranky. Go on and stretch
out for a spell. I'll take the first watch." Pulling her
rifle from its sheath, she stepped off into the gathering darkness.

Victoria lowered herself onto the thin strip of cloth
that Cora had called a bedroll. Associating the comfort
of a proper bed with such a thing seemed absurd, but
Victoria was starting to accept that people out here
took liberties with their language. Rocks and twigs
poked up through the bedroll, jabbing her in more
places than she could count. She shifted from side to
side, trying to find a spot where there weren't as many,
but soon gave up and stretched out on her back.

Above her, thousands of stars filled the sky from
horizon to horizon. Laying there, it seemed as
though the sky would suck her upward at any moment. Or maybe she would fall into it and be
trapped, forever drifting above the earth like a cloud,
unable to return. The thought made her smile.

TEN

A gunshot. Victoria's eyes snapped open. She remained where she was, holding her breath, waiting to see if the danger had passed. As the rolling thunder of the Winchester faded into the desert, the sound of Cora's voice became distinguishable somewhere behind her.

Another shot shook the night air. Pulling herself into a sitting position, Victoria looked toward the sound. The hunter stood some distance off, a shadow in the dim moonlight, her rifle trained on something Victoria couldn't see. She could still hear Cora speaking to someone. Was it her? She opened her mouth to reply, then closed it again. If Cora wasn't speaking to her, calling out might distract the hunter. Victoria's gun belt lay next to her bedroll. Pulling the revolver from its holster, she cradled it in both hands and watched.

Cora's form moved through the scrub. Even in the faint light, Victoria could make out the half-crouch of a predator stalking its prey. The old woman was clearly after something, but whether it was one of their unholy opponents from the night before or just another rabbit to add to the pot, she wasn't sure.

Next to her, the fire had burned low. A few flames still licked the charred wood, but they produced little heat and even less light. Victoria looked around for the pile of wood she and Cora had collected, thinking to build the fire back up so she could see better. The chill of the desert night was sharper than she had expected; her arm shook with it as she reached for a branch.

Something was watching her.

It wasn't human, but that didn't mean it wasn't a threat. The American frontier was as full of deadly animals as it was of ungoverned men. Her fingers tightened around the revolver's grip.

After a few minutes of staring one another down, Victoria's hand completed its trip to the woodpile. She grabbed the first piece of kindling her fingers touched and tossed it onto the fire. Two more sticks, and the fire began burning eagerly. Victoria kept her eyes on the animal, ready to raise her gun and pull the trigger if it so much as inched toward her, but it remained where it was. In the light from the growing fire, she could make out a head with small, triangular ears attached to a long body. She took it for a cat at first, but it seemed too large.

A report from Cora's rifle made her jump. The shadow flinched as well, its head turning toward the sound. Victoria stole a glance in the same direction, but her ears already told her that the sound was farther away. The hunter's quarry was taking her farther out into the darkness. The thought made her nervous, but she shrugged it away. Whatever was out there, animal or monster, Cora knew what she was doing.

The sound of fur hissing through the brush broke into her thoughts. She inhaled sharply as she brought the gun up. Step by step, the animal was making its way toward her. It kept its head low, a predatory stance, and Victoria took that as her cue to center the revolver's barrel on its head.

The creature halted its advance. A furry ear twitched. It stood no more than ten feet away, yet she still couldn't see its face. This close to the fire, she expected to at least see the gleam of the flames in its eyes, but she could only make out the vague shape of a long, slender muzzle. The gun trembled in her grip. She forced her hands to steady it. It was only a fox, a creature her father and his colleagues hunted for sport. It had far more to fear from her than she had from it.

"What you got there?"

Victoria spun in place, bringing the gun around. Cora ducked to one side, raising her free hand. "Mary mother of God, girl. I ain't no spook."

The air left Victoria's lungs in a rush, and her gun arm fell to her side. "Don't do that."

"Ain't got to be so damn jittery," Cora said. "What's got you so wound up, anyhow?"

Victoria looked back to where the fox had been, but the animal had vanished. "There was a fox over there. I thought it might attack me."

Cora howled a laugh at the night sky. "So you was planning on blowing his little fox brains all over the desert with my gun?" she asked. "Wouldn't have done you no good if you had. Ain't no meat on a fox that's fit for eating unless you got nothing else."

"I wasn't going to shoot it for food," Victoria said, rising to her feet. "I just didn't enjoy the thought of a wild animal tearing me to bits is all."

"Let me tell you something, Vicky."

"My name is—"

"If you got yourself ate up by a fox, you'd deserve it," Cora said. Stepping over to the fire, she hunkered down. It snapped in reply. "Ain't never seen nobody get ate by a fox while they was alive, you follow? You was scared for nothing."

"Yes, well, forgive me if my knowledge of the wilderness is somewhat incomplete," Victoria said. "I haven't exactly spent the best of my years traipsing around the back country."

"Ain't nobody perfect," Cora said. She pulled her rifle back out of its scabbard and laid it beside her bedroll. "Now, why don't you go have yourself a turn at keeping watch? I aim to get at least a wink or two before that old sun comes rolling on back up."

"What were you chasing?" Victoria asked.

The hunter looked up at her. "Thought I saw that blue-eyed bastard skulking around out there, but I think my eyes was just playing tricks on me."

Victoria's gaze grew hard. "What? You're expecting me to keep watch by myself when he's out there somewhere?"

"Keeping watch is easy," Cora replied. "All you got to do is yell if he jumps you." Before Victoria could protest, Cora rolled away from her and promptly began snoring.

Victoria sighed and shook her head. Tossing another piece of wood onto the fire, she started searching for a tolerable place to hold her vigil. The desert landscape offered precious few choices, but she finally found one atop a flat stone not too far from the camp. Brushing it off as best she could, she sat down and set her gaze outward into the desert.

Soon, she began to wish her vantage point was closer to the fire. The night air greedily sucked warmth from her arms and legs, and the slightest breeze was enough to make her shiver despite her coat. She stomped her boots on the ground. She opened and closed her fists. She twisted her back around, first one way, then the other. Finally, she stood and stretched her arms. Nothing worked.

To pass the time, she imagined she was a fox herself, running through the endless desert, searching for field mice and other things to eat. Her thick grey coat would keep her warm as she bounded beneath the stars, smelling the sweet breath of the slumbering wilderness.

Above her head, the stars grew dim for a moment.

The ground passed beneath her in a blur. She could hear the rushing of the wind, but the air was not cold on her face. Pausing to look about herself, she saw the light from the fire in the distance, an orange pinprick of light among the sea of blue shadows. It seemed so far away.

A presence flickered through her mind. Somewhere out there, she could sense her fox, but something was wrong. It felt different, unclean, not the pure simple instinct and cunning she felt from the other animals around her. She turned toward the unclean feeling, and suddenly she was moving again, flying over the desert floor like a swallow skimming a lake's surface before a storm. The fire disappeared behind a hill as she moved, but she found she could see perfectly well without it. Light from the waning moon outlined the shape of every rock and plant she passed.

Voices.

She stopped, her feet hovering above the ground as if she were floating in water. Yes, there were people speaking somewhere out in the darkness, and they were nearby. Feeling no fear, she moved toward the sound, following it to the base of a cliff. The voices drifted down from above her. Grasping the stone wall before her, she found she could easily pull herself up along it. Higher and higher she climbed, her body as light as a cotton sheet.

Pulling herself over the edge, she held still for a moment. The voices were much nearer now. There were two, a man's and a woman's, and she recognized both. For the first time, a vague sensation of fear passed through her. The presence of the fox, dark and unnatural, loomed large in her mind. Alighting on the sandy rock beneath her, she willed herself forward, step by step, toward the voices and the presence both.

As she drew near to the far edge of the mesa, she could see two figures standing upright in the moonlight. Moving as close to them as she dared, she stopped to listen.

"You really ain't all that bright, is you?"

"My intention was not to harm her."

"Then why did you have me distract the old woman? Just so you could go have a peek?"

"The young one is as dangerous as the old, but she does not know her power. I had to be sure she has not yet awakened to that knowledge."

"That sprout ain't no threat. I would have had her body and soul both if the other bitch hadn't showed up. She talks big, sure, but she's just a kitten behind them guns and such."

"You speak in ignorance, demon."

"Ain't the first time."

"Victoria Dawes is—" The woman fell silent. Her eyes gleamed. "She is here."

The Indian's red gaze shifted from her companion, sweeping the barren rock for signs of the intruder. When her eyes swept over her, Victoria shuddered.

The woman took a step toward her.

Victoria backed up.

The woman advanced again, her eyes passing over Victoria but not seeing her. She sniffed the air. "She is very close."

"You're out of your gourd, woman. Ain't nobody here but us."

"Be silent." She took another step. "She is here and not here. Her power has stirred inside her."

The woman cast off the blanket covering her body. As before, she was naked save for a fur mantle wrapped around her throat. She crouched and bowed her head, fingers splayed out on the rock. The edges of her figure blurred in the moonlight. Her black hair faded to the grey of old ashes. Her body grew smaller. Ears sprouted from her skull. Her nose stretched forward and her eyes sank backward.

*In the space of a heartbeat, the Indian witch had van-
ished, and a grey fox stood in her place.*

*Wonder filled Victoria, but it turned to terror as the fox's
eyes settled on her. The creature broke into a run. Before
she could react, it leaped at her, teeth bared.*

Victoria jumped to her feet. Her cold limbs ached
at the movement, but she could barely feel them. Her
head swung this way and that, searching for the fox-
that-was-not-a-fox, but it was nowhere to be seen.

Behind her, something snapped. Spinning around,
gun in hand, she took aim at the sound. The campfire burned cheerfully back at her. Beyond it, Cora
still lay wrapped in her blanket. Seconds ticked by,
marked by the frantic rush of her breathing, but
nothing stirred. The dark presence of the witch was
gone from her mind.

Slowly, Victoria allowed herself to relax. The revolver's barrel drifted downward as she sat back down
onto her perch. Her head spun. She massaged her
temples with her free hand, trying to sort reality from
what surely must have been a dream. A fever dream
brought on by the long day she had spent walking
through the desert, back bent beneath the sun's
wrath. Her brain had roasted like a honeyed ham in
the heat, and now it was playing tricks on her.

She couldn't shrug off how real it had felt, though.
The sensation of flying over the hard-packed desert
soil, the coolness of the rocks beneath her fingers as
she climbed up the mesa, the voices of their two ad-
versaries as they held their council; if dream it was,
it was the most vivid one of her life. Even the dreams

she suffered as a child did not possess the same level of clarity this one did, even if they had frightened her more.

Victoria rubbed her arms. Until her parents died, she hadn't given those dreams a second thought since childhood. Even now, they still held some power over her, but such was the case with all childhood fears. No amount of rationalization could rid one of that deep-seated, primal terror of the unknown, the stranger, the dark. Facing them as a child was better, in a way. When she woke from her dreams, frightened and crying, her mother was always there with whispered comfort and a cool cloth for her forehead. Sitting there in the desert, alone but for the sleeping form of a half-mad gunfighter, she was swept up by a sudden longing for her mother's face and soft white fingers.

A chorus of screams rose up in the night, giving her a shock. Eyes wide, she brought the Colt up, ready to fire if the fox so much as poked an ear out of hiding. The cries echoed off the nearby cliffs and rolled through the brush, eerie in their near-human voices. Despite herself, Victoria imagined a legion of fork-tailed imps creeping in the shadows around her, laughing and calling to each other as they encircled the camp. Once planted, the fear grew inside her with alarming speed, threading its black tendrils through her ribs. Panic clutched at her throat. The cries drew nearer. She drew her revolver, pointing it this way and that at echoes and shadows. They were all around her.

She saw a shadow move and fired. The Colt's voice roared into the night, cutting off the eerie cries. Victoria blinked, blinded by the muzzle's flash. When the gunshot stopped ringing in her ears, the desert was silent.

"What is it?" Cora's voice, thick with sleep, broke the silence.

"Nothing," Victoria replied. Holstering her revolver, she turned back toward the campfire. "Just thought I saw something."

"Well, don't go wasting my bullets," Cora grumbled as she rolled toward the fire.

"I'm sorry," Victoria said, but the hunter's eyes were already closed.

Tossing a few sticks onto the fire, Victoria sat by the crackling flames and crossed her legs. Beyond the ring of light, the desert slept beneath its blanket of shadows. She breathed a sigh and looked toward the stars.

ELEVEN

"I never thought I could be so grateful to see such a pathetic group of buildings."

"Hey, now," Cora said, "this here group happens to be my hearth and home. I'll thank you not to make light of it."

"On the contrary," Victoria said, offering the hunter a smile, "it looks finer than Buckingham Palace."

They stood on the hard-packed earth of Albuquerque's streets. Behind them, the sun flooded the desert with weary red light from its place near the horizon. Victoria's face felt flushed and hot, her shirt stuck to her back, and her blisters throbbed. Swaying on her feet, she could think of nothing but the comfort awaiting her in the hotel.

"Ain't got to tell you how I ache in places I can't mention in front of a fine lady," Cora said.

Victoria's laugh sounded more like a groan. She pressed her hands into the small of her back and stretched. Her spine popped like the campfire from the previous night. "I'm afraid this fine lady shares your misery. I don't know if I've ever wanted a proper bath more than I do at this very moment."

"Right, then. Go get yourself washed up and come on over to the Print Shop when you finish."

"Tonight?" Victoria asked, her heart sinking.

"Yes ma'am," Cora said. "We got us some plans to lay out, and I'll warrant you ain't got no protection up in that room of yours."

"Protection?"

"Garlic and crucifixes and the like," Cora replied. "Ain't rightly sure if they're any good at keeping that squaw away, but they'll do against the vampire feller sure enough."

"I still have the one you gave me," Victoria said. "That will be enough."

Cora shrugged. "Suit yourself, then. I know I ain't planning on turning in without a bit of holy water under my pillow. Nothing short of a miracle that they didn't take us last night when we was vulnera-ble-like. Could be they was off someplace else, but I'd put a good bottle of whiskey on them having some big scheme. Anyhow, I ain't going to give that pair a second chance like that."

Before Victoria could reply, the hunter turned and started down the street, her boots kicking up dust. Victoria watched her black braid grow smaller for a few moments, then turned and climbed the hotel's front steps.

Soon, clad in a modest grey dress with tiny roses stitched into the bust, Victoria stepped back out onto the street. Her gunfighter outfit hung from a clothesline in her room, dripping dark circles onto the floorboards. She'd made a point of strapping her gun belt around the waist of her dress, no matter how silly it made her look. Judging from the glances and stares passersby tossed her way, it must have made her look very silly indeed. She hurried toward the saloon.

Pushing through the batwing doors, Victoria found Cora propped up behind the bar. A few tables were occupied by the town's layabouts and drunkards as they bet away what money they had on hands of poker. Victoria thought she saw the man called Wilson seated at one of the games, but he made a point not to make eye contact. In fact, all of the men seemed slightly unsettled about her presence in the saloon. Their conversations were muted, as if they were afraid of her overhearing.

Victoria smiled to herself as she walked up to the bar. Let them fret; they had good reason to fear her now. The weight of the gun around her waist made her saunter a bit as she walked over to the bar.

Cora offered her a lazy wave. "Ain't you all slicked up and back to your fancy self?"

"I'd say the same, but..." Victoria replied, trailing off. In truth, she couldn't tell if Cora had washed up at all. The hunter's leathery face looked much the same as it had that morning, and all of the clothes Victoria had seen her wear were stained from years of use.

"I'm always fancy," Cora said. Her braid flipped over her shoulder as she tossed her head. "Now, then, we got a lot to do and not much time to get it done."

"What shall we do first?"

"Come on upstairs for a spell. I got some tools of the trade stashed away up there."

Victoria followed the hunter to the back of the saloon. Their boots thumped in unison on the worn stairs. Behind them, the hushed conversations rose in volume, and Victoria smiled again.

The stairs ended at a balcony that encircled the entire bar. Cora led her down one side, passing three doors before opening a fourth. Victoria gave the men below one last glance before following the hunter into the small room beyond.

"Home sweet home," Cora said, waving her arm in a semi-circle.

Victoria took two small steps into the room, taking stock of the little place Cora Oglesby called her own. It wasn't much. A bed dressed with rough linen sheets stood beneath the room's sole window. Beneath their feet, a hide rug faded with sunlight and the tread of Cora's boots covered much of the floor. Standing at attention opposite the bed was a dresser hewn from unfinished wood. A collection of books sat on top of it, their spines facing outward invitingly. They looked to be old and well-loved; Victoria could not make out the titles on some of them.

"I never pictured you as an avid reader," she remarked, nodding at the collection.

"I ain't," Cora said. The hunter did not explain further, and Victoria felt it wiser not to ask. Instead, she waited in silence as the hunter rummaged through the top drawer of the dresser. After a few moments, Cora turned back to her.

"First, you're going to put these in your bag and never let them get away from you." Cora held up two vials of clear liquid.

Victoria reached for her satchel. Her hand brushed against her dress before she remembered that she had left it in her hotel room. Blushing at her own forgetfulness, she took the vials from the old hunter and examined them.

"Holy water," Cora explained. "Blessed by a Catholic priest. That stuff is like boiling hot tar to vampires and other critters of dark. Ain't rightly sure how it will fare against that squaw witch, but it should at least get her wet."

"I can't see how that would be to our advantage."

Cora shrugged. "We got to make do with what we got." She reached into the drawer again and produced a handful of small white objects.

"What are they?" Victoria asked, but her nose answered before Cora did.

"Garlic. Keeps vampires out of your hair while you sleep. Ain't much use as a weapon, but them suckers can't stand being around it. No, I don't got any idea why they take such a disliking to it, but they do."

Victoria took the cloves in her free hand, careful not to let them too near her nose. "So all I need to do is put these somewhere in my room, and that Fodor Glava person won't be able to enter?"

"That ain't his name," Cora said, "but yes. Again,

I got no idea whether any of this truck will matter one whit to that squaw, but I wouldn't bet nothing on it. She didn't seem to have no issue with the crucifix or the rosary we had with us, so I reckon she ain't going to balk at a bit of garlic. Best we can hope for is that it will keep the other feller out of the way long enough for us to deal with the witch first."

"What's our plan for that?" Victoria asked.

Cora folded her arms across her chest. "Afraid it ain't got much past praying them Indian fellers that come in regular to the Print Shop know about squaw witches."

"And if they don't?"

"Well," Cora said, "she did light out right quick when I started shooting at her, so maybe that's all there is to it."

"But you missed," Victoria said.

"I know that. If I hadn't, we wouldn't be jawing about it right now."

Victoria flushed and looked down at the cloves in her hand. "What I meant to say was, what if she performs that hex again, the one where she stopped your gun from functioning?"

"Way I figure it, if she ain't keen on bullets, mayhap she won't be too keen on blessed steel, either. Swords don't got to fire, so there ain't no machinery to put a curse on. She's a witch, but I ain't seen nothing to make me think she's undead or a demon or anything of the sort. I reckon she'd bleed when stuck just like me or you."

"Somehow, I doubt it's that simple," Victoria said.

"Why's that?"

"Just a feeling I have." She felt awkward still holding the cloves and the vials, but she wasn't sure where to put them. After a moment's hesitation, she gingerly tucked the holy water into her bodice. The garlic she slipped under her gun belt. When she finished, she looked up to find the hunter's eyes still looking at her steadily, expecting an answer. "It just seems to me that a woman capable of changing into an animal would be more difficult to kill."

Cora shrugged. "Maybe so. I reckon them Indian boys will know for sure."

"When will you speak to them?"

"Tomorrow. They always show up mid-morning like clockwork. Can't get enough of my fire water."

The hunter grinned, and Victoria was struck by a sudden curiosity. "By 'fire water' you mean alcohol, correct?"

"Sure do," Cora replied. "What, you got another kind in mind?"

Victoria shook her head. The reasonable part of her mind told her to keep her mouth shut. She knew it would be unpleasant, that Cora would laugh at her when it was over, but a larger part had to know. "If it's not too much trouble," she began, "I would like to try some of it for myself."

A look of genuine surprise spread across Cora's face. "Come again?" she said, leaning forward.

"I would like to try some," Victoria said in a louder voice.

The hunter watched her for a moment, then shook her head. "Well, if you insist." Pushing the drawer shut, she took a look around the room before moving toward the door. She motioned for Victoria to go through. The young woman obeyed, and Cora shut the door behind them.

"What's your poison?" Cora asked over her shoulder as they made their way back toward the stairs.

"I'm not sure," Victoria replied. "I've sampled a few wines from my father's cellar, but I couldn't really tell you the difference between them. I do prefer reds to whites, however."

"Only thing I got is brown."

Victoria frowned. "Brown? I've never heard of a brown wine. Is it a vintage unique to America?"

Cora's laughter shook the walls. Several of the poker players looked up from their cards. "No, I reckon you got rotgut over yonder. Ain't a place in the world without its own version, or so I've found."

"Rotgut?"

"Whiskey," Cora said as they thumped down the stairs. "Stuff here's trained in from out East. Tennessee, to be particular. Them folk out there know how to brew a fine batch, let me tell you."

"You don't make your own, then?" Victoria asked.

Cora shook her head as she walked behind the bar. "Don't got the proper know-how or the proper set-up here. Besides, can't get no desert to grow enough grain to make it. We're lucky if we can pull enough wheat to make our daily bread out of the soil here. Ain't like back home. Soil was as rich and black as sin, and so thick you could damn near eat it with your hands."

Victoria grimaced at the thought. "Where is your home?"

"Back in Virginia. Pa had himself a nice stead on the river, and me and Ma kept him company while he tilled the soil. Nothing big and fancy, mind you, but he raised enough as kept us fed. Least, he did until the damn Yankees took to burning us farm folk out of house and home."

"They did what?"

"Don't matter none now." Cora heaved a large jug up onto the bar. "This here's what matters. Now then, you want yourself a fancy glass as fits a proper lady or the hog troughs we locals use?"

Victoria blinked at the jug. "I believe I'll try blending in for once," she said after some consideration.

"Ain't much chance of that, specially now," Cora remarked. Her head disappeared below the bar for a moment. Victoria heard clinking, and the hunter reappeared with two short glasses clasped in her fingers. "You look like you ain't got all your cows in the pen with that getup."

"It couldn't be helped," Victoria replied, taking the offered glass. "My new clothes needed washing, and this was in my trunk."

"Not many women in these here parts fancy six shooters as decoration," Cora said.

Victoria straightened the gun belt around her waist. "I'd rather look a fool than be one. After what nearly happened in here last time, I refuse to walk these streets without a means of defending myself."

"Well, now," Cora said, favoring her with a grin, "it seems the lady's got herself a shred of sense in that pretty little head of hers after all. I'll drink to that." The cork popped from the jug with a hollow sound. Cora sloshed brown, foul-smelling liquid into the glasses. Setting the jug down, she picked up the glass closest to her and raised it. "To sense!"

Victoria delicately mimicked her gestures. Whiskey spilled onto her fingers as Cora rammed the glasses together. The hunter tossed hers back without missing a beat, but Victoria raised the liquid to her face for inspection. This close, the smell burned her nostrils, bringing tears to her eyes. Blinking them away, she took a deep breath. She'd gotten herself into this with her own foolish curiosity, so it was best to see it through. Keeping her eyes fixed on her reflection in the bar's mirror, she took a sip.

At first, she couldn't distinguish Cora's laughter from her own coughing. One soon died out before the other, however, and she glared at the hunter until the laughter finally stopped.

"This ain't tea, little missie," Cora said, wiping tears from the corners of her eyes. "Faster you drink, the less you taste."

"So the idea isn't to savor it?"

Another laugh shook the hunter's shoulders. "Not any more than folk savor anything else in these parts. Thing is, this here whiskey's good at getting the other disagreeable parts of life to not be quite so disagreeable, you follow me?"

Victoria nodded, studying the remaining liquid in her glass. With a swiftness that surprised even her, she brought it to her lips and threw her head back. Fire blossomed in her mouth, but she forced herself to swallow it. A burning trail lined her throat. Eyes watering, she fought the urge to cough as the flames spread through her torso. After a few seconds, the worst of it passed. The fire became a pleasant warmth in her belly. She shook her head once, then offered the hunter a smile.

Cora returned it. "That's how it's done proper."

"Now I know why," Victoria replied hoarsely. She cleared her throat. "It does make me curious who first thought to drink such a foul-tasting concoction, though."

"I'm just glad they did," Cora said. "You want another?"

Victoria nodded, surprising herself again. Cora refilled both glasses. "What should we drink to this time?" she asked.

Running her fingers around the rim of the glass, Victoria pondered the question. Several ideas floated to the top of her mind: victory, vengeance, the destruction of their foes. While certainly worth drinking to, she felt it might be somewhat premature. She'd never exactly believed in luck, good or bad, but she'd never believed in vampires until a few days ago. If they existed, luck and jinxes on that luck might, too. Not willing to take the risk, she chose something safer if more mundane.

"To surviving the desert!"

Glass clinked against glass, and Victoria added the second inferno to the first. It went down easier this time, and she set the glass back on the bar with an air of conquest.

Cora nodded approvingly. "A right fine toast. Seeing as how you is just a green horn, it really ain't no small feat that we made it through with what little trouble we had. There was a few times there that I wasn't so sure we would."

"Nonsense," Victoria said. Her head felt loose on her shoulders. "I'm not half as bad as all that. I killed the vampire in the barn all on my own, after all."

"Sure, while I was off whipping the other two. You ain't proved yourself as a hunter until you bag yourself at least a half-dozen of them critters. Why, Ben and I had us hellhounds and Satanists all on our first job."

"Your first job?"

Cora nodded. "Wasn't quite as bad as some of the ones we had, but it still wasn't none too easy. Had to fix a whole coven of witches that had got it in their heads to summon up a hellhound from the world below."

"Seems like a harsh introduction to the trade," Victoria said.

"Ain't no easy way to get into this sort of work," Cora said. "Only reason Ben and I took it up is because we was living off the charity of the Church at the time. Priest there asked us if we wouldn't mind helping him sort them witches out, seeing as how Ben used to be a soldier and all. We felt like we should do what we could to repay him for letting us sleep on his floor, so we agreed.

"Once we had that mess sorted out, the priest asked us if we wouldn't mind doing it regular for the Church and others as needed help with critters. Didn't see any reason not to, so we went ahead and said yes. Best decision of our lives, I reckon. Still, it ain't nearly so dramatic as your story. Parents killed, running halfway around the world to find an old coot, and getting yourself caught up with an Indian witch. Now that's a right fine way to start a career."

"In case you've forgotten, I do not seek a job in this particular line of work."

"Shame, that," Cora said. "If you got yourself enough time to practice, you might not be half-bad at it. World could always use another one of me around, and the pay ain't nothing to sneeze at, neither."

"Money is hardly enough incentive to risk life and limb like that," Victoria said. "In any case, I suppose I should retire for the evening. It's been a rather trying day."

The hunter nodded. "Might close up early my own self. Bob ain't going to be none too happy about it, but he can go hang himself. I'm so beat, I can barely keep myself upright."

"Until the morrow, then," Victoria said. She pushed the empty glass toward the hunter.

"Yes, ma'am," Cora replied. "Don't forget to put them wards out, or you're liable to wake up a vampire your own self."

TWELVE

The shapes of her mother and her husband swam through her vision, their voices faint and far away. She shook her head. They were not there. They had rejoined the Great Cycle, their souls finding new bodies to dwell in. She knew this. The phantoms she saw were only tricks of her mind.

The woman pushed them away. They brought nothing but sorrow and longing, and she could not use those feelings. She needed the anger, the hatred. Those were easy enough to find; they lived very close to her heart. She called upon them now to lend her courage to do what must be done. Even in their burning embrace, she was still afraid. Afraid of the ruined walls and ancient stone that surrounded her. Afraid of the spirits that walked in this place. Afraid of the old woman who brought her here.

Her companion stood before her, back stooped with many years, scratching symbols into the dirt with an old branch. The woman watched her with a mixture of fascination and dread. The darkness that clung to the crone's robes was thick and black, but the power she wielded was palpable. With such power, the woman could take revenge on the men who killed the ones she loved most. She could stop them from hurting the Diné for all time.

A faint shout echoed from behind her. Turning to look, she bit back a cry. Her mother's face stood at the edge of the firelight, features etched with love and fear. Her lips moved, but the woman could not understand her words. She blinked back tears. It was just a phantom of her guilt and her fear. Were she here, her mother would surely want her to go through with this. She had been a strong woman in life; she would have understood this desire to protect her people. The American soldiers had guns and numbers, but they did not have knowledge of these arts.

"Now," the old woman croaked.

The woman turned back to her. "Yes?"

The crone's eyes flashed red in the darkness. "You are ready?"

"Yes," the woman said again, trying to give more strength to her voice than she felt.

"You may never go back," the old woman said. "No-one may turn from the Witchery Way once they begin walking it. It will be with you and you with it until you die."

"I am ready."

A dry cackle spilled from those ancient lips. "So be it, girl. Come," she said, beckoning with a withered claw. "Come and take the power you desire."

The woman swallowed back her doubts, closing her ears to her mother's faint cries. Keeping the image of the American soldier's face in her mind, she stepped forward. The scratchings in the dirt were unreadable in the flickering light, but the woman knew the meaning of the animal skin laid next to them. Letting her anger fuel her need, she

*slipped out of the doeskin tunic she wore and knelt next to
the hide.*

Above her, the old woman's lips spread in a toothless grin.

The next morning, Victoria pulled on her clean shirt
and denim trousers, ate a quick breakfast of flapjacks,
and stepped outside. The sun had just climbed above
the tops of the buildings, but a slight chill hung in the
air. Victoria relished it, knowing that the hellish
swelter would soon smother the dusty streets. The
townsfolk moved sluggishly around her, as if they
could not move properly unless their limbs were
greased by sweat.

When she reached the saloon, Victoria found
Cora's business partner Robert behind the bar. He
wore a button-up shirt and tie beneath his jaunty,
small-brimmed hat. Had he been in a bank or office
tower in London or New York City, he might have
looked right at home. Standing behind the bar of a
dusty saloon, he seemed displaced and vulnerable.
For the first time since her arrival, Victoria thought
she might not be the most awkwardly-dressed person in the room.

Robert's face brightened when he caught sight of
her. "Ah, Miss Dawes. Wonderful to see you again."

"Likewise," she said, returning his smile. "How
have you been?"

"Much the same as ever," he replied. He looked
her up and down. "I'm guessing the getup was
Cora's idea?"

"Quite right," Victoria said, stepping up to the

bar. "Speaking of whom, has she been about this morning? I'm rather surprised not to find her where you are."

Frustration creased Robert's face. "I was, too. You wouldn't think it would be difficult for someone who lived in the saloon to open it on time, would you?"

"Certainly not," Victoria said.

"Yet here I am," he said, turning his palms upward, "and here I will remain until she remembers where she belongs."

"I don't expect Cora is a particularly easy woman to keep in line."

"Heaven spare me," Robert said, shaking his head. "I don't think any man anywhere has ever been able to keep her in line. Those who tried at one point or another aren't among the living anymore, or so I imagine."

The memory of Cora facing down the blue-eyed monster came to Victoria's mind, and she laughed. "Somehow, that seems all too likely."

"My other partners figured I'd lost my mind when I agreed to help Cora open this place," he said, looking around the near-empty saloon. "Truth is, had she wanted to start any other kind of business, I would have turned her down in a blink, but I knew she would be reliable so long as there was whiskey and poker involved. She's got enough of a reputation that I knew she'd pull in a crowd. Can't say I understand the name, though."

"Did she not explain it to you?" Victoria asked.

"Don't see why it matters none."

Both Victoria and Robert started and turned at the sound of Cora's voice. The hunter stood in the doorway, silhouetted by the morning light. Her spurs chimed as she strode over to the bar. "Ain't like most of the folk what pass through here can read the sign, anyhow."

Robert smirked. "That's truer than you know," he said to Victoria. "The people around here aren't what you'd call educated."

"Yeah, yeah," Cora said. "We ain't nothing but a bunch of ignorant frontier folk. Ain't got enough sense to wash or dress ourselves or take a proper squat." Robert opened his mouth to reply, but Cora didn't pause. "Last I checked, us frontier folk was keeping you in a steady means of living, Bob."

Robert dropped his gaze to his shoes, leaving Cora and Victoria looking at the top of his hat. "Yes, well," came his voice, quiet with embarrassment, "I wasn't going to go quite that far with it."

"You can stew about it till that hat of yours wears clean through for all I care," Cora said. "I'd just thank you to do your stewing right here for a spell."

That brought Robert's head back up. "Here? Why? Where are you going?"

"Got me some business with Morgan."

"What did you do this time?" Robert asked, rolling his eyes

"Nothing that you need to worry your city-fied head over," Cora said. She turned to Victoria. "You ready?"

Victoria blinked. "Ready?"

"Good." Cora headed back toward the door. Victoria exchanged a look with Robert. He shrugged and offered her an apologetic smile. She nodded in return, then followed Cora out onto the street.

"Where are we going?" Victoria asked.

"Off to see old Morgan," Cora replied. "Ain't you been listening?"

"Who's Morgan?"

"Sheriff in these parts." Above the edge of its scabbard, the butt of Cora's rifle caught the morning sunlight as she walked. "Seems he had himself a killing last night that ain't quite what he's used to."

"What do you mean?"

"Stiffs are drained dry," Cora said.

"Dry?" The two women paused on a corner to let a carriage thunder past. "You mean they've been drained of their blood?"

"Yes ma'am. He's all in a tizzy about it, says it's the worst thing he's seen in fifteen years of sheriffing. Can't see how that is, being as he don't look a day over thirty his own self, but I reckon it ain't smart to question a lawman on his numbers."

Cora strode toward a three-story building that stood near the end of the main street. Unlike the smaller buildings around it, whose shiplap walls were in various states of decay, this edifice boasted stone walls that glowed with the color of carnelians in the sunlight. Rows of windows, their curtains drawn, faced outward into the street. The building's crown thrust a triangular wedge toward the sky like a cockscomb.

As they approached, Victoria saw a small crowd gathered around the building's pillared entrance. Cora pushed her way through the throng, and Victoria followed close on her heels. A man stood in front of the doorway, arms folded, a gun hanging from his hip. The hunter marched right past him with a curt nod. The man returned the nod, a silver star gleaming on his chest.

Cora didn't slow her march when they entered the building. Desks, chairs, and people passed in a blur as Victoria followed her to the back of the building, where they clambered back and forth up a staircase until they reached the top floor. Stepping through an open doorway, they found a man with deep-set brown eyes waiting in the hall.

"Thanks for coming," he said, extending his hand.

Cora shook it. "You know this ain't my business no more, right?"

"Sure do," the man said. A mustache the color of ripe chestnuts covered his upper lip. "Don't expect you to do nothing beyond telling us your opinion of the matter, neither."

"So long as we're clear on that." Cora stepped aside and held her hand out toward Victoria. "This here's Vicky Dawes. Vicky, this is Sheriff Morgan."

"A pleasure, ma'am."

"My name is Victoria," she replied, giving Cora a look as she shook the sheriff's hand.

"You ain't from around here, are you?" the sheriff asked.

"No, she's from England somewhere," Cora said

before Victoria could answer. "Came all the way out here so she could have a chance to ride with the legendary Cora Oglesby. Wasn't none too happy to learn I ain't the riding type no more."

"You sure on that count?" Morgan asked with a pointed look at Cora's rifle.

"Sure as shit. This here's just for protection. I may have given up my spurs, but that don't mean I gave up my sense with them."

Morgan nodded and motioned for them to follow him. The trio made their way down the hall, their boots drumming a cacophony on the worn floorboards. Opening the last door on the right, Morgan led them into a small office. A window dominated the far wall, curtains drawn back just enough to allow a modest stream of sunlight in. Documents and legal books were piled high on the bookshelves standing at attention behind a large desk. Two comfortable-looking chairs faced the desk, their stained feet nestled into a thick green carpet.

Victoria absorbed all of this in a flash. Her eyes fixed on the slumped bodies of two men in business suits. One man was positioned behind the desk, and the other faced him in one of the two chairs. Both corpses were the color of old milk, their skin drawn tightly over their bones. Victoria's stomach gave a flop.

"Ain't seen nothing like it," Morgan said. He and Cora bent down on either side of the body behind the desk. "I ain't even sure how it was managed, sucking these sorry fools like they was oranges."

"I got a notion," Cora said, "but I don't reckon it's one you'll take to."

"Try me." Morgan stood upright and folded his arms. "I didn't call you here to give you a free gander. You got an opinion, I want to hear it."

"Vampires."

The sheriff leaned forward. "Come again?"

"Vampires," Cora repeated. "Blood-sucking living corpses what go about doing just this sort of thing. What's more, these fellers will start moving about again come sundown looking for some blood of their own. Were I you, I'd set them out where the sun can shine on them nice and good and leave them there."

"Propping up stiffs that look like these is like to put folks right off their feed," Morgan said. "Ain't like these two was outlaws or some such so folks'd be glad to see them done in. I put a pair of fine businessmen on display like sacks of potatoes, this town is liable to string me up from my own gallows."

"Putting them out on the street's a better idea than letting them run about once the change sets in," Cora said. "You do that, you'll have another few stiffs on your hands come tomorrow morning, and that's if you're lucky."

"Forget it," the sheriff said, shaking his head. "I always figured you was a loon, but when the talk in town is that you got a knack for strange cases, I thought you'd have something worthwhile to say about this here situation, but all you got is kid stories. Go on and take your fancy lady friend with you and leave the real work to the men folk."

"Seems to me like the sheriff needs some hard ev-
idence," Cora said to Victoria. "You got that holy
water I gave you?"

"Yes," Victoria said.

"Go on and pour a little on this feller's head," she
said, nodding toward the corpse.

Hand suddenly shaking, Victoria reached into her
satchel. She could feel the sheriff's eyes on her as she
pulled the vial out. The glass was cool to the touch.
Gripping the stopper with her thumb and forefinger,
she twisted to one side. It wouldn't budge. Smiling
nervously, she tried again. The rubber squeaked
against the glass. One more try, and the stopper came
out with a small popping sound.

Careful to keep as much distance between herself
and the corpse as she could, she held the vial over
the dead man's head and tilted it enough to let a few
drops fall.

The result surprised her as much as it did the sheriff. Where the water fell, plumes of smoke billowed
from the desiccated skin. It was as though someone
had poured vinegar on a hot stove. A sound like sizzling fatback filled the room. Alarmed, Victoria took
a hasty step backward, bumping into Cora. The
hunter held out a hand to steady her companion, a
smirk playing about her lips. She nodded toward the
sheriff, and Victoria followed her gaze.

Morgan's eyes were wide in his lean face, and his
cheeks had gone deathly pale. His lips moved without sound. Brown eyes stole a quick, bewildered
glance at the two women.

"What in tarnation is this?" he finally asked.

"This," Cora said, "is what happens when you throw holy water on something that's been cursed with unholy blood. Vampire, hellhound, werewolf, they all go up in steam and screams when you give them a good bathing." She folded her arms and cocked her head. "Still think I'm an old fool?"

The sheriff gaped at her for a moment before turning his gaze back to the smoking corpse. The trails of smoke were thinning out, resembling cigarette smoke instead of blacksmith's steam. Morgan took a step toward the body. Crouching down beside it, he craned his neck this way and that. Finally, he shook his head. "You is still a fool in my book, but maybe you got your head screwed on right about this here case."

"See?" Cora said, arching an eyebrow at Victoria. "The men here ain't nothing but a big old herd of sweet-talkers."

The sheriff stood and brushed his hands on his trousers. "How'd they get this way in the first place?"

"Another vampire had himself a drink," Cora said. "Given that they're all nice and tidy, I'd put good money on it being the same one we've been chasing lately."

"You know who did this?"

"Got a strong notion, though we can't be sure about it with things as they are here. Could be there's another vampire feller out there somewhere causing his own bit of ruckus, and it's just a coincidence that he turned up right when we was chasing the other one."

Brow furrowed, Morgan studied the two corpses. "So we might have two on our hands? What's the best way of handling these things?"

Cora patted the butt of her rifle. "Holy weapons, mostly. Silver bullets and blessed swords and the like. I got me some leftovers from when I was in this business, but it ain't going to be enough if you got a full infestation brewing on your hands. Best advice is to make friends with them monks out at the old Spanish mission. They ain't equipped for fighting, but they might have enough holy water and crosses as can offer the townsfolk some protection."

"Can't you go after the one that started this?"

"That's our plan," Cora said, "but you'd best have something else up your sleeve in case we can't find and whip the son of a bitch in time."

"I'll lend you one of my deputies if you like," Morgan said. "Got me a good tracker in the bunch, knows this here country powerful well."

Cora shook her head. "Keep him. Don't need me two greenhorns on the trail, or they're like to trip me up." Victoria blushed and looked down at her boots, but Cora didn't miss a beat. "Better your boys stay here and do what they can to protect folk.

"As for hunting down the bastard as did this, I got an idea." She stepped over to the other corpse and took a good look at its face. "I don't reckon those two will hide out on that ranch after what happened," she said to Victoria. "Was I them, I'd have lit out for another place to lay low for awhile."

"This isn't what I would call laying low," Victoria said.

"Me, either, but I did catch that feller in the leg with my rifle," Cora said. "I reckon he got himself a powerful hunger after that. Fresh blood keeps him strong and helps that wound of his to heal. Held off for a day or two, either out of fear or because that squaw wouldn't let him feed, but his need finally got the better of him.

"Second thing is, we done shot up his troops out at the farm. I reckon he's feeling a mite naked without critters at his heels, so he's looking to make him some new ones." She poked a grey cheek. "This feller's one of his new recruits. When he wakes up, I'd put good money on him running straight back to that blue-eyed bastard. Might not even feed before he goes if we're lucky."

"So we follow it back, just like that?" Victoria asked. "Won't he know what we're about and lead us back out into the desert, or ambush us?"

"Could be," Cora said, "but ain't like we got any other trails to follow. For all we know, this sucker will get right up and start feeding on folk as soon as the sun goes down. Then again, he might not. It might just be a pair of sixes, but it's the hand we was dealt, and we got to play it or fold."

"I'd rather not gamble our lives on it."

"You don't got to tag along. I reckon old Bob would be pleased as all get out if you decided to keep him company at the Print Shop tonight instead of riding out with me. Might even make it so he don't come grumping at me in the morning."

Hot blood coursed through Victoria's cheeks. She could feel the sheriff's eyes on her. "I'll ride," she said quietly.

"I knew you'd come around." Cora's grin lasted only a moment. "Now then, we got a lot to get done and not much time. First thing, we make for the Print Shop and wait for them Indian boys to wander in. Sheriff, I'll thank you to leave one of these fellers – this one, the one that's dry – right where he is so we can take our gamble with him."

"Just the one?" Morgan asked. "Why not both?"

"We went and made a sorry sight of the other one's face. Even if he did wake up, and I ain't sure he would now, I don't reckon old blue eyes would have much of a use for him. Best to just drag him into the sun and have done with it."

When the sheriff hesitated, Cora rolled her eyes. Placing a hand on the hilt of her saber, she leaned toward the ruined corpse. "Or, if you'd rather, I can just have off with his head right here, and you can go about explaining to his widow why he's a head shorter than he ought to be."

"Don't make much difference, way I see it," Morgan replied. "Ain't like saying it was spooks that did it will make a damn lick of sense, anyhow."

"Well, you ain't been elected just to slick down that mustache of yours," Cora said. "If you don't like my explanation good enough, go on and spin your own yarn about how these poor fools got themselves killed. Maybe they gone and got themselves done in by being too greedy."

Cora laughed at her own joke, but the sheriff didn't join in. In the dim light, his face seemed to redden, but whether it was from anger or embarrassment, Victoria couldn't tell. His right hand curled into a fist, then relaxed and smoothed down his mustache.

"I do believe we've places to be," Victoria reminded Cora.

"Right, right," she replied. "Much obliged for the tour here, sheriff. Now, if you'll excuse us, we got to go ask some Indian boys about a witch."

Morgan's eyebrows twitched. "A what?"

"Never you mind. Come on, Vicky, let's make tracks."

Victoria followed the hunter down the stairs and out through the building's front entrance. The deputy still stood at his post, arms folded, as if he were carved from stone. Cora ignored him, pushing her way through the crowd of onlookers. The sun had climbed higher into the sky, and the temperature was beginning to rise. Victoria sighed at the thought of another sweltering day.

"I reckon I might need your help with these here Indians," Cora said.

"What do you mean?" Victoria asked. "I'm not exactly an expert on their culture. I'd never even seen an Indian before I arrived here."

"No," Cora admitted, "but you are an expert at sitting still and looking pretty."

"What does that have to do with anything?" Even before the question passed through her lips, she was dreading the answer.

Cora shot her a look. "You ain't as thick as all that. Woman your age, specially one as doll-faced as you is, ought to know by now just how to make a man go all weak in the knees with a smile or a wink."

"You expect me to be coy with them?"

"Damn straight I do. Ain't like I'm asking you to let them have a poke with you, so simmer down. All I need you to do is look sweet and scared, like you ain't got a hope in the world if they don't tell us everything they know about witches. Men plumb lose their wits when they think there's a pretty girl that needs their saving."

"What if they don't think I'm pretty?" Victoria asked. "For all I know, they may find blue eyes or blond hair repulsive."

"Maybe so," Cora said, "but there ain't no harm in trying."

"Save to my dignity," Victoria muttered.

When they arrived at the saloon, Cora pushed through the batwing doors. Robert glared at her from behind the bar. "Took you long enough."

"I reckon so," Cora said.

"Morgan didn't see the need to arrest you after all?"

Cora shook her head. "Just wanted my expertise on a case he's got brewing. Couldn't help him none, though, so I told him I'd send you over instead."

"Very funny," Robert said. "Are you going to mind the saloon now, or should I stand here all day?"

"You're welcome to," Cora replied. "Me and Vicky got business here with them Indian boys what drop by in the mornings, so you can stay and look after the other folk if you got a mind to."

Robert looked at her suspiciously. "What business do you have with Indians?"

"Ain't none of yours, that's what. If you ain't going to help, best you just get. I don't need you looking all prickly and scaring off the decent folk what come in for a little morning poker. Vicky's doing enough of that as it is."

Victoria gave her a scowl. "I beg your pardon?"

"See? There you go again. I swear I'm the only person here who ain't sat on a cactus this morning."

With that, Cora took up her usual place behind the bar. Robert twisted a rag around his fingers, his face alternating shades of red and white, but he didn't move. Victoria remained where she was for a moment, then sat down at the nearest unoccupied table. Her blisters wailed in agony. Despite the pain, she fought the impulse to pull off her boots and give them some relief. The sight of her bare, bleeding feet would probably undermine whatever charm Cora expected her to use on the two men they were expecting.

The thought still made her furious. What did she know about seducing men? Her parents hadn't raised her to be wanton, winking at every man that crossed her path. Perhaps she enjoyed the occasional attention she garnered from young men, but what of that? She still had her dignity. Even if she didn't, she knew she would only end up embarrassing herself. Heaven knew her riding clothes weren't exactly alluring, and what guarantee did she have that these two Indians would even be able to understand her? They could very well not speak English. A fine sight that would be.

The batwing doors creaked as two men entered. Victoria knew right away that they were the men Cora was expecting. Both had broad faces, raven-colored hair, and black eyes that seemed to spark in the smoky air. To her surprise, however, they wore denim pants and flannel button-up shirts. Red kerchiefs hung around their necks. She had expected them to come dressed in skins and face paint and feathers, like the stories she'd heard of such men, but they looked more at home in the saloon than she had when she first arrived. But for their long braids, they might have passed for dark-skinned Mexican cowboys.

After giving the room a brief glance, the Indians stepped up to the bar. Cora set a pair of glasses in front of them and pulled out a familiar jug. Victoria could feel the fire in the back of her own throat as she watched the brown liquid flow. The two men nodded their thanks and drained their glasses.

"You boys care for another?" Cora asked. "It's on the house."

Robert started to sputter a protest, but she silenced him with a look. The two men nodded. Cora refilled their glasses with a grin. "Drink on up."

They obliged. Cora watched the whiskey disappear down their throats, her grin widening. Behind her, Robert deflated with a shake of his head. He moved down to the other end of the bar and settled in to watch a game of poker.

"Say, you fellers got a minute?" Cora asked. "I was wondering if you might answer some questions I got for you."

The two men exchanged glances. "What questions?" one finally asked.

"Nothing incriminating," Cora said, holding up her hands in surrender. "I ain't looking to get you all in trouble or nothing. Wouldn't be no kind of business owner if I went around getting my own customers locked up, anyhow."

Another glance. "What questions?" the one repeated.

Cora nodded in Victoria's direction. "See that pretty little thing over there?" Two sets of black eyes settled on her. Victoria returned what she hoped was a shy-yet-inviting smile. "You might have seen her around town lately. She's got herself in a bit of a fix, and she done came to me for help. Sorry to say, but I ain't got the know-how necessary to help her out, but then I thought of you two fellers and figured you might be able to lend her a hand."

Their eyes lingered on her. Victoria willed herself not to squirm under their gaze. Instead, she raised her eyebrows in a hopeful expression, as if her life really did hang in the balance. Then again, maybe it did.

Faces betraying no hint of emotion, they sized her up for a minute longer before one of them – the one who had spoken earlier – finally nodded. "We will hear your questions," he said. His accent was thick, but it was not foreign to Victoria's ears: the Indian woman hunting her spoke in the same manner.

"Glad to hear it, boys," Cora said. "Come on over to the table and we'll have us a little pow-wow. Bob, keep an eye on the rest of the place for a spell, would you?"

Robert nodded absently as the two men walked toward Victoria's table. They stopped short of sitting down, but that was fine with her. She offered them another smile, inwardly screaming at Cora to hurry up and join them. The two men didn't exactly frighten her, but their unreadable faces made her uneasy.

Thumping boots announced Cora's approach. "Go on and have a seat, boys," she said, claiming a chair next to Victoria. The men exchanged glances again, and the one who had spoken to them nodded. Their chairs skidded across the floorboards as they sat.

"You boys got names?" Cora asked. "It don't feel right just calling you boys all the time."

The first man nodded. "I am Naalnish. He is Ata'halne."

"Fine names, if you ask me." Cora grinned at them. "I reckon you already know who I am. This here's Vicky Dawes."

Victoria was about to correct her, but before she had a chance, Naalnish spoke to his companion in their native tongue. Victoria listened, fascinated. The words flowing out of him sounded like the bubbling of a small river. The man called Ata'halne nodded and said something in reply.

"What does this name 'Vicky' mean?" Naalnish asked, looking at Victoria.

"My name is Victoria," she said. "My parents named me for Queen Victoria – that's our queen where I'm from – and I never gave it much thought. I suppose it has something to do with victory and being victorious."

Naalnish said something to Ata'halne, and the other nodded. "It is a strong name. Your parents chose well," Naalnish said.

"Thank you," Victoria said.

"You got meanings for your names, too, right?" Cora asked. "All you Indians do, I hear."

Naalnish nodded. "Yes. In your tongue, my name means 'He Works'. His name means 'He Interrupts'."

Cora laughed. "He sure ain't living up to his name today. I don't think he's said a word but to you. Did you all name him that as a joke?"

"No," Naalnish said. "He does not know your language and so does not speak to you."

"Fair enough." Cora placed both hands on the table. "So, are you and him ready to help us out?" Naalnish nodded again, so she continued. "Well, as it turns out, Vicky here got herself into a bind with one of your folk, and she ain't quite sure how to go about getting out of it."

"She has been injured by one of our people, or she has injured one of our people?"

"Not injured, exactly. At least, not hurt or nothing. See, a lady Indian took her from her hotel room here in town, carried her out to an old ranch west of here, and gave her quite a scare. Then, when Vicky and I rode out to that same ranch, this here lady killed our horses and left us in the middle of the desert to starve or die of sunstroke."

Strange words flowed between the two men. Cora folded across her chest and waited. Victoria listened to them speak, hoping to catch any hint of meaning or emotion, but she soon gave up. Though their words were at once as graceful and earthy as the mesas in the desert, she couldn't make any sense of them. The Indians seemed intent on their conversation; they spoke for several minutes, occasionally glancing at the two women.

Naalnish suddenly turned back to them. "What reason would one of our people have to do these things?"

"I ain't rightly sure, myself," Cora replied. "Vicky didn't go picking any fights, if that what you mean. She was minding her own business when she got snatched up."

"That is not good," Naalnish said. "Our people do not wish to fight with yours." His dark eyes fixed on Victoria with startling intensity. "You did not give her reason?"

"No," Victoria said. "I had never seen her before she kidnapped me. I'm sure of it."

Naalnish relayed her words to Ata'halne. The other man replied with something that made both of them laugh. Victoria shot a glance at Cora, not sure what to make of their laughter, but the hunter's eyes remained on their companions.

"Why do you come to us with this?" Naalnish asked. "Surely your laws can deal with this woman. You do not need our help."

"Well, this woman ain't exactly normal," Cora said.

Naalnish's brow twitched. "What do you mean?"

"You Navajo folk got religion, right? Not like Catholics or Protestants or whatnot, but you all have spirits and magic and such?"

"Yes," Naalnish said.

"That's what I figured," Cora said. "See, this here woman what's been giving poor Vicky so much trouble uses that spirit magic of yours to pull off her tricks, I reckon. Spooky stuff, what's more. She made it where my gun didn't work, and said she even turned into my horse to trick us."

As she spoke, the man's face clouded over. He leaned back in his chair. When Cora finished, he turned to his friend and spoke in a low, hurried voice. Ata'halne's eyes locked onto the hunter as he listened. Like Naalnish, his face betrayed a deep concern at what he was hearing. He responded to the other man, his voice hushed as though he was afraid the two women would overhear.

Naalnish abruptly stood. "We cannot speak of this."

"What's that, now?" Cora asked.

"To speak of this evil is to call to it," he said. "We can say no more."

"Now, you just wait one minute," Cora said, rising to her feet. "How can you call yourself a man if you just light out and leave this poor girl to her fate?"

"She is not of our people," Naalnish replied. He met Cora's gaze without flinching. "We have women and children, brothers and sisters. Why should we risk their lives for her? The evil that you speak of will devour them all. We will not help you."

"Please." The look of distress on Victoria's face was genuine. "I don't know what to do."

The Indian turned away from them, placing a hand on Ata'halne's shoulder before walking toward the door. Ata'halne rose to follow his companion. His black eyes lingered on Victoria's face for a moment before he, too, turned and left the saloon.

Cora sat back down as the batwing doors creaked shut. "Well, that puts a burr under our saddle, don't it?"

"You do not seem all that concerned."

"Well, what to do about it?" Cora said. "Ain't like we can go clinging to their boots and begging. Indians don't take kindly to that sort of display, and that's one thing we happen to agree on. I ain't exactly the begging type."

"You aren't the smart type either, are you?" Victoria asked.

Cora held up a hand. "Hey, now, no need to get nasty about it. So these two fellers are too yellow to lend us a hand. They ain't the only two Indians in the world. We'll find us a one that ain't such a coward."

"Why? So you can drive them off again?" Victoria's chair nearly fell over as she stood. "What if none of them offer to help us? How will we get ourselves out of this mess?" Cora started to speak, but Victoria was too angry and too frightened to slow down. "I'll tell you. We won't. We won't because you have the diplomatic subtlety of a cannon. You have condemned us to death, but I refuse to just sit about and wait for it. If this witch woman wants to kill me, I will make her catch me first. I'm going back to England. Even if you refuse to come. I have had enough of your insults, your condescension, and your recklessness, and I won't stand for another minute of it. Goodbye, Cora Oglesby."

Victoria turned on her heel, ignoring the spikes of pain shooting through her feet. She half-expected to hear Cora's voice calling her back, but the hunter remained silent. Not that it mattered. Cora could scream and beg for her to stop. Her mind was made up. It had been a mistake to come out here in the first place, the mad delusion of a girl lost to grief. She should have listened to her doubts and abandoned this quest before it had ever gone this far. The sooner she boarded a train bound for New York, the sooner she could begin forgetting this miserable little town and its horrible hero.

Outside, the sun had already transformed the streets of Albuquerque into dust-lined ovens. Victoria pulled her hat down against the glare and stormed down the wooden sidewalk. With every painful step, her longing to see the cobblestone streets and green pastures of Oxford increased. She could have been seated in her father's study that morning, learning all she could about managing the investments he had left to her. In the afternoon, she might have taken a carriage to a friend's estate to take tea and watch children play in the garden. Nightfall would have seen her return to her own bedchamber for a deep, dreamless sleep beneath her silk sheets.

A hand grabbed her shoulder.

She let out a short scream and whirled around, hand reaching for her revolver. It was halfway out of its holster before she stopped. The Indian called Naalnish stood before her. The sun shone in his black hair as he regarded her in silence.

"Yes?" she asked after a few awkward moments. "What is it?"

Naalnish looked over his shoulder as Ata'halne appeared behind him. Naalnish asked the other man something in their native tongue. Ata'halne nodded.

"You would know why he is called 'He Interrupts'?" Naalnish asked, turning back to Victoria.

"Not particu–"

"It is not because he speaks too much or too loudly. He was given that name because he interrupts the speech of wisdom."

"What do you mean?" Victoria asked.

The Indian sighed. "He spoke to me of his great worry for you. He says you are young and do not understand this world. He asked me if I would have my own daughter receive help if she journeyed to your lands and found trouble. I could not say no."

He paused. Victoria said nothing, afraid of somehow changing his mind again.

"I cannot help you to fight this evil," Naalnish said, "but I know of one who can."

Hope fluttered in her chest. "Who is he?"

"A singer," he replied. "He has seen many things in his long years, and he knows much of the Holy People. He has led many ceremonies in our clan. I will ask him to help you, but he may say no. If he will not help you, you must find your way alone."

"Where is this man?"

"He is near," Naalnish said. "It will not be a long journey."

Victoria studied the man's face. He seemed sincere, as did his friend. If what Naalnish said was true, she might not need to return home in shame, defeated by powers beyond her ability to overcome. Still, could she trust these two men? They seemed honest and decent, but she knew nothing of them or their ways. They could be planning to kidnap, rape, or even kill her, abandoning her body for the desert animals to scavenge. Or perhaps their people kept slaves, and they would sell her to this singer man they spoke of.

The thought of spending the rest of her days in this god-forsaken desert almost brought the refusal to her lips. She opened her mouth to say as much when her gaze met Ata'halne's. The Indian's eyes sparked at her from beneath his thick brows. This man had convinced his friend to turn back and offer her their help, even at the risk of endangering his own family. If their offer was sincere and she turned it down, she would make a fool of him. Besides, she still had her gun and her knife. Abrasive though she was, Cora had taught her how to handle herself. She could at least give them a fight if their intentions proved less than honorable.

"Take me to him."

THIRTEEN

"Welcome to our home."

Victoria leaned out from behind Ata'halne, her arms clamped around his waist. Naalnish nodded toward a small group of structures rising out of the desert floor. They were conical shapes built of sticks and mud. As they rode closer, she could see that each hut had a large, colorful blanket covering its entrance. A few women sat in a small circle, talking and laughing in the same strange language Naalnish and Ata'halne spoke. They raised their voices in greeting when they caught sight of them. The two men raised their hands in return.

Victoria could feel eyes staring at her with great interest, but she avoided their gaze. She shifted her leg to feel the pressure of the revolver against it. Her two escorts had not demanded she remove her weapons, which gave her a small measure of comfort.

They had ridden for no more than a few hours. The sun had continued its journey into the fathomless blue sky and now hung near its peak, raining down its relentless heat in earnest. Victoria's shirt stuck to her back again, and she knew she would need to have it washed when she returned to town. The aching in her body had become a constant companion, one she had learned to ignore.

Ata'halne guided their horse up to a larger building. Unlike the other huts, this one had a small extension protruding from its side. Had it been of any notable size, Victoria might have likened it to a hallway leading into a sitting room, but the "hallway" was scarcely taller than a man.

The two men dismounted. Ata'halne turned to help her down, but she slid off the horse's back with little trouble. Naalnish led them up to the building's entrance. A woven blanket covered the opening, its pattern full of squares and triangles in white and black and red. Victoria had never seen a blanket like it, even among the British aristocracy. How these primitive people could produce such work was beyond her.

"The singer is inside," Naalnish said. "He is the one that can help you. He may not help you, and if he does not, you must leave at once. You will bring evil to us all if you do not."

Victoria nodded. "Even if he chooses not to, I thank you for your help."

The Indian looked uncomfortable. He gave a quick nod and pulled the blanket aside. Victoria stepped through the doorway into the darkness beyond. Smoke swirled around her, burning her eyes and throat. She tried to hold in the coughs that rose up in her chest but failed. Covering her mouth with her hand, she took a painful breath.

Naalnish placed a hand on her shoulder, encouraging her to go farther in. She took a few more steps and entered a small, circular room. Sunlight streamed in through holes in the walls and roof, forming smoky rays that cut across the shadows. The remains of a fire smoldered in a circular pit. Sitting on the far side of it was the dim figure of a man. She watched him for a moment, unsure if his eyes were open or not. Naalnish slipped into the room behind her, taking a seat to the man's right. He motioned for her to sit opposite them. She nodded and eased herself into the packed earth.

Victoria sat in the darkness watching the two Indians. She wondered why Ata'halne did not follow them inside, but did not think it would be polite to ask. Naalnish was looking at the elderly man, who hadn't moved since they first entered. After a few moments of silence, Naalnish spoke softly in the Indian tongue. The singer turned his head to listen.

"I have told him your name," Naalnish said to her, "and why you have come."

The old man's eyes glittered in the dim light. He spoke in a voice of dry leaves and wind, but it filled the small room with authority.

"He feels shame for the actions of this woman who has injured you," Naalnish said. "He says no *Diné* should behave in such ways."

"Oh, he shouldn't feel sorry for that," Victoria said. "Tell him it is not his fault."

Naalnish relayed her words to the singer, who replied without taking his eyes off her. "He says this woman should have known better than to act as she did. We do not wish for any fight with your people."

Victoria hesitated, not sure how to respond. "Not everyone is a good person," she finally said. "Perhaps this woman is just given to hurting others."

"It is true," the old man said through Naalnish. "But you did not come here to speak of good and evil in men. You came for help, and I will give it."

A smile spread across Victoria's face. "Thank you, sir."

The singer held up his hand. "Before I start, you must promise to only speak of this when you need. When you speak of this evil, it hears. Naalnish put himself in danger by speaking of it to you. Those who walk the Witchery Way silence talk of them, and their ears are sharp. What is more, after learning these things, you may want this power for yourself. It is believed that one who knows much of the Witchery Way must walk that path."

"You know much," Victoria said, "and you are not an evil man."

"Are you certain?" The light caught the old man's eye in a queer gleam, and a chill skittered up Victoria's spine.

A grin deepened his wrinkles. "Yes, you are right. I know more than I could tell you in a hundred nights, and yet I know little of the Holy People and all their ways. I know also of the Witchery Way, and it has not corrupted me. I will tell you enough so you may fight this woman that seeks to do evil to you.

"The Witchery Way is a very old path given to us by First Man and First Woman. We do not know why they created it, but we endure its evils as we enjoy their blessings. Those who walk this path we call *ánt'įįhnii*."

"What does that mean?"

"It means 'witch people'."

"Are all witches women, then?" Victoria asked. "Can men ever follow this path?"

The old man smiled. "You would know much. If we spoke of other things, I would tell you with a glad heart. Of this, I will only say what you need to hear."

"I understand," Victoria said.

"Good." He shifted his weight. "Now, to choose the wise path, I must know what this woman has done to you."

Victoria recounted both her encounter with the woman on the first night and the subsequent confrontations with her. Wanting to leave nothing out, she even told the old man of her dream in which she flew across the desert and came upon the two pursuers on the mesa. As she spoke, Naalnish grew visibly more agitated. He hesitated to translate her words, and when he did, his words were hushed and hurried. His distress fed her own uneasiness.

When she finished, the singer studied the embers between them for a long time. Beads of sweat glistened on his forehead, and Victoria could feel her

own running down her cheeks. The air in the tiny
room was still and thick. It made breathing difficult.
Her shirt peeled away from her skin as she shifted
her weight, waiting for the old man's reply.

At last, his gaze lifted from the fire. "It is strange,"
Naalnish translated. "This woman says she can become an animal, and you say you have seen this."

"I did not witness it, exactly," Victoria said. "I only
dreamed I did."

"That you say it was a dream is not strange," the Indian said. "Your people have no stories of such things,
but I can tell you that your dream was not a dream."

Victoria blinked. "How is that possible? I most certainly did not grow wings and teach myself to fly, nor
could I have instantly moved from the top of the
mesa back to our camp."

"Your body did not move," he said, nodding, "but
you moved across the land all the same."

"I don't understand."

The singer smiled. "As I said, your people have no
stories of such things, but my people do. The *Diné*
have long known that the spirit can leave the body,
moving over the land and seeing things that the
body's eyes may not. You are not *Diné*, so it is strange
for you to do this, but you did."

"So my dream wasn't a dream?" Victoria asked.
"What happened to me that night, what I felt and
what I saw, was real?"

"Yes," he replied.

Victoria couldn't quite grasp what she was hearing. Surely this old man, wise though he was, had

somehow confused the world of dreams with the real world. Maybe his tribe did have stories to explain dreams as something other than they were, but they were just stories. It wasn't possible for the spirit to leave the body prior to a person's death, when it was sent to paradise or damnation for all eternity. To say otherwise was absurd and heretical.

"I see on your face that you do not believe me. Tell me this: in your dream, when you saw the *ánt'įįhnii*, how did she see you if you were not there?"

"I'm not sure," Victoria said. "She just seemed to sense me somehow."

"The *ánt'įįhnii* knows of the spirit world, and she sees those that walk in it. When you came close, she felt you. When she took the form of the fox, her eyes could see you."

Victoria's stomach grew slightly ill. "What would have happened if I hadn't returned to my body?"

"She would have wounded your spirit," the singer said. "If her spirit was stronger, yours may have been broken. You would have been lost."

"I would have died?"

"Your body, yes. Your spirit may have found a new body, but maybe not."

"What do you mean, found a new body? I might have possessed someone else?"

"Now you ask of the Great Cycle. I would gladly tell you more, but it must wait. We must keep our words on the *ánt'įįhnii*."

Victoria looked into Naalnish's eyes. They were round with fear. "Yes, I'm sorry. Please tell me about her."

"Like the *Diné*, the *ánt'įįhnii* do not all walk the same path. I am a singer, and Naalnish is a strong worker. They have their own skills also. We call them all *ánt'įįhnii,* but they have other names. The one that hunts you is called..."

"What? What is it called?"

Naalnish looked away. The singer watched him for a moment, then turned to Victoria. "*Yee naaldlooshii,*" he said.

The younger Indian cringed at the words. Speaking in soft tones, the singer placed his hand on Naalnish's shoulder. Victoria's heart filled with sympathy. The things the old man said terrified her, and she had only come to know of them in the past few days. For Naalnish, who surely had heard stories of such creatures since infancy, it was as though his childhood fears were coming to life around him. If she had come across a man in Oxford who claimed to have witnessed Frankenstein's monster with his own eyes, Victoria knew she would feel much the same.

Naalnish nodded at the old man's words and turned back to Victoria. "I am sorry," he said. "It is forbidden for us to speak of such things."

"I understand," Victoria said, offering what comfort she could with her eyes. "I am truly grateful for all your help, and I will pray that this woman will not harm you or your family for it."

"Thank you," he said. He took a deep breath, then continued. "The word he spoke would be 'skin-walker' in your tongue."

"Skin-walker," Victoria said, testing it out. The words sounded ominous, and yet it seemed to fit. "What does a skin-walker do?"

"What you have seen," Naalnish translated. "They take the shape of animals. They do this to hunt, to hide, to play tricks, and to attack people. To take an animal's shape, they must wear the skin of the animal and no other clothing."

"That explains why she was naked in the barn that night," Victoria said, mostly to herself, but Naalnish translated her words anyway.

The singer nodded. "And why she wore nothing in your dream that was not a dream."

"Still," Victoria said, "that doesn't quite explain everything. Why is she able to control the man she travels with, the one Cora calls a vampire? Is that also a power of the skin-walker?"

"Yes and no," he replied. "The *ánt'įįhnii* are of many paths, as I have said. Some walk more than one. If she can do this thing, she must also walk The Frenzy Way. This way gives *ánt'įįhnii* the power of will over others."

Victoria remembered her strange feelings when the skin-walker first questioned her in the barn. "So they can control someone's mind?"

"No," the old man said, shaking his head. "Not control, but pressing on the will like a stone on corn. If your will is strong, you may keep it, but you will still feel the pressing."

"That vampire must be weak-willed, then," Victoria said. "An odd thing to think about such a creature." She shook her head, then moved on to the most important question of the day. "So how do we protect ourselves from this skin-walker? Can she be killed?"

The singer inhaled deeply. "Our stories say it can be done," he said, "but it is not easy. The *ánt'įįhnii* protects itself well. When it is in an animal shape, it may be wounded, but it is very quick. When it is human, it has magic to make bowstrings break and guns fail."

Victoria's heart sank. His words were filling the holes in her understanding of their encounters with this skin-walker. Cora didn't seem to know any other way of dealing with a threat besides shooting at it, and that clearly wouldn't work. "So what can we do?"

"She has shown her face to you," he replied. "Skin-walkers will not do this unless they must, for it puts them in danger. If one sees her face and calls her by name, her magic will not work. You have seen her face. If you learn her name, you may do this."

"I don't know that we will," Victoria said dejectedly. "I wouldn't even know where to start looking for her."

"I cannot help you with that. Many *Diné* were lost in *Hwéeldi*, and those that returned spread like dust in the wind. The skin-walker may travel far in her animal shape, so she could sleep in a place far away.

"Still," he said, "even without her name, you may wound her."

"How?" Victoria's eyes became clear and bright, her spirit eager for the old Indian's words.

The singer reached toward the embers. His gnarled fingers curled around a handful of ashes near the fire's edge. Lifting his hand up, he nodded to her. She cupped her own hands and held them out. The ash filled them, soft and weightless. When she pulled her hands back, a ghostly cloud hung in the air between her and the Navajo men.

"That is ash from the fire of a singer and healer," Naalnish said before the old man could speak. "It is the best weapon you can use against *ánt'įįhnii*."

"How do I use it? Do I throw it on her?"

Naalnish translated, and the old man shook his head. "No. You will not get close enough. Put it on your bullets before you shoot them at her. The ash will break her magic and wound her body. In the stories, men would fight skin-walkers in this way, by dipping their arrows into ashes. Shoot at her head or heart. If you do not, your bullets may not kill her."

Victoria tucked the ash into her satchel. "Thank you. I will."

"And now, young one," he said, "you have what you need, and I cannot aid you more. Naalnish will take you back to the white town. May the Holy People watch over you."

"Thank you," Victoria said again. "If there is anything I may do to repay you for your kindness, please ask."

The old man shook his head. "It is enough that I

have helped stop the evil of an *ánt'įįhnii,* even if she is one of our people."

Victoria thanked him again, then rose to her feet. Her hands instinctively pinched at her sides, looking for a dress to curtsey with. Too late, she remembered she was wearing her denim riding trousers. Blushing, she nodded at the singer – who returned the gesture – and made her way down the hallway and into the desert sun.

Naalnish emerged from the building behind her. "Remember what you have heard."

"I will," Victoria said.

His flinty eyes fixed on her. "Do not speak of it to anyone."

"I need to tell Cora what I learned. She and I will be fighting together."

"Only tell her what you must," he said. "If you speak too much or too openly, it will draw evil attention."

"I understand," Victoria said. She walked over to the two horses, then paused and looked around. "Where is Ata'halne? Will he be joining us for the ride back?"

Naalnish smiled and shook his head. "He is with that woman again, I think."

"A woman?" Victoria asked, surprised. "He has a wife?"

"No," Naalnish replied, "but he wants to change that. He has been speaking a lot with a woman in the village."

Victoria pulled herself up onto the horse's back. "Is she nice?"

"She is quiet," he said, mounting his own horse and nudging it in the direction of Albuquerque. "If they marry, he will not be able to interrupt her."

A smile spread across Victoria's face. "Men in my country value a quiet wife, or so I'm told. I am not married myself, though my parents did their best to change that. I suppose I speak too much for men to fall in love with me."

"Anaba is not like you, then," Naalnish said.

"Anaba? Is that her name?" The Indian nodded. "What does it mean?"

"She Returns From War."

"She Returns From War?" Victoria wrinkled her nose. "That seems like rather a violent name to give a woman. Is she a soldier?"

"No," Naalnish said, his hips swaying with the rhythm of his horse's steps. "Our women do not fight. She received this name when she returned to the village without her husband."

"Her husband?" Victoria asked. "So she has been married before."

"Yes, but her husband was killed by men from your army."

Victoria's back stiffened at his tacit accusation. "You mean the United States Army. I can assure you that Her Majesty's soldiers had nothing to do with it."

"This is so," Naalnish agreed. "I am sorry."

"Quite all right," Victoria said. "Please continue."

"Her husband died three years ago," Naalnish said. "When she returned to the village and told us her story, we gave to her the name Anaba."

"Why did the army kill her husband?"

Naalnish shrugged. "This is not known. I believe it was for no other reason than he was *Diné*. The white man's soldiers do not fear to kill our people without cause. It is not often, but it is so."

"I'm sorry," Victoria said. "Men can be such monsters."

"Yes."

The pair rode in silence for a few moments before another question came to her. "You and the singer both said the word '*Diné*'. What does this word mean?"

"It is our name for ourselves," Naalnish replied. "You call us Navajo, but we have always been *Diné*. It means 'The People'."

"Practical enough," Victoria said.

The Indian looked to their left and raised his hand. "There is Ata'halne now."

Victoria followed his gaze to a figure standing outside a hut some way off. The figure raised his hand in reply, and Victoria waved at him. The blanket behind Ata'halne moved aside as a woman emerged. She wore a smaller blanket around her shoulders, and silver medallions flashed about her waist. Thick hair framed her face and flowed over her shoulders in a waterfall of shimmering sable. The woman raised her hand toward them as well. Victoria smiled as she waved back.

Then nearly fell off her horse.

Victoria gripped the saddle horn with her free hand, trying to steady herself. The blood drained from her face. Once she had waved long enough to be polite, she turned her head away. Fear twisted inside her, even in the light of the noonday sun. It was all she could do to keep herself from spurring her horse into a gallop.

Naalnish looked at her. "What is wrong?"

"This Anaba," Victoria said, "how much do you know about her?"

"Not much," Naalnish replied. "She is not a young woman like you, but she is not old. She has no mother, but I do not know how her mother died. She has no children."

"And that was her? With Ata'halne?"

"Yes."

"Naalnish," Victoria said, "I believe the woman that has been hunting us is this Anaba."

"This is not possible," he said. "We have no people of that kind in our village."

Victoria couldn't help stealing a glance over her shoulder. The woman had turned away from them, but Victoria knew she hadn't been mistaken. The woman's face had haunted her in dreams and the waking world; she knew it all too well. "But what if she is?" Victoria asked. "What if this woman has been living with you all this time?"

Naalnish shook his head. "No," he said. "She is quiet and sad, but she is not..."

"A witch?" Naalnish refused to look at her. "I am not lying. That woman back there is the one who kidnapped me."

"No," he said again, but his voice was weaker. His eyes did not leave the horizon. "Anaba is the

daughter of the singer. She would not choose...
that path."

"Are you certain of that?" His silence was reply
enough. "I think I can find my way from here if you
want to go back and speak to the singer."

Naalnish dropped his gaze. "I do not want you to
get lost."

"No need to worry," Victoria said more confidently
than she felt. Her mind was exploding from the implications. Cora needed to know, and Naalnish
needed to warn his village. Now that the skin-
walker, this Anaba, knew that they were on to her,
she might become more aggressive and unpre-
dictable. Victoria didn't want any harm to come to
Naalnish, the singer, or any of the other innocent
people in their village.

What if she was wrong, though? The poor widow
could simply be that, a woman whose husband had
been heartlessly killed by the U.S. Army. Maybe Victoria had been mistaken. Maybe she was just afraid,
seeing the witch in every Indian woman's face. She
had been so certain when she first saw Ata'halne's
friend, but now she wasn't as confident. If Naalnish
accused Anaba of being a witch, they might shun her
or kill her. Victoria knew history well enough to understand that such accusations were seldom taken
lightly, and they almost always resulted in death or
some other form of punishment. By speaking her
mind, she may have well just condemned an innocent
woman to be burned at the stake, or whatever form
of execution the Navajo used for their own witches.

Naalnish turned his horse around.

"Naalnish," she said. He looked over his shoulder. "Don't hurt her if she isn't a witch."

"We can show her no kindness."

"But only if she is a witch," she said. "Promise me you won't if she isn't."

"The singer will decide," he replied, then turned away.

Victoria watched him recede into the distance. Her hands twitched, eager to spur her horse after him, to ensure that the woman would be safe from any unjust punishment. She wouldn't be able to live with herself if Anaba died because of a guess made through a fog of heat and fear.

The skin-walker and her vampire pet had to be stopped, though. If they weren't, more innocent people would die. Pride firmly swallowed, she would ride back to Ben's Print Shop, tell Cora what she'd learned from Naalnish and the Navajo singer, and ask her to ride against their enemies that night. They would need new horses, fresh supplies, and the handful of ash she carried in her satchel. God willing, they might bring this all to an end that very night, and then they could be on their way back to England.

Pulling her hat down, she urged her horse forward, in the direction of Albuquerque.

FOURTEEN

"Well, ain't that strange? Seems we got us five aces on the table." Cora sized up each man in turn. "Which one of you all is funning around with my cards?"

The men didn't answer. Nervous glances flicked around the table like frenzied ants. From her seat near the batwing doors, Victoria couldn't see the hunter's face, but she could see the faces of the other gamblers. They were all playing the part of innocence accused well enough that she couldn't have picked out the guilty party. Whoever the cheater was, he'd done it enough times to make a convincing display of suspicion.

"Wilson, I've got a hankering to see what you got under that shirt of yours," Cora said. "Why don't you show the other fellers here."

Victoria's breath caught in her throat when she recognized the man who had threatened her before. His ears were crimson with anger again, but his gaze wasn't directed at her. He stared at the old hunter, as if he could make her take back her accusation through sheer force of will. Victoria lifted her hand to her mouth to hide her grin. Strong and quick to anger though he was, it seemed that Wilson was none too quick to realize when he was fighting a losing battle.

The other men at the table sat in silence, eyes darting between Cora and Wilson. Around them, other conversations carried on. Victoria caught snatches of them, tales of exploits and adventures too wild to be true. In the back of the room, the piano marched its way through an off-key melody.

Wilson slowly stood to his feet. "Reckon I'm done for the day," he said, his tone flat.

"Don't be a stranger, now," Cora said. "Go on and help yourself to a drink. Ain't on the house, mind you, but might help to settle you down some."

"Ain't so riled up as all that," Wilson replied. "Just need some air is all."

Wilson walked around the table, each step deliberate, his eyes never leaving the hunter's face. Cora shook her head and reached for an ace. "This one here's yours. Ain't got no need for two aces of hearts at my table."

She held it above her head, not turning to look at the man. Victoria watched his fingers curl into fists. At the table, one of the men looked up at Wilson and nodded.

The ace drifted to the floor. "I ain't going to hold it for you till sundown, Wilson. Pick it up if you like."

Wilson bent down to retrieve the card. As he straightened up, the man who nodded shoved the table toward Cora. The edge caught her in the chest, knocking her chair backward. She went with it, cards scattering like leaves. Her elbows hit the floor with a thud Victoria felt in her teeth. Before the hunter could recover, Wilson stepped over her and clamped a hand around her throat. The other man was standing now, too, his eyes watching the other two players, hand hovering near the butt of his gun.

"Call me a cheater, do you?" Wilson asked, lowering his face toward Cora. The hunter's fingers clutched at his hand, trying to pull it away and failing. "You ought to know by now that you never call a man on his word in a card game. Goes against agreement between gentlemen and all, but I guess a fool woman like you ain't got the sense for such things."

Around them, the room had fallen silent. Victoria could hear Cora's desperate, wheezing breaths and the scraping of her boots across the floor. She tried to bring her knees up into Wilson's back. He held up his other hand to block her blows, putting more of his weight on the hand around her throat.

"You ain't nothing but an old bitch past her prime," Wilson said, "and I reckon it's time somebody put you down for good."

His shoulder moving to block her flailing legs, he drew a revolver from his belt. The barrel pressed against the skin beneath Cora's chin.

"Hey, now," somebody said.

Wilson's accomplice whirled toward the voice, pulling his own gun. "Shut your trap, boy." The man put up his hands and backed up a step. Nobody else moved.

"Hear that, bitch?" Wilson asked, a sneer stretched across his sweating face. "Ain't a man here willing to help you out of a bind."

The hard, pointed toe of a riding boot smashed into Wilson's face. His revolver clattered to the floor as he rolled to one side, hands holding his cheek. The other man spun toward the sound to find himself staring down the business end of a Colt .38. At the other end of the barrel, cold blue eyes regarded him.

"I'm consistently amazed at the lack of proper manners in this country," Victoria said. "Really, is this how one should conduct oneself around a lady?"

Wilson's accomplice stared at her, his own revolver still in his hand. "Little thing like you ain't got the guts to shoot a man."

"I've shot worse," Victoria said.

"Better believe her," Cora's voice rasped more than usual. "Girl ain't shy about using that gun of hers. Why, not two nights ago, she had a pudding-headed lump like your own self at gunpoint, and it was only my word that stopped her from pulling the trigger."

Victoria stole a glance to her right. Cora stood beside her, Wilson's gun in her hand. "Now, why don't you set that gun down nice and easy," the hunter said, "or I might not be able to call off my friend."

The man's eyes darted between the two women. Somewhere behind them, Victoria heard Wilson groan. She kept her eyes on the other man, finger tense on the gun's trigger. If his weapon moved an inch higher, he was a dead man.

After a few seconds, the man dropped his gun and raised his hands. "There's a good boy," Cora said. "Now then, why don't you take your buddy Wilson and get before Vicky here loses her patience and shoots the both of you."

"She wouldn't dare," the man said, but he started moving. Wilson groaned again as his friend helped him to his feet. Throwing a nervous look over his shoulder, the man half-led, half-carried the injured gunman through the batwing doors. Victoria listened to the thumping of their footsteps move down the wooden sidewalk. Only when she could no longer hear them did she let herself relax.

"You all are white as ghosts," Cora said, turning to look at the rest of the Print Shop's afternoon patrons. "Ain't you never seen folks dust up in a saloon before?" Shaking her head, she walked around behind the bar. The big jug of whiskey made its appearance, and she waved Victoria over.

"This one's on the house, little lady," Cora said, pouring out a glass. "Ain't every day I get to serve a drink to somebody what saved my hide, and you got yourself the honor of being the first lady ever to do it."

Victoria picked up the glass. "I will drink to that."

Cora raised her own drink. Glass clinked against glass, and the two women tossed back the whiskey. The taste still made Victoria grimace, but she managed to keep from coughing. She set the empty glass down on the bar and eyed the hunter. "Does this make up for earlier, then?"

"What's that, now?"

"Our...altercation?" Victoria asked.

"Oh, that?" Cora snorted a laugh. "You call that an altercation? That wasn't nothing but a bit of yelling. What happened just now with Wilson, now, that was a right proper altercation."

"So no hard feelings, then?"

"Wilson ain't got nothing but hard feelings," Cora said.

"I meant–"

"I know what you meant," Cora said. She looked Victoria in the eye. "Way I figure, stepping in with me against them thugs done washed away any transgressions between the two of us. I ain't the type to let a few hot words get to me, anyhow."

"Well, I suppose that's all well and good, then." Victoria toyed with her empty glass, which Cora took as a request for a refill. The second shot followed the first, and Victoria shook her head at the burning in her throat. "I never thought you would turn me into a whiskey bibber. Or a gunfighter, for that matter."

"The frontier makes folk into all sorts of things," Cora said. "Thieves out of honest men, cowards out of soldiers, and monster killers out of fine young ladies."

"I don't rightly know if the blame can be placed on your frontier," Victoria said. "That fault lies at the door of black shuck, I'm afraid. It gave me the heart, and you gave me the means."

"Speaking of, we ought to go buy some more of them means before the sun goes down," Cora said. "We only got one revolver between the both of us now."

Victoria reached for the gun at her belt. "Yes, I suppose this is yours by rights."

"Nah, go ahead and hang on to it." Cora jammed the stopper back into the bottle. "Ain't like there's anything special about it. One we buy over at the gunsmith will work just as well, I reckon."

"Are you sure?" Victoria asked. "It doesn't hold any sentimental value for you?"

The hunter shrugged. "Ain't rightly sure, but I don't bet on it. Go ahead and ride with it tonight, and I'll go fetch me a new one. If I get to missing the one you got, we can switch."

"Deal," Victoria said. She slapped her palm on the bar. "Shall we?"

"Yes ma'am. Why don't you mosey on down to the gunsmith and pick me out a shiny one. I'll stop in to the livery and see if I can't get that old fool to lend us a pair for the night, seeing as how Our Lady was killed on his watch and all."

Cora walked around the bar and toward the door, hollering at one of the tables as she did. A young man, his face dark with stubble, jumped to his feet. "Mind the bar, would you?" she said. The man nodded, settling back down to his game. Cora turned back to Victoria and grinned. "Let's get a move on."

• • • •

Victoria lay on the hotel mattress, eyes fixed on the ceiling. Outside, she could picture the sun still hanging in the empty sky, white-hot in its unyielding fury. The hotel's roof hid her from its rays, but they couldn't hold the heat at bay. Sweat glistened on her forehead, trickling through her hair like stray raindrops on a windowpane. Her riding clothes lay in a heap on the floor, a disorderly reminder of her vain attempt to escape the soul-draining swelter.

Not much longer to wait, she reminded herself. Purchasing a new revolver for Cora had not taken half an hour. Returning to the saloon with revolver in hand, she made small talk with Robert until Cora blew through the batwing doors a few minutes later. Her negotiations with the livery owner had been brief as well, and Victoria had no trouble imagining why. With that, there was nothing more but to wait until sundown. Cora told her to get some rest in case it ended up being a long night. Victoria agreed and retired, never imagining that her room could be hot enough to prevent sleep altogether.

She rolled onto her side with a sigh. In lieu of rest, her mind kept returning to her conversation with the Navajo singer. Most of what he said made sense in its own way, but she couldn't quite figure out the part regarding her dream. It seemed so absurd, so contrary to everything she knew about spirituality. There was no place in God's design for such a thing, and yet she couldn't so easily disregard her experience. The memory of it was too clear. What, then, had happened to her?

Victoria had a thought. Stretching out on her back again, she folded her hands on her stomach and closed her eyes. If she did have the ability to separate her spirit from her body, she should be able to do it at will. There was time enough before sunset to try. When she failed, she would know that the old Indian had been mistaken.

How to try, though? The singer hadn't elaborated on how the separation was done. When – if – she had done it last time, it had felt like falling asleep. That was out of the question in this heat. She had been keeping watch over their camp, thinking about the strange fox she saw in the bushes. The fox that was not a fox if the Navajo man was correct. Victoria tried to imagine the fox again, running free beneath the stars in the cool of the night, but the wooden oven surrounding her made it impossible. No matter how she tried, all she could picture was an endless line of heat waves shimmering against the horizon.

Frustrated, Victoria soon let her concentration slip. Instead of trying to imagine the starlit desert, she began focusing on her own discomfort. Somehow, despite the heat and the dry air, the sheet beneath her was damp with sweat. It made her feel disgusting, like one of the unwashed men in Cora's saloon. They probably didn't bathe more than once a fortnight. Some of them probably used water from the horse troughs. She could picture them seated around one of the misshapen structures that passed for tables in the Print Shop, their sweat-stained clothing sticking to them as they gambled away what little money they had.

The rapid slap of cards shuffling made her blink. It came sharp and crisp, as though she was standing in the room. Victoria looked around. Robert still stood behind the bar, but Cora was nowhere to be seen. What few patrons there were clustered around a greasy deck of cards. From the dark circles on their shirts, she could tell that the saloon was no cooler than her room.

Her room.

The realization hit her like a crack from a riding crop. She hadn't left the hotel, yet she stood in the Print Shop, watching a game of poker. It wasn't a dream. The sights, the sounds, and the smells were all too vivid to be a dream. Somehow, without conscious effort, she had managed to do exactly what the Navajo singer had said she could do: she was in the spirit world.

Cautiously, she reached toward the nearest poker player. He didn't flinch or give any indication at all that he was aware of her presence, even as her hand passed in front of his face. She waved it back and forth, but the man only flipped a card onto the table and reached for another.

Victoria shivered as a thrill ran through her. Part fear and part excitement, it made her non-existent limbs prickle. Her mind spun as the implications of this ability began crashing into her, one after another. She could travel where she wanted at will, listen in on conversation without fear of discovery, and that was just what she knew. It might carry with it other possibilities, ones even more powerful. Surely this was what the skin-walker Anaba had meant when she said Victoria had the power of witches. If this ability was something a person as dangerous as Anaba feared, it must be formidable indeed.

But how had she done it? Returning for a moment to the present, Victoria frowned. There had been no sense of travel, no chanting of spells over a bubbling cauldron. If this was magic, it was apparently uncon-scious. One minute, she had been imagining the gamblers in the saloon, and the next, she had traveled there in spirit. The same had happened in the desert the first time: after imagining herself a fox, she had freed herself from her body and followed it through the desert. Perhaps it really was as simple as focusing her thoughts outside of herself.

Another question deepened her frown. Why now? She had imagined being in other places and times on many occasions without any such result. What had changed? Was it that she was now an orphan? Or did the desert have a role to play? Perhaps being so close to the magicks of the Navajo people somehow awakened this ability in her. The old singer would know. Before she left for home, she would be sure to stop by the Navajo village and ask him.

The sound of Cora's voice made her turn. The old hunter came striding out of the storeroom where they had their first altercation, her fingers through the loop of another clay jug. Her boots thumped right past Victoria, but her pace didn't slow. Lifting the jug onto the bar, she barked something at Robert and pulled out the stopper. Robert held two glasses out, and Cora filled them with dark liquid.

"Drinking our profits again," Robert muttered as he lifted the whiskey to his lips.

"Worth every drop," Cora said, refilling her glass. "Business partners ought to drink together, I say."

"No harm in sampling the stock, I guess."

"There you go." Cora tossed back the second drink. "Besides, this could be the last time we have the chance. Me and Vicky ride out tonight, and we might not ride back in. Reckon you'd like that just fine, though. You'd get the place all to yourself."

Robert laughed. "That would be a sight, me trying to handle this lot. No, I'll thank you to stick around awhile longer."

"Well, if you say so. Ain't the first spook I've settled, anyhow, so I don't see no reason it should be my last ride. Now that Vicky ain't like to shoot her own foot off, I reckon we got ourselves a fair shot at living through the night."

With that, Cora straightened. "Best be making tracks. Almost sundown, and I still got to wrangle them horses from the livery. Don't want to keep Miss Proper waiting."

The hunter started for the staircase that led up to her room. Victoria gave a thought to following her, then decided against it. She felt slightly guilty about eavesdropping on the conversation, and watching Cora prepare for the hunt without her knowledge would only worsen the feeling. Besides, she had to get ready herself. Her body must still be lying in the hotel room in her smallclothes, and she could hardly go riding out dressed in such a fashion.

Victoria was through the door and halfway to the hotel before she realized that she was moving without effort. Like that night in the desert, she seemed to float along the ground instead of walking on it. She gave a moment's thought to experimenting with the possibility of flight, then decided against it. There would be time enough for such exploration later. Best to get back to the room and prepare for the coming battle.

Victoria's horse stomped a hoof on the dusty street. The mare had once been black, but age had faded the luster from her coat. Victoria thought about patting the horse's neck but decided against it. The horses would be returning to the livery in the morning, so there was no point in getting attached.

Pale clouds floated in the purple sky above their heads. The sunset had set them awash in pink fire, but their glory had slipped away with the daylight. Victoria watched them drift along, wishing that a breeze would kick up to cool her face. Her wish wasn't granted. Turning toward Cora, she pantomimed a panting dog.

Cora grinned. "Give yourself a few months, you get used to it."

"God willing, I won't have the time," Victoria said. She looked up at the building looming against the evening sky. "Do you think this will work?"

"Ain't any more sure than I was this morning," Cora replied with a shrug. "Either it lights out for our boy, or it starts looking to fill its belly. Either way, we got to keep an eye out."

"What happened to the other body?"

"Lawmen hauled it out," Cora said. "Didn't do all like I said, but so long as the stiff was exposed to sunlight, it'll stay dead for good."

"One would think the constables might have done something about the people here," Victoria said, casting a dubious eye at the horses and people milling through the street. "I don't relish the thought of chasing a living corpse through this crowd."

Cora laughed. "Oh, I reckon they'll clear out right quick when they see that stiff running through town."

"Won't we lose it, though? I imagine it will blend in with the townsfolk."

"No worry about that," Cora replied. "Feller might still look human enough, but you can bet the rest of your fortune on that he won't just stroll about all casual-like. Ain't got it in him no more. He'll conduct himself just like them ones out at the farm, and he'll look like them with the teeth and all after a week or so. King George told me all about that process back in Leadville."

The mention of James Townsend stirred a sudden homesickness in Victoria. She pictured his round, jolly face as he sipped at his cider, and she could almost smell the inviting, intellectual scent of the many books lining his study. Victoria watched the

SHE RETURNS FROM WAR

townsfolk mull around her, wondering how many of them could even read. In all likelihood, some of them would live their entire lives in this dusty little town, never seeing a proper garden or a grove of trees garbed in the green of summer.

Whatever pity she felt for them evaporated when a familiar face emerged from the bustle. Wilson rode toward them at the head of a group of rough-looking men. A sneer bared his teeth when their eyes met, made all the more hideous by the swelling bruise on the cheek. Victoria touched Cora's wrist and nodded toward the approaching men.

"Howdy," Wilson said, tipping his hat. His posse spread out in a rough semi-circle, fencing the two women in against the row of buildings.

"Didn't figure you'd show your face on the street after getting it whipped by a sprout of a girl," Cora said. Drawing on the hunter's confidence, Victoria straightened up in the saddle and met Wilson's gaze.

Wilson raised a hand to his injured cheek. "This ain't nothing but a whore's love tap." His men chuckled. "I just reckoned I ought to return the favor, seeing as how she's so keen on me and all."

Despite her fear, Victoria laughed. "You bring half a dozen men to administer this retribution? Such courage."

"Ain't you just stuffed full of guts?" Wilson said. "Best keep that tongue in your head, or somebody might get a notion to pull all them guts out and see what they look like. If I wasn't such a gentleman my own self, I might have already had myself a look.

Some of these fellers, though, they ain't so man-
nered."

The ruffian to Wilson's left spat in the dirt. Another piped up, his voice like muddy gravel. "I
reckon that one's got a few things I'd have a gander
at afore taking her guts out."

A roll of wanton laughter rolled through the
group. It made Victoria's skin crawl. She stole a look
at Cora. The hunter might have been watching a cow
scratching its hindquarters, her face was so indiffer-
ent. Her casual demeanor only worsened Victoria's
apprehension. They had taken Wilson and his friend
by surprise in the saloon, but they were outnum-
bered three to one here. None of the grizzled faces
leering at her would think twice about raping her
and shooting her in the head when they were done.
Victoria's mind jumped to the revolver at her belt,
but she knew she wasn't fast enough to draw on all
of them at once. They were gunfighters of the American West; she was just the daughter of a British
aristocrat.

"So that's your game, then?" Cora asked. "You're
just going to take her right here in the street, right
in full view of the town and the law?"

Wilson's puffy cheek plumped up even more as
he sneered. "We ain't so stupid as all that," he said.
"No, we aim to take you two someplace nice and
private for what we got planned. You ladies is going
to come without a peep if you know what's good
for you, too."

"And if we don't?" Victoria asked.

"Well, then," Wilson said, "the both of you is going to be right sorry for it. My boys'll see to that, don't you worry none. We got ways, see?"

"All right, you got yourselves a deal," Cora said.

Victoria's blue eyes went wide. "What?"

"I said they got themselves a deal," Cora said. Her face was unreadable, a stone carving staring back at Victoria's incredulous gaping. "Ain't no point in fighting now, is there? They got us outmatched, and I'd rather not make it worse than it's got to be. Should go easier for you, too."

"How can you–"

"Cause I know these fellers, and I know their type. Ain't no good comes from making a fuss when you're outgunned, plain and simple. Just makes the rotten things they got in mind go more rotten. We go along quiet-like, they go easy on us." She turned to Wilson, whose grin had transformed his cheek into a ripe plum. "Ain't that right, boy?"

"Sure is," the man replied. "Listen to the old bitch, little missie. She's got enough sense to save you both a world of hurt."

Cora reached out and covered Victoria's hands with her own. "Don't fret none. Ain't so bad as all that, you'll see."

Victoria fought back tears. Whatever else they would do to her tonight, she would not give them the satisfaction of seeing her cry. Her blue eyes filled with rage and pain at Cora's betrayal, and she directed all of it at the old hunter. How could she just go along with this? Surely Cora knew what men like this would do to a young woman like her. Even as sheltered as she had been in Oxford, Victoria still knew enough to stay away from the roughnecks in the pubs when she was running errands by herself. Fat lot of good her precaution had done her now.

The thought of using her newfound power to escape came to her, but she dismissed it almost as quickly. Her spirit might be able to flee, but her body would remain behind, and that would be enough for monsters such as these. Besides, if they killed her while her spirit was away, she wasn't sure what would happen to her. God might not welcome her if she came to His threshold by way of witchcraft. No, it was better to remain inside her body and prepare her spirit for eternity.

Victoria lowered her head as the weight of her fate settled on her. After everything Cora had told her about the dangers of the American frontier, it was the old hunter herself who would sell her into the hands of bandits just to make things easier on herself. So much for the great loyalty of companions who have shared the horrors of war. It was just another romantic illusion that this God-forsaken place had seen fit to dismantle.

Cora must have taken her bowed head for acquiescence. "Knew you'd come around," she said. Her brown eyes squinted at Wilson. "See, now? We ain't going to give you no trouble."

"Glad to see you ain't put your sense out to pasture after all," Wilson said. "Now then, about time we got a move on. Don't want to be wasting any precious time we have with you ladies."

Cora's gaze shifted pointedly to the streets around them. "Right this minute? Ain't sure that's the best time for it, seeing as how you still got a lot of witnesses wandering about. Maybe we ought to wait a spell, give ourselves more dark for cover before we ride out."

"My boys is impatient," Wilson said. "Ain't no good comes out of them waiting any longer than they need to."

"Ain't no good comes out of getting caught by Morgan and his posse, neither. You want to have your fun or rot in his jail?"

Wilson made a show of rolling his eyes. "That sheriff ain't got the wits God gave a turnip. He sees us riding through the streets, he'll reckon my boys is making sure you ladies get to where you is going safe and sound, like the proper gentlemen we is."

Spurring his horse forward, he rode between the two women. His fingers clamped onto Victoria's arm. Startled, she looked into his swollen, filthy face for only a moment before her rage exploded. Her palm smashed into his bruised cheek with a wet smack, sending fresh drops of blood sailing through the air. The blow nearly knocked Wilson from his saddle. He recovered quickly, his free hand pulling the revolver from his belt. Other guns flashed into view, and Victoria found herself looking down four different barrels. Her own was pointed at the bridge of Wilson's nose.

"Well, now," Cora said, "ain't this awkward?"

Before anyone could reply, something shattered above their heads. Shards of glass rained down on the group. It felt like someone had tossed a handful of pebbles on them. As one, they all ducked and pulled their hats low, shielding themselves from the myriad of sharp fragments.

When the shower stopped, the whole group looked toward the source. Victoria drew in a breath, and she heard crude exclamations of surprise from the bandits around her.

Above them, a man crouched in the ruined remains of a third-story window, looking for all the world like a human-shaped gargoyle brought to life by some dark magic. He was peering down at the street, his head lolling this way and that. The movements were unsettling, too exaggerated and jerky to be natural. His naked fingers curled around the jagged pieces of glass still lingering in the window. In the stunned silence, Victoria could hear air hissing between the man's teeth.

"What in the hell is that?" Wilson finally said.

The creature's gaze locked onto the bandit, and its nostrils flared. Before anyone could react, it leapt head-first from the window, fingers curled like claws. A grunt exploded from Wilson's lips as they collided. The impact knocked him from his horse, and the other men hollered in surprise. When Wilson's grunts became screams, they took aim at the creature. Had the struggle not already encouraged the street traffic to give them a wide berth, the chorus of gunshots would have done it.

Wilson's attacker jerked this way and that under the hail of gunfire, but it remained intent on its victim. Victoria couldn't imagine all of those shots hitting their mark without a few hitting Wilson, and the gunman's ebbing cries confirmed her speculation. One or two of Wilson's posse reached the same conclusion and pointed their guns skyward. Others fired their weapons empty and paused to reload.

By the time they took aim again, Wilson had stopped screaming.

Victoria could see gun barrels shaking in unsteady hands as the men watched the creature feed. In the absence of thundering gunshots, the air filled with a slurping sound. Blood seeped onto the street, mixing with the dust to create a thick red mud. Stealing a glance at Cora, Victoria wasn't surprised to see a look of smug satisfaction on the hunter's face. She felt a little of it herself, watching this brute and would-be rapist become food for a true creature of nightmare.

The monster raised its head. Red streaks ran down its chin and stained the collar of the suit it still wore. Its eyes darted between the onlookers, already searching for its next meal. Before it could settle on one of them, Cora shouted and raised her rosary. "Get out of here!" she yelled at the men. "Get before this thing settles on you for its next drink."

Wilson's posse needed no further urging. They fled in all directions, horses pounding up clouds of dust. The few onlookers not among their number also heeded her advice and took to their heels.

Soon, the area around Wilson's body was empty

but for the creature and the two hunters. It eyed them with hatred and desire, but the rosary in Cora's outstretched fist held it at bay. Snarls bubbled through the blood on its lips. Staring into its feral face, Victoria almost found it more frightening than the monsters they had fought at the ranch. Those, at least, had lost their humanity enough to look like monsters. This one still clung to vestiges of his human appearance, making the inhuman fury in his eyes all the more unnatural.

"Back, you damned thing!" Cora's voice rang out dry and tough in the hot evening air. "Run your scrawny ass out of my town, or I'll do it for you!"

The creature hissed in reply, bearing bloodstained teeth that still looked too human. It backed away from the hunter like a wildcat, spine arched and limbs trembling. Cora urged her frightened mare forward. The horse tossed its head and whinnied. Turning her spurs inward, the hunter punched her heels into the animal's ribs. It sprang forward, bearing down on the creature and its victim. Victoria heard Wilson's bones snap like dry branches beneath the mare's hooves. The vampire darted to one side and fled down the street.

"Wake up, girl!" Cora yelled at her. "We got us a spook on the run!"

Without thinking, Victoria spurred her own mare forward. The two women thundered down the street – now quite empty – in pursuit of their quarry. Even at a gallop, they had trouble keeping up with the vampire; its arms and legs were dark blurs beneath its body as it fled from them.

They quickly reached the outskirts of Albuquerque. Victoria knew the train station was somewhere off to their left, but the vampire was leading them eastward. Once again, the New Mexico desert opened up before her eyes, its thirsty plants nothing but silhouettes in the dwindling light. The vampire charged headlong into the wilderness, gravel flying from its heels. Even after the creature itself disappeared into the scrub, the cloud of dust it kicked up was all the trail they needed.

Cora took the lead, guiding her galloping mare around hidden obstacles with practiced ease. Riding just far enough behind her to avoid the hunter's dust cloud, Victoria bent low over her mare's neck. Around them, the desert had become a smear of dark blues and greens and browns. She did not have any idea what lay in this direction, but somewhere out there, far beyond the horizon, was the Atlantic Ocean. Each drumming stride of her mare's hooves brought her a little closer to home. The thought gave her a small measure of comfort. If Cora's plan worked, they would be heading this way again in the next day or two, relaxing in a rail carriage as they discussed a strategy for bringing justice to the black shucks.

Lost in thoughts of home, she nearly rode into Cora. Only the hunter's panicked hollering brought her back to the present. Victoria pulled on the reins as hard as she dared, her mare voicing its objections loudly. The animal stopped less than a foot from Cora's mount and champed on its bit in protest.

"Got us a problem," Cora said.

Looking beyond the hunter, Victoria's heart sank. The two of them stood at the edge of a small cliff. Below them, the desert stretched out like a great dark ocean. From the look on Cora's face, Victoria could guess what the problem was.

"It went down there?" she asked.

The hunter nodded. "All lickety-split. Ain't rightly sure if it climbed down, jumped off, or sprouted a damn pair of wings, but this is where the trail ends."

"Vampires can fly?"

"Some say so," Cora said. "Turn into bats or some such. Ain't never seen it myself."

"So what do we do now?"

"Ain't much we can do, way I see it. This here cliff don't taper off for a spell in either direction. By the time we got to the bottom, all we'd find is a bunch of scrub and a cold trail."

"What of the dust cloud?" Victoria asked. "Surely we could follow that."

The hunter shook her head. "We'd still take too long getting down there. Dust will have settled by then."

"You aren't suggesting we abandon the chase?"

"Afraid so," Cora said. "Can't say I like it myself. That blue-eyed bastard still owes me answers, and that squaw's got to answer for killing Our Lady. I don't want nothing more in the world than to settle them both, but we can't do that if we get ourselves lost in the desert. Best thing we can do now is head on back to town, settle in for some drinks, and lay plans for when that skin-walker of yours to make a move."

"Have you learned nothing of tracking bounties in all your years of hunting them?"

Cora's eyes gleamed with the last of the daylight. "I know more about it than your fancy fox hunters could shake a stick at, but ain't no good in the dark, see? Sun's gone down, and moon won't show herself for another few hours. Maybe you got some fancy cat eyes that let you track a body at night, but I don't."

"I refuse to accept that waiting for our enemies to come after us is the wisest course of action," Victoria said.

"Worked just fine back in town when them outlaws was fixing for trouble."

The incident hadn't left Victoria's memory. "A splendid plan, certainly. I can't believe you so easily bargained with them – using my honesty as your currency, no less – to spare yourself some unpleasantness. Will that be the order of the day when the skin-walker comes calling? Trade me to her so you can have yourself a comfortable time playing cards?"

"You really are thick sometimes, you know that?"

"What do you mean by that?"

The hunter's silhouette shook its head. "Ain't no point in explaining it if you ain't figured it out by now. Just like there ain't no point in riding around after a monster we can't find without some hounds."

Cora turned her mare back the way they had come and nudged her into a walk. Victoria remained where she was, staring helplessly at the endless desert below her. Somewhere in that gathering darkness, their only hope of finding the skin-walker and the blue-eyed vampire was fading into the distance. With it went their best chance of catching their enemies by surprise and ending the fight before the sun rose. Frustration boiled in her chest, threatening to overflow from her eyes.

Victoria slammed the heel of her hand into the saddle horn. "No."

Behind her, the sound of hooves stopped. "What's that, now?"

"I refuse to accept it," Victoria said. "We aren't going to give up now."

"Maybe you ain't," Cora replied, "but I am. Ain't too keen on wandering around in the desert again so quick after our last outing. Maybe in a week or so, but no way I'm doing it tonight."

"What if we weren't roaming aimlessly?"

The hunter's cackle rolled down the cliff. "Only way we'd manage that is if we was headed back to town, which is the way I'm pointing."

Victoria's heart raced. She didn't know if what she was thinking was even possible, much less if she should tell Cora about it. The Navajo singer's voice echoed in her memory, telling her that her dream was not a dream, that she had the power to separate her body and her spirit. It had seemed preposterous to her. It still did. Even now, her rational mind belittled her for even considering it as a possibility. With everything else that had happened to her, though, why should this come as a surprise? Skin-walkers were real; she had seen one with her own eyes. If such creatures existed, it wasn't so much of a stretch to believe other Navajo folk tales could have truth behind them.

"I can track them."

"Sure, and I'm the Queen of England," Cora said.

Victoria turned her mare to face the hunter. "I mean it."

"So you followed along after your daddy on his fox hunts, then?" Cora asked. "Or maybe you just got the eyes of a cougar and ain't never told nobody about it."

"Neither." Victoria's ire at the hunter's ridicule set her resolve. "I can walk in the spirit world."

A silence fell between them. Victoria watched Cora's silhouette with a strange mixture of anxiety and anger. Her mare snorted and lowered her head to graze. In the distance, an unseen animal raised its voice in a yipping cry.

"You can do what now?" Cora finally asked.

"Walk in the spirit world," Victoria said. When the words passed through her lips a second time, their absurdity nearly drove her to laughter. She took a deep breath to steady herself. "You recall what I told you of my conversation with the Indian singer?"

"About them skin-walkers and the ashes and all that, sure," Cora said. "Don't recollect you saying nothing about walking in no spirit world."

Victoria lifted her chin. "Because I didn't see any reason to mention it, and I did not wish to endure your mockery." The hunter made no reply, so she continued. "While I was keeping watch in the desert during our expedition, I dreamt I could fly over the desert like a bird. I flew to a nearby hill and saw both the skin-walker and your Fodor Glava impostor. They spoke of us."

"Ain't a week goes by but I get a dream of running down one monster or another, even after all this time. Don't mean I'm actually doing it in my sleep."

"That was my conclusion at first, too," Victoria said, "but the singer believed that my spirit left my body and traveled across the desert freely. I have given it a good deal of thought, and I'm not entirely sure I disbelieve him anymore."

"Why's that?"

"Because everything else he told me appears to be accurate."

Cora's hat moved up and down as she nodded. "Wise men is wise men, and I reckon they're the same anywhere you go. Don't matter if he calls himself a professor or a singer or a shaman. Thing is, all them wise folk got a funny way of mixing in what really is with what they think is, and the two don't always match up. Could be this singer of yours is spot-on about the skin-walker woman, but that don't mean every word he says is true."

"Yes, I realize that," Victoria said, "but what choice do we have?"

"We can ride on back to town and play a few hands, maybe win us some drinking money."

"You truly care only for gambling and tippling." Victoria shook her head and sighed. "Go on, then, if you wish. I shall track down this menace myself and kill it if I can. Should I come across your blue-eyed

vampire, I will kill him as well, and you will be forever left to wonder who he really was."

"Suit yourself," Cora said.

With that, the hunter resumed her course back the
way they had come. Victoria watched her form melt
into the evening's shadows, her insides a knot of con-
flicting emotions. Anger at Cora's belittlement, fear at
being left alone in the desert, determination to prove
the hunter wrong, to see her boast through and come
back alive. Each rose to the surface and slipped beneath it again like onions in a simmering stew. Part of
her wanted nothing more than to prod the old mare
beneath her into a canter and follow Cora back to
town. An evening spent indoors, warm and comfortable, safe from the horrors roaming through the
desert, was the loveliest thing she could imagine at
that moment.

A breeze hissed through the scrub around her
horse's hooves, carrying the promise of a chilly
night. Victoria shivered. She could no longer see the
hunter's retreating form or hear the steady crunch-
ing of her mare's steps on the hard-packed earth.
The hunt was hers and hers alone now. She ran a
finger along the grip of the revolver on her hip.
Cora's revolver. It brought her comfort. The gun had
shot and killed more monsters than she could imagine. It would do so once more, even if her hand was
not as skilled or practiced at its previous owner.

Straightening up in the saddle, Victoria let her gaze
sweep over the landscape sprawled out beneath her.
She drew a deep breath. Now was the moment of

truth. If she couldn't free her spirit as she had before, she would have to return to town, defeated and humiliated. Worse, their quarry would escape, making a living return to Oxford that much more unlikely.

Victoria bowed her head, closed her eyes, and pictured the world as it would appear through a falcon's eyes.

FIFTEEN

A frown passed over the woman's face. Somewhere nearby, skulking beneath the faint moonlight, she could feel a presence. Like her, it was at once human and inhuman, but it was not ánt'įįhnii. Closing her eyes, she slipped her skin and rose above the ruined city. Yes, there was a new creature in the desert, one she had never before encountered.

The woman shaped her aura and extended it toward the presence. Black as burnt wood, the channel of energy stretched out over the desert. The creature took notice of it, and the woman filled its heart with a desire to seek her out. Once the seed of thought had taken root, she returned to her body and waited.

She did not need to wait long. As the creature approached, she could feel its intense hunger, its desire to feed on her, but she did not fear it. Not here, in this ancient place once inhabited by the ancestral enemies of her people. Here, the veil between worlds was thin; the ruins hummed with spiritual power. Other Diné *feared and shunned this place, calling it dangerous and evil, but to her, it was a place of power.*

When the monster stepped into view across the remains
of the kiva, she opened her eyes. It looked like a man, but
its eyes burned with an inhuman radiance.

"Stay, demon," she said in the American tongue.

The figure halted.

"What do you want of me?" she asked.

"Your blood," the demon replied.

"You will not have it," the woman said.

The demon snarled at her. In response, the woman
bent her will around it, testing the strength of its mind.
Finding it weak, she smiled again. This creature could be
of use.

"You will help me."

The blue eyes flickered with hesitation for only a moment. "How?"

"We are both creatures of the night," the woman said,
her own eyes gleaming red. "There is a woman who lives
near this place. She hunts those such as us. I must kill her,
and you will help me."

"A woman hunter?" the demon asked. "Just so happens
I'm looking for one, myself. Yours got a name?"

The woman felt anger flowing from the creature in great
dark waves. Perhaps controlling him would be easier than
she thought.

Her elation was short-lived, vanishing beneath an unexpected shadow of regret. How would her father look at
her if he knew what she was? The daughter of a singer,
now a skin-walker and companion of demons. Could she
make him believe that it was for the protection of all Diné
that she did these things? Surely the warrior spirit in him
would admire her bravery and determination to right the

SHE RETURNS FROM WAR

wrongs done to them. Yet all she could see at that moment were his eyes, filled with disappointment.

The demon was waiting for her answer.

She drew herself up to her full height and looked into his eyes. "Her name is Cora Oglesby."

The ground dropped away as Victoria rushed upward. The air whistled around her, but she could not feel its chill. She spun around, ecstatic in the giddy weightlessness, the absolute freedom. Her eyes drank in the view, marveling at how the world changed when one saw it from the sky. The rational aristocrat in her mind still insisted it was a dream. Maybe it was, maybe it wasn't; she no longer cared.

She wanted to continue sailing through the sky, a hawk drifting effortlessly on the night air, but time was short. Taking herself in hand, she turned her gaze eastward, down the cliff and on toward the horizon. A panic filled her when she realized she felt nothing in that direction. No familiar sense of darkness, no ominous shadow on her mind. She waited for a few minutes, hoping that the sensation would come to her in time. When it didn't, her heart sank. How had she done it before? It wasn't through any conscious act that she could remember, but she had believed it all to be a dream then, acting with the carefree trust that comes naturally in dreams. If only she could recover that same instinct.

Perhaps she was too high up. She swooped toward the earth, picturing herself as a bird with wings swept backward in a graceful dive. The ground rose to meet her. Banking this way and that, she skimmed along just above the tallest bushes. Whimsy guided her course as she lost herself again in the wondrous sensations.

Mesas, dark and brooding, loomed against the horizon ahead. Below her, the ground swelled and receded like ocean waves as she flew over dry riverbeds and small, rolling hills. She wondered how others with this gift, the Navajo spirit walkers mentioned by the old Indian, ever thought of returning to themselves. The spirit world was so free, so invigorating and limitless. She never wanted to trap herself in her small, confined prison of a body again.

Her body.

The thought halted her carefree flight beneath the stars. What was her body doing without her? She imagined it slumped in the saddle as if asleep, perhaps drooling out of drooped lips. If a wild animal, one of the many creatures she had heard calling and screaming and laughing in the night, came upon her like that, would she realize it? Would she know to return to her body in time to save herself? If she didn't, the animals could very well kill her body and leave her stranded, a nomad of the spirit world. The idea washed over her like cold water on naked flesh. Despite her earlier wish, she found herself not at all eager to learn what such an existence would be like.

Victoria's worry blossomed into full-blown panic when she realized she no longer knew where her body was. She may very well have traveled miles from the small cliff where she and Cora parted ways.

The desert landscape, now barely discernible in the advancing gloom of the night, offered her no clues. Desperate, she began zipping to and fro, hoping for something – a prominent rock formation or odd-looking hill – to jump out at her as a familiar sight.

So great was her panic that she did not notice the creeping shadow on her mind at first. When it finally caught her attention, she dismissed it as a product of her own mounting fear. It burrowed deeper into her awareness, pricking and poking at her mind like a grain of sand in her undergarments. Finally pulling her mind away from her frantic search, Victoria paused to consider the growing sensation. It only took her a moment to recognize it. A thrill of excitement and fear ran through her. It was the skin-walker's aura; she was certain of it.

The dark energy flowed out from beneath the approaching night to the east. It would be easy enough to follow, but Victoria had to find her way back to her body first. Shutting the skin-walker's power out of her mind, she envisioned her own aura as a sphere around herself. She willed the sphere to expand, to envelop the landscape beneath her. The radiating power from the witch became a visible stream in her mind, but she turned her attention away from it, stretching her energy westward.

After a few minutes, her growing alarm broke her concentration. Maybe the Navajo spirit walkers could navigate the world in such a manner, but she didn't seem to have the power herself, and now she would be forever trapped in the spirit world. Worse,

the skin-walker might find her in this state and de-
vise some method of torturing or enslaving her spirit.
The singer had been vague on what sort of interac-
tions could happen between spirits, but Victoria's
imagination was more than willing to supply various
outcomes, all of them terrifying.

The skin-walker's ripples of energy abruptly
changed. They became waves, large and full of purpose. Victoria could sense them closing in on her like
the jaws of an animal trap. She dove for the desert
floor, hoping to somehow hide herself from the
witch's awareness. Pressing herself as close to a large
rock as she could, she watched and waited.

Above her, the waves began forming a narrow
cone of darkness against the evening sky. They swept
through the space she had just occupied like an animal sniffing after some escaped prey. Had her spirit
needed breath, she surely would have been holding
it. She didn't know what she would do if the skin-
walker discovered her. Flee, most likely, but to
where? The desert's endless march of shrubs and
rocks had already defeated her sense of direction; a
blind flight through it would destroy any hope she
had of finding her body again. If only she could
stumble upon that same instinctive reflex that trans-
ported her back in an instant during her last journey.
Somehow, though, she figured it wouldn't work if
she was expecting it to, much like a kettle refusing
to boil until she looked away.

Giving herself a mental shake, Victoria pulled upon
the rational side of herself that even now insisted that

she was only dreaming. Her body was somewhere west of her, and the skin-walker was somewhere to the east. She didn't know how far the dark waves – now looming scarcely twenty feet overhead – could reach, but she knew it wasn't forever. Their power had to fade over distance, or she would have sensed them when she first left her body.

Could she risk moving with the skin-walker's attention so close to discovering her? What would happen if that sinister, pulsing energy enveloped her fragile spirit form? Looking upward, she realized that she would soon discover the answer whether she moved or not. The cone of shadow swept back and forth no more than ten feet above her hiding place.

Victoria gathered her resolve, took one last look at the dark predator, and ran.

She felt the attention, the malice, the raw power of the skin-walker descend upon her immediately. The shadow energy filled her vision, swirling like the murky trails of a fever dream. Unbearable heat swept through her. She fled before it, hoping that the witch could not take a spirit form herself and pursue her. For all she knew, her damnation had been guaranteed when she first made her move, and it was only a matter of time before she was overrun and devoured. The skin-walker had no doubt mastered more than the art of transformation that gave her that name. If an ignorant foreigner like Victoria could walk so easily in the spirit world, her enemy must know every path and every crevice it contained.

The desert flora whisked by beneath her, hardy plants dozing in the cool of the evening. Stars grew brighter in the sky as Victoria's vision began to clear. Soon, the burning sensation faded to a dull heat, and even that vanished over the next ridge. Relief washed through her in its place, but she dared not stop just yet. Even if the witch's power was fading, Victoria wanted to put as much distance between the two of them as she could.

Finally, when the lights of Albuquerque became visible on the horizon, she allowed herself to stop. The cone of darkness had faded into the night behind her along with any sensation of the skin-walker's awareness. Even better, she could see the route she and Cora had taken out of town, meaning she could find her body again. Assuming she had a body to return to, anyway.

Finding it was even easier than Victoria expected. It sat slumped in the saddle just as she expected. She took a moment to marvel at seeing her own body from this perspective. If she didn't know better, she would have taken herself for a man at first glance, some young American frontiersman searching for his fortune among the lawless towns and endless horizons. Mounted on his trusty steed like some time-displaced knight from the court of King Arthur, he rode forth with a gun on his hip and a swagger in his stride. How her parents would have started to see her dressed in such a fashion.

Victoria laughed at the thought, then jerked her head upright. The laughter came from her own lips.

Blinking in surprise, she lifted her hands for inspection. Somehow, without intending to do so, she had slipped back into her body in the midst of her musing. She stretched her arms toward the stars with a groan. Her joints were stiff and cold, and she massaged life back into them with her fingers.

The cliff still blocked her way. Rubbing her eyes, she peered to either side, looking for the shortest way down. To her right, the cliff stretched on for several hundred yards before arching back westward. The opposite direction saw it slope gently downward for some distance before meeting the ground below. That seemed the more likely route, so she turned her mare left and tapped her heels into the animal's ribs. The mare responded with a shake of its mane as it began plodding forward. Victoria's legs ached with the motion, but she gritted her teeth and shifted her weight in the saddle.

The daylight had waned to nothing but a thin yellow ribbon on the western horizon. Victoria looked at it as she rode, wishing for a moment that she had followed Cora back to town. The hunter was undoubtedly planted at one of her tables, a jug of whiskey within easy reach, fleecing some local cowboys for their month's wages. Victoria wondered if she'd gotten into another fight and if she'd survived it with all of her parts intact.

Reaching the bottom of the slope, she turned her mare eastward and eased her into a trot. The night was young, but she didn't know how many miles she had to cover before reaching her destination or what she would find there. If it was only the skin-walker and her vampire accomplice, she would consider herself lucky. Her satchel rested against the horse's flank, and she reached for it with one hand to reassure herself it was still there. It contained the special weapons – holy water and sacred ash – that she would need to overcome her foes. Much too late, she remembered she had given some of the ashes to her erstwhile companion before they rode out that evening. Nothing could be done about it now. She would just have to pray that her remaining supply would be enough.

The grip of Cora's revolver lightly pressed into her belly as the horse moved beneath her. Alone and in-experienced though she was, she was as ready for the coming battle as she could be. Her will was set: she would not turn back or give up until she de-feated them or they killed her.

Behind her, standing at the edge of the cliff, a shadow watched her ride into the gathering night.

SIXTEEN

The walls stood before her in the darkness, sudden and out of place in the desolation that surrounded them. They were not the castle walls she was accustomed to seeing, great grey barriers rising out of the green of the English countryside. These were smaller – no more than ten feet high in most places – and didn't look as though they had been built to keep armies out. The crumbling structure nearest her appeared to have once been a small house. Further down, a larger ruin stood against the stars, perhaps a temple or some sort of market.

Victoria wondered what sort of world this land had been, where ancient cities didn't build walls to keep invaders at bay. Guiding her mare up to the nearest ruin, she reached out and ran her hand along it. The stone was slightly warm to the touch. She thought it strange that the wall would retain its heat so many hours after the sundown, but the New Mexico sun had a lot of heat to give. Maybe it wasn't so unnatural after all.

Taking a deep breath, Victoria braced herself for another look into the spirit world. She had found her
way to the ruin by stealing quick glimpses as she
rode, feeling for all the world like a spiritual rodent
poking its head out of some burrow. It was anybody's
guess whether such a tactic had kept the skin-walker
from noticing her as she approached. Whenever she
slipped out for a look, she could sense the evil presence, but she didn't feel any indication of awareness
on the other's part. She took that to be a good sign,
but she knew her assumption was really nothing
more than an educated guess.

Victoria closed her eyes once more and slipped out
of her body. Her mare didn't seem to notice or care
about the change; the animal simply lowered its
head and began grazing on the long, dry grasses
growing at the base of the wall. Victoria resisted the
temptation to stare at her own form slumped in the
saddle. She reached out with her awareness instead,
searching for the dark presence. It was very close
now, hiding somewhere in the ruins ahead.

Satisfied, Victoria ducked back into herself and sat
up. Looking up and down the crumbling wall in
front of her, she spied a shadow not too far away.
Possibly an entrance. She gave her mare a single pat
on the neck, then slipped out of the saddle as quietly
as she could.

A faint chiming broke the stillness of the night.

Dropping into a crouch, she held her breath and
waited for it to come again. After a few moments,
she risked a look over her shoulder. Nothing. She

took a tentative step, then nearly fell over from relief. The sound had been her own spurs jingling as
she dismounted. Fighting an urge to burst out laughing, she bent over and pulled them free of her boot
heels. Her horse regarded her with one large black
eye as she tucked the spurs into a saddlebag.

"Stay here," she whispered.

The animal blinked in reply. Taking that for an af-
firmative, Victoria turned and cautiously approached
the shadow in the stone wall. Her fingers itched to
draw her revolver. She curled them into a fist instead. As much comfort as the weight of the gun in
her hand would bring her, she didn't trust her own
nerves. She might shoot at a bird, a rat, or even
nothing at all, throwing out whatever small chance
she had of catching her enemies off-guard. No, it
was best to approach empty-handed until she had a
clear shot.

The opening loomed ahead of her. Victoria
crouched next to it and tried to calm her pounding
heart. She'd lost count of how many times she'd
thought herself mad for coming out here alone. Even
now, in the shadow of that ancient wall, she had to
fight to keep from climbing back onto her mare and
galloping back to town. After all, Cora had insisted
on doing that very thing, and the old hunter's sense
had kept her alive for a long time.

The thought of Cora's dry voice and condescend-
ing glances hardened Victoria's resolve. She was out
here to kill a skin-walker and a vampire, and she
would do exactly that. If that old bat didn't want to

help, she could drown herself with that horrid drink of hers. Victoria raised her blue eyes to the stars, nodded to herself, and turned toward the opening.

Red eyes gleamed at her.

Victoria screamed and jumped backward. Her boot caught on a rock, and her hands flew out to either side as she fought to keep her balance. In an instant, strong fingers wrapped around her wrists and yanked her arms around her back.

"You just don't learn, do you, darlin?" came a familiar, loathsome voice.

Victoria twisted against his grip, trying to free herself. He laughed in her ear and bent her arms until she cried out in pain. Straightening up as best she could, Victoria looked into the woman's face.

"You did not listen," the woman said, her tone almost remorseful.

Despite the pain, a gleam came into Victoria's eyes. "I do not need to run from you," she said. "I know who and what you are. You are a skin-walker, and your name is Anaba."

Victoria watched Anaba's face, waiting for the flash of realization and fear to flicker through those inhuman eyes. Once the witch woman's powers were gone, she would lose control over her pet vampire. Victoria couldn't know for sure what would happen when he broke free of the spell, but she didn't think it would bode well for the skin-walker.

Anaba nodded slowly. "You have spoken with my father."

"Yes," Victoria said, her confidence wavering. "He taught me much of your kind."

"He did not tell you enough."

Victoria swallowed. "What do you mean?"

"You have named me, but it is not enough. Not here. The spirits in this place are powerful, and they protect me from such trickery."

Victoria wilted a little in the man's cold grip. Her fingers were tingling. She tried to flex them as her mind raced. The skin-walker could not be weakened by the calling out of her name. Would the sacred ash also fail to stop her? The silver bullets might still kill the vampire, but what good would that be while the witch lived?

"I hope you were kind to my people," Anaba said.

"I tried to be," Victoria said. "They were very kind to me."

The skin-walker smiled. "They are a kind people. They did not deserve what your people did to them."

"My people?"

"Yes," Anaba said. Her brow drew downward. "They killed many, and made the rest of us walk many miles and sleep inside their strange walls. For no crime but that we live."

"Anaba," Victoria said, "my people did not harm you. I am not from America."

"You come from the east," Anaba said. "So did the men that took my family and made my mother walk until she died. The men who shot my husband laughed in your tongue. Your speech is their speech, your skin is their skin, and your eyes their eyes. It is enough."

"No." Fear burrowed deeper into Victoria's mind, robbing her of words. "No, it isn't."

"Enough talk. You were given a chance, and you did not take it. Now—"

The skin-walker paused. Her eyes gleamed in the waning moonlight as she cocked her head to one side as if listening. Victoria wanted nothing more than to lunge at her, taking advantage of her sudden distraction, but the vampire still held her fast. Pulling against his grip would only hurt her wrists more, so she remained still and silent.

Anaba's gaze fixed on her again. "Your idea was clever."

"What idea?"

"To arrive ahead of the hunter," Anaba said. "To make me believe you came alone."

"Cora?" Victoria's look of confusion twisted into disdain. "Cora left me alone out here and went back to her absurd little pub."

"Your lie is wasted. I feel her approach on the wind."

A swell of hope surged in Victoria's stomach, but it quickly faded. Cora may have been planning to catch them off-guard, but it wouldn't do any good. Now that Victoria had gotten herself captured, Cora would face both the skin-walker and vampire alone.

The red eyes glanced at the creature behind her. "Demon, I will leave this one to you. Do with her as you see fit, but she must be dead when you are finished."

"Sure thing." Victoria didn't need to see the man's face to hear his leer. "I ain't got to play nice no more, do I?"

The skin-walker shook her head. Victoria felt as though she might vomit. Anguish twisted her insides as she berated herself for her own foolishness. Why had she ever thought she could overcome two powerful, supernatural creatures by herself? The sacred ash and silver bullets might as well have been back in England for all the good they had done her. Even with the holy weapons, she was still just a human, an ordinary girl playing at being something that she would never be.

And now she was going to die for it.

The vampire twisted her arms ruthlessly. Pain exploded through her body as she writhed against him, trying to ease the agony, but it only grew worse. He laughed at her efforts. "That's right, ain't it? Don't matter how uppity you women think you is. Sooner or later, you can't control yourselves no more, and you're plumb crawling all over me."

Victoria's stomach heaved at his words, but the pain in her arms left her without the breath for a retort. She had never in her life imagined that such agony could exist, and it was only a taste of what the man would surely do before the end. Tears burned in her eyes. The world faded away, leaving her alone with the pain and the monster.

"Be fast with her." Anaba's voice came from a great distance, echoing down a long, dark tunnel of despair. "I may need your help with the hunter."

"Ain't no fun if it's quick," the man said. The pain in Victoria's arms lessened, and she sagged against his grip. "You got to give me at least ten minutes or it just ain't worth it."

"No more," the skin-walker said. Before the vampire could respond, Anaba lowered herself into a crouch, her hands coming to rest on the desert floor. Victoria forgot the pain in her arms for a moment as she watched the witch's dark skin melt into a silvery grey. It was over in the space of a single breath, and the fox-that-was-not-a-fox stood before them. The creature looked at Victoria, intelligence burning in its black eyes, then loped off into the underbrush.

"There now," came the man's voice. "Nice and quiet for us to do our business."

He laughed and shoved her forward. Her arms, asleep from their imprisonment, could not break the fall in time. Pebbles bloodied her cheeks as she slammed into the ground face first. She gasped from the pain and inhaled a lungful of dirt. Her knees came up to her chest as violent coughs shook her frame.

Something hard and pointed drove into her back, sending her skidding across the ground. More shocks of pain ripped through her as she rolled over the rough terrain. Coming to rest on her stomach, she pushed herself up on her hands and knees. The coughing fit began to subside, and she raised her head. The man stood before her, fingers hooked through his belt loops and a smirk spread beneath his flashing blue eyes.

"Ain't never had me a British lady before."

Victoria's hand darted toward her belt. The smooth, firm grip of Cora's revolver filled her palm. She leaned backward and brought the weapon up in a single motion. The man's smirk vanished. Victoria allowed herself one of her own as she squeezed the trigger, eager for the thunderclap that would end this wretched creature's existence once and for all.

It didn't come.

The vampire's boot came up, knocking the Colt from Victoria's grip. She fell backward as a second kick swept toward her. It missed her nose by mere inches. Turning away from him, she pulled her feet under her and broke into a dead run. Her boots crashed through the scrub, raw terror giving them speed. She knew she could never hope to escape the monster, but her instincts had taken over. On she ran into the night, expecting to feel those cold, crushing fingers around her neck with every step.

Cora's mare plodded along, head bobbing up and down to the rhythm of her hooves. Around them, the desert slept beneath the waning moon. Cora could hear the echoes of its nightmares on the wind, given voice by the animals that lived and died beneath the stars. The old hunter had spent so many years riding on such nights that she scarcely heard their cries at all. She slouched in the saddle, hips swaying with the motion of the horse beneath her, lost in thoughts and memories of better days.

Her lips moved beneath the brim of her hat, cracked voice drifting into the darkness as she spoke to someone who wasn't there. Laughs would occasionally burst forth from her like quiet gunshots. A metal flask gleamed in one hand; the other held the reins in relaxed fingers. Moonlight winked on the tips of silver spurs.

Something small skittered across the ground under the mare's nose. The animal whinnied and reared, taking Cora by surprise. She kept her seat as the animal bucked beneath her. Curses joined the chorus of the night's voices as she fought with the reins. After a few moments, the mare calmed down. Cora leaned forward, speaking quiet words into the mare's twitching ears as she rubbed her neck. The animal snorted in reply.

Cora straightened up in the saddle. A long, low shadow spread out on the horizon in front of her. It rose in sharp angles and staggered arches, blotting out the starlight in rigid shapes. She'd heard of the ancient ruins in the desert, but she'd never had occasion to explore one in all her long years of hunting. Had she been a younger woman when she moved to Albuquerque, she might have ventured into one in search of excitement, her husband tagging along in the hope of discovering long-forgotten myths. The thought made her heart sink. She pushed it aside, her fingers toying with the lid of her flask.

"Why did you follow us here?"

The voice was quiet but clear. Cora's new revolver appeared in her hand as she turned toward the sound. Dry branches and jagged rocks covered the ground with shadows, but the voice's owner was nowhere to be seen.

"Funny you should ask," Cora said. "I was just thinking how I'd always wanted to see one of these ruins up close. Figured I might as well get to it while I ain't dead."

Nothing rose up out of the underbrush to answer. Cora turned in a slow circle, the revolver's barrel sweeping along the horizon. She had recognized the voice that asked the question, and her entire body was on alert.

"I gave you the gift of mercy. Why did you not accept it?"

Cora spun around. She thought she caught a faint red shine in the shadows and fired. Her mare flinched at the sudden fire and thunder. Cora tightened her grip on the reins with her other hand. She could feel the kill approaching like a thunderstorm; the last thing she needed was for the livery's horse to spook and take off into the night.

A shadow darted through the brush, a glimmer of silver in the shadows. Cora spurred her mare into a gallop and gave chase. The night filled with the rumbling of the horse's hooves as she rode after the animal. Ahead of her, the ruins grew larger, their dark shadows consuming more stars with each stride.

Soon, the ancient walls echoed the sound of the mare's pounding feet. Cora saw the flitting shadow of her mark slip through a small gap in the wall. She pulled back on the reins, easing her mount to a standstill. Bullets winked in the blue-white light of the rising moon as the hunter replaced the spent shells in her revolver. Giving the horse a quick pat on the neck, she slipped out of the saddle and approached the wall. The hole where the animal had disappeared was too small for her to follow. Grumbling at the inconvenience, she began making her way along the structure, looking for an opening large enough to accommodate her. Behind her, she could hear the heavy, lathered breathing of her mare.

Rounding a corner, Cora took a dozen more steps and found an opening. She kept her gun in hand as she peered into it. The moonlight painted soft shadows in the narrow alley, outlining the round stones in the walls. Cora adjusted the strap of her satchel, listening to the soft clinking of vials and spare shells. Taking one last look at the desert behind her, she entered the alleyway.

The ruins closed in behind her as she ventured into their maze, footsteps echoing off the dilapidated walls. Above her, the moon was rising toward its zenith. Cora took note of its position with a quick prayer of gratitude. Navigating by starlight might have been possible in the open desert, but it would have been impossible in the ruins. The creatures she hunted already held the advantage over her. Without the moon, it would have been all but impossible to hunt them down.

Somewhere nearby, a cry broke the stillness of the night. The hunter instinctively dropped into a crouch. The scream had sounded human, but Cora couldn't tell if it was the voice of a man or a woman. Whichever it was, she knew it meant that Victoria was in danger. Ignoring the protests in her joints and muscles, she raised her revolver and crept farther into the ruins.

The walls soon opened up on either side, ushering her into a wide, circular space. She swept the area with her Colt before venturing past the opening. Directly in front of her was a large, shallow pit. A crude wooden ladder rested on the far edge, poking above the stone lip like the last rotten tooth in some dead giant's maw. Stepping up to the nearest edge, Cora peered down.

"You are not welcome here."

Every muscle in Cora's body snapped to attention. The voice rolled around the open area, making it difficult to pinpoint its source. She backed away from the pit until she felt warm stone at her back, her eyes watching for the slightest hint of movement.

"You and the girl should not have come."

Cora looked around for the speaker. "We never would have if you and that feller you're riding with wasn't so keen on ending us."

"Why did you not listen to my warning and go east?"

"And leave you two out here to do God knows what to these poor folk?" Cora asked. "Ain't fitting, no matter how you cut it."

"Liars and thieves and killers," the voice of the skin-walker replied. "Their deaths would be justice."

"Maybe so, but you ain't the one to say who lives and dies." Cora's fingers dug into her satchel as she spoke. "Best leave that up to the Almighty and get on with your life as best you can."

"You do not live by your own words. A demon killed your husband, and for that crime, you killed him. Can I not have the same justice? Why should I not kill the demons that killed my husband?"

A soft click as the Colt's cylinder swung open. "Well, I ain't perfect neither. Besides, the feller that killed my Ben had no other aim in life but to go about killing people. Somebody had to put him down before he killed every last man, woman, and child there is."

"And so must your soldiers be stopped, before they kill the last of my people."

"They ain't so bad as all that," Cora said, letting the bullets fall into her cupped palm. Puffs of grey swirled around her fingers. "Sure, they ain't all angels, but they ain't no different from regular men."

"They are different from our men," came the reply.

Cora slipped the rounds back into the chambers and swung the cylinder closed. "Maybe so. Your folk seem nice enough when they come through, which is more than I can say for a lot of white folk in these parts. Never took much to Yankee soldiers my own self, truth be told. Bastards done burned my family out of our farm during the war, but I ain't hell bent on killing every last one of them for what they did. Maybe I should be, but I never was too keen on picking fights I can't win."

"You are here."

"So I am," Cora said, "and I got a question for you before we get to dusting up."

A pause. "Ask."

"Where'd you come by that blue-eyed bastard that follows you about?"

"The demon came to me from the north with knowledge of you."

"I figured that much," Cora said. "Got him a name, does he?"

"He bears the name of your great paper chief, the one you call Washington."

The name washed over Cora like a bucket of icy water. Washington. She'd met several men by that name during her travels, but only one would have had any intimate knowledge of her past. That smug grin, his self-assured swagger, and his keen blue eyes jumped into her memory like a thunderclap. Her hands trembled as blind fury filled her.

"That bastard," she muttered. Lifting her head, she unleashed the full power of her voice at the stars. "Washington Jones!" The walls echoed her shout back at her, filling the ruins with her rage. "You low-down yellow bastard!"

So great was the sound of her wrath that she did not hear the rushing of bare feet behind her until it was too late. When it reached her ears, Cora turned on her heel, the revolver's barrel sweeping across the crumbling heart of the ancient city.

Something hit her in the chest with a sound like a punch. The animal eyes of the skin-walker filled Cora's vision as a wetness began seeping into her shirt. Looking down, she saw the witch's fingers wrapped around a bone hilt. The hunter's brow furrowed. Why could she only see the hilt? Where had the rest of the knife gone?

Another scream rose from somewhere beyond the ruins. Cora tried to take a breath. Her lungs filled with excruciating fire. Brown eyes, now rimmed with white, found her enemy's gaze once again.

"What...?"

The word burned in her throat. A cough burst from her lips, sending the world into a white haze of agony. Her body suddenly felt very heavy. She needed to sit down for a moment. The jolt as she fell to her knees unleashed another crippling wave of pain through her chest. Cora coughed again, dimly aware of the blood that now dotted the skin-walker's legs.

"You should have stayed away."

The voice rang in her ears, offering the hunter an anchor in the vortex of pain and confusion. Her brown eyes cleared, focusing on her enemy's face. Words formed on blood-spattered lips, but she couldn't find the breath to say them. More coughing, more drops of red on the witch's skin.

Cora swayed for a moment, struggling to stay up-right. The world around her descended into a murky haze of dust and starlight. She was swept away by the maelstrom, pitching backward onto the packed earth. The impact made her draw in an uneven gasp only to expel it in another thick, wet fit of coughing. Rolling into her side, she doubled up against the pain, covering her mouth with her hand as the spasms ran their course.

When they finally subsided, Cora forced herself up

onto her elbow. Her gun had fallen nearby. She could still finish the job if she could just find it. There was still time. Her eye caught on a faint glimmer of silver in the moonlight, and she reached for it.

A hand grabbed her wrist, pulling her backward. Cora fought against it, but the agony in her chest stole her strength. Forced onto her back, she watched in a daze as the hand curled around the hilt of the knife and pulled. Fresh waves of agony flooded the world as her wail returned to her ears again and again, magnified by the unfeeling stone. Her hands covered the wound as if it were an indecency, blood seeping between her fingers.

Mustering the last of her strength, Cora looked up at the skin-walker. "Damn....bitch...."

Those animal eyes regarded her. "You would have done the same." Kneeling down, the witch wiped the knife on the hem of Cora's pants. Cora tried to kick her, but she could only manage a feeble stirring of her boot. It was just too heavy for her to move.

When the weapon was clean, the skin-walker rose and turned her back on the fallen hunter. "You fought well," she said. Cora tried to answer, but the words drowned in the fluid welling up from her lungs.

The witch walked away in silence. Eyes fixed on the back of her enemy, Cora tried once more to rise, to recover her gun and take the life of the woman who had taken hers, but her body refused to respond. Another coughing fit took hold of her, and all awareness disappeared beneath a fresh blossom of pain. Cora could feel her life leaving her with every agonizing spasm as blood from her wound and her lips mingled with the ancient dust.

When the coughs faded away once more, Cora looked up at the stars. They seemed dimmer now, as though they were dying with her. A surge of anger swept through her. This wasn't how it was supposed to go. She was Cora Oglesby. No squaw could lay her out, especially with nothing more than a stone knife. Her fingers curled into a weak fist. She held it for a moment, intending to raise it and pound the ground in anger, but it was such an effort, and she was getting so tired. The anger flowed out with her blood, soaking into the dry earth beneath her.

Relaxing her hand, Cora forced the skin-walker from her mind. She would not let her last thoughts be of that woman. Instead, she called up memories of younger days, riding along dusty back trails that wound through endless deserts with Ben at her side. They had camped beneath the same stars that hung above her now. She could still see the firelight dancing in his eyes as he laughed at some jest of hers, the sound seeming to carry to the very end of the world. His hand, calloused and forever stained black with ink, covered hers as he leaned over and kissed her cheek. She laughed then, scrunching her face up against his mustache as it tickled her ear.

Opening her eyes, Cora found she could still see his face. Her lips parted in a bloody smile. He smiled back, a sight she hadn't seen in far too long.

"About time you showed up."

• • • •

The monster crouched in front of Victoria, still looking far too human for the savage hunger burning in its eyes. They watched her now with murderous intent.

"That's what you got to look forward to, darlin."

Tearing her gaze away from the feral businessman lurking in the scrub, Victoria forced a look of disdain through her fear. "Compared to hearing your endless prattle, such a fate is a blessing."

The vampire laughed. "You got spunk enough to fill a wagon, all right. I reckon your blood will be a sight sweeter for it. Strong souls always got the most flavor, I've found. Wish I could have had me a taste of that Oglesby bitch before the squaw puts her down for good, but yours'll do just fine."

"Are you certain of that?"

"Only one way to find out." He stepped toward her, blue eyes aflame with lust.

The fire vanished an instant later as the vampire recoiled from his victim, shielding his eyes. Victoria took a small step forward, Cora's wooden crucifix held high.

"Nearly forgot about this little treasure," she said. "A gift from Cora, and a useful one at that. Who knew such a little thing could have so much power over filthy vermin like you?"

Victoria took another step toward him, enjoying the sight of his agony. Her attention was so thoroughly fixed on him that at first she didn't feel the hand grab her ankle. Realization set in just as it yanked her leg out from under her. She fell to the desert floor, branches snapping beneath her. The monster's fingers were like steel rods. She drove the heel of her other boot into the creature's head with a crunch, but it scarcely seemed to feel the blow. Somewhere nearby, she could hear boots scraping on the ground. The man was recovering. She didn't have much time.

In a single, swift motion, Victoria swept the crucifix toward the cold hands gripping her leg. The wood brushed against the grey skin with a sound like sizzling meat. Smoke filled the air between them as the monster shrieked and pulled away.

Her leg now free, Victoria scrambled to her feet, looking for the blue-eyed man. He stood a few yards away, hand gripping his head as if in pain. She didn't wait to see how quickly he might recover from whatever ailed him. Crucifix held forward, she charged at him, a cry rising from her lungs. He looked up at the sound and began stumbling backward.

The fear in those wicked eyes spurred Victoria onward. Too late, she realized she couldn't stop herself in time. Vampire and hunter tumbled to the ground in a cloud of smoke. A roar of agony echoed in the night air as Victoria held the crucifix to his chest. His limbs flailed in the dirt as he writhed beneath her, trying to shrink away from the holy object, but she leaned on her outstretched arm, pinning him to the ground with her weight.

She might have stayed there until sunrise, relishing the sound of his suffering, but the smoke belching from his skin blinded her. Reluctantly, she rose to her feet and stepped to one side. She kept the crucifix pointed toward the thick grey cloud as she blinked back the tears stinging her eyes.

When the smoke cleared, the vampire lay on the ground in a fetal position. Victoria stood over him, not daring to lower the crucifix for even a moment. In the shadows nearby, she could make out the shape of the feral vampire. Its eyes on her made her uneasy. The crucifix held it at bay, but for how long?

Victoria's mind raced. Without her gun, she had no way of killing either monster. Her knife was made of ordinary steel and did not have the blessing of Cora's saber. Only the blessed silver bullets would work, and the revolver still lay near the ruins where the man had kicked it from her grip. Stealing a glance over her shoulder, she estimated the distance back to the ruins. No more than a few hundred yards; she hadn't made it far before the savage one cut off her escape. She could make it back without too much difficulty, but finding the gun would be another matter completely.

Facing the vampire again, Victoria began backing away. After a few steps, she could see him beginning to revive. His hands pressed into the dirt as he rose to his hands and knees, head still hanging between his shoulders.

Heart hammering in her chest, she thought better of her plan and reversed direction, approaching him again. His arms began trembled beneath his weight. Raising his head, he aimed a helpless glare at her before falling back into the dust. She planted a sound kick between his shoulder blades and smiled at the resulting moan.

An idea came to her, and she acted on it at once. Switching the crucifix to her left hand, she began digging through her satchel with the other. Her fingers touched on cool glass and closed around it. The scrub rustled as the other creature stirred nearby, not willing to face the pain of the crucifix to save its master.

Victoria clamped her teeth around the vial's stopper and twisted. There was a satisfying pop as it came free. Stepping forward, she bent over the blue-eyed man, bringing the crucifix close to his head. He groaned and pulled himself into a tighter ball, cringing at the nearness of the holy object. A sudden urge to pull his hair or ear seized her, and she only managed to overcome it with great effort. She didn't know what might happen, what sort of desperate attack he might attempt if she took things too far. Besides, both her hands were full.

At that moment, a shout rose from somewhere behind her. Victoria spun around, nearly spilling the vial as the echoes rolled out into the desert. A chill skittered down her spine. Although she couldn't quite make out the words in the cry, she knew the voice belonged to Cora.

Behind her, she heard the vampire give a delirious chuckle. Pointing the crucifix at him again, she smiled as the laughter became another moan. "Is something amusing you, monster?" she asked.

The man sucked in a breath. "Sounds like that

bitch figured out who I really is," he said, his voice slurring.

"Is that so?" Victoria said, moving the crucifix closer to him. "And who might that be?"

"Washington Jones." The last word ended in a hiss as he curled away from her.

"Well, Mr. Jones, you may consider this a gift from the good Mrs. Oglesby," Victoria said. Leaning over him, she emptied the contents of the vial onto his head. A scream of pain erupted from the center of the resulting cloud of smoke. It stopped suddenly a few seconds after it began, but Victoria did not stop to see the reason why. She was already running back toward the ruins as fast as she could, her knuckles white around the crucifix. The image of the savage ghoul galloping somewhere behind her lent speed to her heels.

Although it was only a short distance, she was gasping for breath by the time she reached the outskirts of the ruined village. Her lungs burned, demanding that she stop for a moment to calm her racing heart, but she knew she didn't have the time. Washington Jones might recover from the holy water at any moment, and she didn't know where the feral creature had gone. She needed her gun.

Her boots kicked branches and stones aside as she frantically searched through the scrub. She thought she was near where she and the vampire had their first confrontation of the night, but she couldn't be sure. The fear-driven need to steal glances over her shoulder slowed the search. So far, there was no sign of the man Washington Jones, but she knew it was only a matter of time before he came for her again. Her only hope lay hidden by the stubborn desert growth.

Not her only hope, she reminded herself. Cora was nearby, presumably introducing the skin-walker to new worlds of pain. Although Victoria hadn't been able to understand what the hunter had yelled, she recognized the anger in Cora's voice. Anyone or anything on the receiving end of that anger could not hope to survive the night.

The thought made Victoria smile. As if in reply, a small glimmer of moonlight winked at her from the bushes. Pushing a branch aside, she felt her smile widen. Never had the sight of a firearm brought such comfort to her heart. Kneeling down, she picked it up reverently. The weight of the gleaming cylinder, each chamber housing a sacred silver bullet, promised a swift death to Washington Jones and his pet monster. With any luck, the vampire was still reeling from the holy water and wouldn't be able to defend himself. One clean shot, and Victoria would be free to return home with Cora in tow. The thought of England made her ache with longing. Closing her eyes, she let herself slip far away from this scorched wasteland for a moment. A warm green light filtered down through poplar leaves as a breeze carried the scent of grass and blooming daisies. She was back under her favorite tree, a book and a packed lunch beside her, ready to let another lazy afternoon pass by around her. The promise of such days ahead gave her courage. Once she silenced these nightmares once and for all, she could return to that world. Her world. Victoria opened her eyes, ready to send Washington Jones home to the devil.

Red eyes gleamed back at her.

Victoria let out a short shriek and jumped to her feet. The revolver seemed to come up of its own will, its barrel pointing between those animal eyes. Her finger pressed against the trigger, but she didn't pull through.

"Where is Cora?"

"The hunter has rejoined the cycle."

"What the devil does that mean?" Victoria asked, ignoring the shadow of dread growing in her mind.

"She lost herself for only a moment, but it was enough," Anaba said. "When two hunters circle each other, the smallest weakness is death. So it was with her."

"Impossible," Victoria said. "Cora would not let herself lose to the likes of you."

"She did not like to lose, but she did all the same. Her blood will join with this sacred place, and her spirit will return to the Great Cycle. Perhaps she will be reborn as *Diné* and will learn of our ways. That would be a fitting end for one such as her."

The gun sight wavered from its mark. She tried to hold it steady. "So she's dead."

The witch nodded.

"Then this is her vengeance."

Victoria squeezed the trigger, her entire being thirsting for the sight of the skin-walker's blood.

Click.

The ominous silence that followed mirrored her own overwhelming disappointment and confusion. She tried again. The cylinder turned smoothly, moonlight sliding along its nickel finish, but nothing else. No brilliant flame erupted from the barrel to announce the witch's death in the deep rolling thunder of its voice. There was only another terrible silence.

In that silence, Victoria wilted. The revolver hung loosely from her fingers, its barrel pointing at her boots. Her knees threatened to give way; her vision grew blurry. The great dark shadow that had been looming over her spirit now descended, crushing her under its weight. Her holy weapon had failed. Cora Oglesby, the herald of evil's bane, had fallen and left Victoria at the mercy of those who had none. The memory of sunlit fields in Oxford became a poison, taunting her with beauty and peace she would never see again.

"Now I understand."

The skin-walker's voice reached through the haze of despair, pulling Victoria back into the present. Her eyes refocused on her adversary, and she forced her mouth to move. "What do you understand?"

"You have the hunter's gun."

Victoria looked at the revolver in her hand. "Yes," she said after a moment. "Cora...she let me have hers and bought a new one when we rode out today." It seemed like half a lifetime ago, not mere hours.

"Unexpected," Anaba said, "and unlucky for you."

"What do you mean?"

The animal eyes gleamed in the darkness. "The

weapon will not fire. I have seen to it. The one the hunter carried tonight was different. I did not expect it to fire."

Something in the witch's voice stirred the last vestige of Victoria's resolve. She brought the Colt up once more, leveling the barrel at the skin-walker.

"Still you fight," Anaba said, her face betraying no sign of fear. "The hunter, too, fought with the last of her strength. You both will return as warriors. Let that comfort you."

"Let this comfort you," Victoria said. The revolver was heavy in her hand, a solid shape that embodied what remained of her defiance. She knew it was hopeless. The gun had already misfired three times, and the confidence in the skin-walker's eyes removed any doubt that it would do so again. Still, she had to try one more time. Her grandfather's legacy and his blood in her veins demanded it. If she was to die in this hellish place, let it be on her feet with a weapon in her hand.

Victoria squeezed the trigger.

The revolver did not jump in her hands, but the crashing of a gunshot still rolled through the desert night. Victoria blinked. She had seen a flash of light, but it hadn't come from her gun. Confused, she studied the Colt's barrel for a moment, then looked at Anaba.

The skin-walker's red eyes had gone wide. Her hand clutched at her right breast, looking for all the world like a young girl pining for her lover. A word floated from her lips into the night. "How...?"

"I don't know," Victoria replied.

A shadowy lock of Anaba's hair fell across her chest as the witch turned her head. Victoria followed her gaze and saw a shadow standing at the base of a ruined wall. She squinted, unable to believe what she saw. "Cora?"

The hunter's laugh cracked like a whip. "Wasn't expecting me, was you?"

Anaba took a step toward her. "You...died."

"Not quite," Cora said. "Don't you Indian folk know that you got to make sure a cougar's breathed his last before you turn your back on him?"

Before Anaba could reply, another flame erupted from the revolver in Cora's hand. The impact blew Anaba backward. Coming to rest at Victoria's feet, the witch looked up at the young woman. Victoria returned her gaze, overwhelmed by a sudden, powerful sadness.

"I'm sorry," she heard herself say.

The skin-walker's mouth moved. Victoria knelt down, trying to hear her words, but there was only silence. Cora's boots rustled through the scrub as she approached, but Victoria could not look away from the dying woman.

Anaba's eyes were fading, their gleam like the final touches of evening sunlight through a window. They turned their gaze toward the hunter. A queer look, half respect and half hatred, twisted the Indian woman's features. Her lips moved again, offering what Victoria took to be a silent curse, her final act in this world.

Cora nodded as if she understood. "Can't say I blame you for what you done. Might be I'd have done the same if I was in your boots. Only the good Lord could say if you was in the wrong, after all." The Colt's voice roared once more, and the light disappeared from Anaba's eyes.

When the gunshot faded from her ears, Victoria looked up. "She told me you were dead."

"And she was right," Cora said.

"Then how..." Victoria trailed off as she got a good look at the hunter. Blood had soaked through her shirt and spattered her trousers. The hand that clutched the revolver was streaked with the dark fluid. A thrill of fear ran through Victoria, and she felt her hand tighten around her own gun. The woman who stood before her should not be alive. Had she somehow become undead herself?

Cora answered the fear in her eyes. "Turns out this place is like a doorway between this world and the next, kind of like a bit of cloth that's been worn thin. Spirits can pass back and forth all comfortable-like. I reckon that's why our friend here set up shop out here. Good place for all sorts of witchcraft."

"That still doesn't explain–"

"How I'm standing here?" Cora grinned. "Don't add up, do it?" She paused, her eyelids fluttering for a moment. "Well, my Ben could see I was getting ready to die and came through to walk me over. Always was a gentleman like that. I ain't much of a lady, though, so I told him I wasn't going until I'd settled business on this side. He argued some but soon got it through his head that I was serious. Figuring it would speed things up, he gave me what strength he could, and here I am."

"So you've cheated death," Victoria said, a smile spreading across her lips.

"Not exactly," Cora said. She chuckled as Victoria's smile faltered. "Ain't like I just get to waltz on out of here and get back to living. No, this here squaw did her job all right. Ben just stepped in and put it off for a tick."

Victoria swallowed against the lump forming in her throat. "How long do you have?"

The hunter sighed. "Seeing as how we sorted the squaw out, I reckon I should get a move on. Things are getting all foggy, anyhow, and it won't do to keep the good Lord waiting."

With that, Cora sank to her knees and leaned back on her heels. Victoria reached out a hand to steady her. The hunter gripped it with her own, her eyes suddenly intense.

"I ain't going to live up to my end of the bargain," Cora said, her words beginning to slur. "Here you helped me out all this way, and I can't return the favor."

"Don't be silly—"

"Hush up, now. I ain't got but a few more breaths in me." As if to prove it, Cora turned her face away and coughed. The ruins echoed with the ragged sound. Drawing a deep breath, the hunter looked back at her young apprentice. "I can't go with you in body, but don't you think I won't be watching

you. Take my gun on back with you and show them
black things a thing or two about the fear of God. Do
me proud."

"I will," Victoria said, the words threatening to un-
leash a flood of tears. She wouldn't start blubbing
now, not in the last minutes of this battle-hardened
warrior's life. Taking a breath to steady herself, she
gave Cora's hand a squeeze. "I promise."

"That's a good girl," Cora said, easing herself down
onto her back. "You'll be just fine out there. Give old
King George my regards while you're at it."

"What about you?" Victoria asked. "What should
I do when...?"

"Take me on back to Father Baez," Cora replied.
"He can put me next to my Ben like we ought to be.
Tell him what happened out here and what you're
fixing to do over in England. He'll set you up with
some right fine help, see if he don't."

The hunter's breathing grew shallower as the
power warding off her death ebbed away. Her eyes
were half-closed. No longer looking at Victoria, they
seemed to be gazing at something distant, something
beautiful. A faint smile softened her face. Even
though the smile wasn't directed at her, Victoria
smiled back.

Cora's smile vanished, and her eyes opened wide.
"Wash," she whispered.

Something slammed into Victoria's side, sending
her flying. She smashed into a bush a number of
yards away, the branches snapping like bones.
Dazed, she picked her head up. Starlight and shad-

ows spun in a nauseating vortex around her. She closed her eyes and willed the world to stop swirling.

"Looks like you whipped that squaw right proper," came the taunting voice of Washington Jones. "Reckon I owe you for that, but I ain't never been good at paying back favors. Hope becoming immortal seems a fair reward."

Victoria pulled her boots under her and rose to her feet. "I will not serve you, filth."

"Ain't talking to you, darlin," Wash said, blue eyes flashing in his burned face. "You is in for a world of pain for that nasty bit of work back there. See, I ain't no good at paying back favors, but I happen to be an expert when it comes to paying back an eye for an eye."

Moonlight flashed on the Colt's barrel as Victoria raised it. "Is that right?"

Wash laughed. "Go on, keep waving that gun of yours. Maybe one of them bullets will drop out and you can throw it at me."

Victoria's heart sank. Anaba must have told him about the curse she put on Cora's gun, or maybe he simply remembered how it had misfired when she tried to shoot him earlier. Either way, intimidating him into submission was not an option. She still had her crucifix, but there was no way she could reach him before he killed Cora. Nothing could save the huntress now, but she deserved to die in peace instead of being twisted into an undead slave of this monster.

The vampire suddenly reeled backward as if someone had punched him in the jaw. Confused, Victoria watched him stumble for a moment before shifting her gaze toward the hunter. Cora's arm was raised slightly, fist closed around something. Victoria couldn't make out what she was holding, but she didn't need to. Whatever it was, it was buying her the few precious seconds she needed. Her boots crashed through the dry branches, sending stones flying to either side as she sprinted forward. If she could just get to Cora's side and take her gun, she could make an end of Washington Jones.

Without warning, Washington's pet vampire leapt at her from the scrub, powerful arms wrapping around her like constrictors. They squeezed a cry from her lungs as the two of them crashed onto the ground. Jagged rocks punched into Victoria's ribs, sending spikes of pain through her body.

When the two of them came to rest, the vampire was on top of her. Victoria fought to breathe, to free her arms, to throw it off. The demon bared its teeth at her, and she snarled back. Her fingers pulled at her belt, searching for the crucifix but not finding it. Despair flooded her mind. It must have fallen out when the creature slammed into her.

Dead fingers wrapped around her golden braid and gave it a savage tug. Victoria cried out as the creature pulled at her scalp, forcing her chin up. White teeth clamped onto her neck. She punched at its head with her free hand, but she might as well have been beating on a rock. Its jaws were pure agony as they crushed her throat. Soon, she could feel the creature tearing the blood from her veins, slurping it down like a mongrel drinking from a dirty puddle. The pain was unlike anything she could have imagined, at once filling her body with fire and sending tendrils of frostbite through her soul. Her lungs heaved, trying to suck in a breath, but the vampire's jaws clamped her windpipe shut.

Victoria felt herself dying, her essence flowing down the throat of the monster on top of her. Her thoughts grew thin and light, wisps of lace floating through her mind. She felt a twinge of sorrow that their victory had been snatched from them when it had seemed so certain. They had bested the skin-walker only to fall to her servant. There was an irony there, she knew, but she couldn't quite remember what it was.

Air rushed into Victoria's lungs like a flash flood, propelling her back up into the realm of life. She felt as though she would continue to sail upward until she reached the stars. The icy knife that had been digging its way into her soul was gone. She took another breath. Trickles of blood tickled her neck, and she almost giggled.

The laughter died on her lips as the memory of where she was crashed back into her mind. Clapping a hand to her bleeding neck, she raised her head and looked around. A few yards away, the vampire crouched low to the ground, hissing through its bloody teeth. Victoria stared at it in confusion for a moment, wondering why it had suddenly released her. Cora's voice reached her then, thin and scraping like chalk on a blackboard.

"Get up."

Victoria forced her arms and legs into action. As they pulled her into a sitting position, she felt something slide down her shirt. Cora's rosary. Wrapping her fingers around the beads, she groaned. Her whole body ached.

"No time for that," Cora said in response to her moan. "Hump it or we're through."

Nodding in agreement, Victoria stood to her feet. Her legs wobbled beneath her, threatening to collapse. One look at the creature crouching nearby was enough to steady them. Keeping the rosary in plain sight, she made her way to Cora's side. Blue eyes glared at her from the shadows, but the vampire kept his distance.

Victoria half-knelt, half-fell next to the hunter. "Where is your gun?"

"He took it," Cora said, lifting a finger in the direction of Wash Jones.

"What?" The hunter's words sapped Victoria's strength, and she struggled to stay on her feet. "How am I supposed to kill him without it?"

"My gun," the hunter whispered, tapping the holster on Victoria's belt. "Shoot him."

"It doesn't work," Victoria said. "How can I–"

"Do it!" Cora's eyes opened wide, blazing in the moonlight. Victoria thought she saw a flash of white light from deep inside them, but she didn't stop to look twice. The force of the hunter's command propelled her to her feet, her hand reaching for the revolver of its own will.

Washington Jones watched her, his blue eyes alight with amusement. He held the other revolver in his hand, the barrel pointed at Victoria's chest. "Well, now, ain't this a pretty picture?"

"Indeed," Victoria said.

"See, now, I'm trying to decide what's most fitting to do," Wash said. "Here I is pointing a gun at a lady who's pointing a gun at me. Trouble is, your gun don't work, and it ain't proper to shoot an unarmed body. I reckon I could shoot you anyhow on account of you being such a pain, but then you wouldn't get all what's coming to you for doing what you done back there. Now—"

The thundering crash of a pistol shot cut him off. Victoria lowered her smoking revolver, cold blue eyes glittering. Across from her, Washington Jones stared in disbelief. Words started to form on his lips, but they dissolved into a moaning wail that could have arisen from the depths of hell itself. The vampire fell to his knees. Thin, piercing notes shredded the stillness of the night as smoke belched from his nose and mouth. One cry became a multitude, rising in a horrid cacophony that made Victoria wince, but she did not look away. On the ground beside her, Cora lay with her eyes closed, the ghost of a smile on her worn face.

When the desert night had swallowed up the last of the hellish chorus, Victoria allowed herself to breathe. Turning around, she swept her gaze through the brush, searching for the fallen master's minion, but the feral creature had vanished. She took a step toward the ruins when Cora's voice stopped her.

"Take my sword," the hunter said, her voice rattling deep in her chest.

Kneeling down next to Cora, Victoria put a hand on the hilt of the hunter's saber. Starlight glimmered on the blade as she drew it from its sheath.

"Cut off his head."

Victoria stood and turned toward her fallen foe before the hunter's words hit home. "What?" she asked.

Cora merely looked at her and nodded.

Taking a breath, Victoria marched toward the vampire's corpse. Nausea swept through her at the thought of decapitating a man, even this one, but she forced it down. If it was the only way to make sure the monster stayed dead, then she would do it.

Victoria looked down at Washington's face, and her fingers involuntarily tightened around the saber's hilt. The dead man's face was frozen in the rictus of his dying scream, but the fire was gone from his eyes. He looked like an ordinary man, one who might have passed many a hot afternoon in Cora's saloon. A strange sense of pity passed through her. Once, this man had been no different from any other, trying to make his own way in a world as dangerous as it was mad. He had chosen a path of darkness and demons, perhaps beguiled by the man he pretended to be, the one called Fodor Glava. So damned, he had become a monster in soul as well as in body, ultimately leading him to his death by her hand. A tragic end to a tragic tale.

The memory of his hands around her throat, his promises of rape and murder, returned to her, and her pity vanished beneath a landslide of loathing. Her skin crawled at the thought of his icy touch. Gripping the hilt of the saber with both hands, she raised it above her head.

"Bastard."

Moonlight flashed on the polished blade as she brought it down on the vampire's neck. It sliced through the undead flesh as if it were jelly. The head of Washington Jones rolled a few feet before coming to rest, long strands of dirty yellow hair splayed out like the legs of an insect. Victoria shuddered at the thought and turned away.

Retracing her steps, Victoria returned to the hunter's side. "It's done."

Cora did not answer.

Kneeling down next to her, Victoria softly called out her name. The lean, weathered face did not stir. No breath rose and fell beneath her shirt. A smile still lingered on her lips, and the sight brought one to Victoria's own. Despite the blood on her shirt, the carnage that surrounded her, Cora Oglesby was a vision of peace. Her hat lay to one side of her head, the brim painted by threads of her hair. The moonlight softened the hard lines of her face, taking the years away from her. In its bluish hue, Victoria could still see the face of the girl she had been, the face her husband must have seen when they first met. They

were together again at last, after all their long years
of separation. The thought made Victoria's smile
widen, and she felt a tear slide down her cheek.

"Rest well, my friend," she whispered, touching
the hunter's hand. "You've earned it."

Victoria lingered there a moment longer, a captive
of the powerful serenity that had settled over the
ruins. She took a deep breath, drawing the cool
desert air into her lungs. It smelled of dust and blood.
She wanted to carry this place inside her forever, just
as it was, stained with the blood of heroes and monsters. To forget would be a dishonor to the woman
who lay beside her.

Finally, Victoria roused herself. Her cold muscles
creaked in protest as she stood. Moving to wipe her
eyes, she realized she still held Cora's saber in her
hand. Bending down, she wiped the gore on a nearby
bush, then carefully slid the blade back into its
sheath. Metal rasped against metal, sending echoes
bouncing off the nearby walls.

Reaching toward her own belt for the hunter's gun,
she paused. Cora's words came back to her, telling her
to take the gun with her back to England so she could
enact her own vengeance. Victoria smiled again. "I
will wear it with pride," she said, "and I hope to some-
day be worthy of it."

Tipping her hat to her friend, Victoria turned and
started walking toward the ruins. Somewhere near
their weathered walls, she knew her horse must be
waiting. For the first time in her life, she found herself eager to climb into a saddle and ride beneath the

stars, the night flowing around her in dark rivers of purple and blue and brown, forever searching for the break of dawn.

EPILOGUE

Early morning sunlight streamed through the windows, making Victoria's eyes sparkle like a mountain lake in summer. She rested her head against the glass, watching the distant mesas march past beneath the empty sky. The train swayed gently as it clacked and clamored along its route. Victoria could feel sleep coming for her, peering into each row as it stalked up the aisle, eager to cover her in its warm embrace.

Somewhere behind her, another car followed hers over the winding steel rails. Inside, her luggage was doubtlessly bouncing and thumping in time to the clacking and swaying. Beside it sat an ordinary coffin, unadorned and simple. Victoria never imagined herself traveling with such a thing, but she would not refuse Cora her dying wish to be buried next to her husband. Sheriff Morgan had offered little resistance, saying that Victoria was as close to kin as the old hunter had. He seemed eager to rid himself of the whole affair, and Victoria didn't blame him for it. Only a few short months ago, she would have felt the same.

Her thoughts drifted far away from the desert, lingering in a moonlit spring night, one that seemed so long ago now. Instead of the hulking shapes and burning yellow eyes of the hounds, she remembered the fine cut of her father's overcoat and the way her mother's hat seemed to forever teeter on the verge of slipping off. In her drowsy haze, Victoria could almost feel the soft scratching of her favorite scarf, and a dreamy smile spread beneath her tired eyes.

Around her, other passengers spoke in hushed tones, trading gossip and rumors like currency. Sunlight flashed and jumped along the windows, sending brilliant spears dancing through their hair and across their faces. Oblivious to them, the young woman slept, lulled by the gentle rocking of the train as it carried her out of the unforgiving wilderness and back toward the green fields and quiet rivers of her home.

Acknowledgments

Thanks always to my constant companion and best friend, Tori, for standing strong against my legions of writing grumps. Thanks to my wonderful beta readers for their donations of time and invaluable advice, to my AR editors Lee and Marc for their keen eyes and keener cuts, and to Darren, Roland and Mike for their fantastic work. Thanks to everyone at ChiCon 7 for making my first official convention such a lovely experience. Finally, thanks to my brother, Joe, for his enthusiasm, support, and generous gifts of alcohol.

INTRODUCING CORA OGLESBY, MONSTER HUNTER...

LEE COLLINS

TRUE GRIT MEETS TRUE BLOOD

The DEAD of WINTER

"Read it with the lights on – but for damn sure read it."
— CHRIS F HOLM, AUTHOR OF *DEAD HARVEST*

"Read it with the lights on – but for damn sure read it." – CHRIS F HOLM, AUTHOR OF *DEAD HARVEST*